NEW YORK TIMES BESTSELLING AUTHOR
NICHOLAS SANSBURY SMITH

GREAT WAVE INK
PUBLISHING

Books by New York Times Bestselling Author
Nicholas Sansbury Smith

The Sons of War Series
(Offered by Blackstone Publishing)

Sons of War
Sons of War 2: Saints (Coming Fall 2020)
Sons of War 3: Sinners (Coming early 2021)

The Hell Divers Series
(Offered by Blackstone Publishing)

Hell Divers
Hell Divers II: Ghosts
Hell Divers III: Deliverance
Hell Divers IV: Wolves
Hell Divers V: Captives
Hell Divers VI: Allegiance
Hell Divers VII: Warriors

The Extinction Cycle (Season One)
(Offered by Orbit Books)

Extinction Horizon
Extinction Edge
Extinction Age
Extinction Evolution
Extinction End
Extinction Aftermath
Extinction Lost (A Team Ghost short story)
Extinction War

NicholasSansburySmith.com

For my grandfather Angelo 'Jake' Angaran, my grandfather Marvin Smith, and all the other veterans of World War II that risked their lives to fight the Nazis.

We will never forget your bravery and sacrifice.

"The supreme art of war is to subdue the enemy without fighting."

—Sun Tzu

Note from the Author

Dear Reader,

In Spring of 2020 I updated this section to reflect the current international medical crisis. As you all know, we are in the middle of a pandemic with extreme damage being done to the global economy. Trade has come to almost a standstill and the major gears of the supply chain have ground to a halt. We have an overwhelmed medical industry focused on COVID-19 and a shortage of personal protective equipment (PPE). The meat and poultry industry has been hit hard, slowing production, and resulting in shortages. Over thirty million people have filed for unemployment in the United States.

And that isn't even the full picture of just how much has changed in the past five months. An EMP attack now could cripple the United States to the point of no return.

If this attack were to occur, I believe North Korea is the country that would be the most likely to carry it out. Despite international efforts to stop them, they are still advancing their nuclear weapons and ballistic missile programs in defiance of the United Nations Security Council resolutions and sanctions.

At the end of April 2020, there was another twist to this explosive situation, with reports coming out of the Korean peninsula and Japan that North Korean leader Kim Jung Un was either dead or in a vegetative state. If this is true, it adds a new element to the fragile international conflict.

Whoever replaces Kim Jung Un could be worse, furthering the risk of war. On the contrary, they could help bring unification to the peninsula. I've updated this note again in May to reflect reports of Kim Jung Un being spotted in public. Some analysts are saying it's a body double, others say it is indeed the leader. Only time will tell if he is still alive, but either way, the situation remains a powder keg.

And that is exactly what this story is about.

Before you dive in, I've included some background on how this story came to be. In 2016 I was finishing up book five of the Extinction Cycle, and at that time, I thought Extinction End would be the "end" of the series. I decided to write a new type of story—a story without monsters, zombies, or aliens—about a different type of threat.

Rewind ten years. I'm a planner with the State of Iowa sitting in a meeting with other agencies and utility companies talking about solar flares and a weapon called an electromagnetic pulse (EMP). It was there that I realized just how devastating an EMP could be to the United States if it were strategically detonated in the atmosphere. The longer I heard about the effects, the more I started to wonder—why would our enemies poison our soil and destroy our cities with nuclear weapons or waste their troops in a battle they probably couldn't win, when all they had to do is turn off our power and sit back and watch the chaos and death that would ensue?

During this meeting with other agencies, I was shocked to learn there wasn't much being done to harden our utilities and critical facilities to protect against such a threat.

A few years later, I started working for Iowa Homeland Security and Emergency Management. I had several duties as a disaster mitigation project officer, but my primary focus was on protecting infrastructure and working on the state hazard mitigation plan. Near the end of my time at HSEMD, I was also assigned the duty of overseeing the hardening of power lines in rural communities.

After several years of working in the disaster mitigation field, I learned of countless threats from natural disasters to manmade weapons, but the EMP, in my opinion, was still the greatest of them all.

That brings us to today. We're living in tumultuous times, and our enemies are constantly looking for ways to harm us, both domestically and abroad. We already know that cyber security is a major concern for the United States. North Korea, China, and Russia have all been caught tampering with our elections and our systems. We also know other countries are experimenting with cyber technology that can shut down portions of our grid. But imagine a weapon that could shut down our entire grid. The perfectly strategized EMP attack gives our enemies an opportunity to do just that. And that is the premise of the Trackers series.

Before you start reading, I would like to take time to thank everyone who helped make this book a reality. Many people had a hand in the creation of this story. I'm grateful for all their help, criticism, and time. I'd like to start with the people that I wrote this book for—the readers. You are the reason I always try to write something fresh, and the reason I strive to always make each story better than—and different from—its predecessors.

Secondly, I'd like to thank the Estes Park Police Department.

In the spring of 2016, my wife and I spent a few weeks in Estes Park, Colorado, a place I had visited many times growing up. I wanted to show her this gorgeous tourist town that borders Rocky Mountain National Park, and I decided it would also make a good setting for some of the scenes in Trackers.

The police department very graciously allowed me to tour their facilities and ride along with Officer Corey Richards. Department officers and staff explained police procedure for tracking lost people, and their operations and response to natural disasters. Captain Eric Rose, who is in charge of the Emergency Operations Center, described what they went through in the flood of 2013, when Estes Park was quite literally cut off from surrounding communities.

I've spent time with many law enforcement departments over my career in government, and I can tell you Estes Park has one of the finest and most professional staffs I've ever had the pleasure of meeting. Thank you to every officer for serving Estes Park and assisting with Trackers. I hope you find I did your community justice.

I'd also like to thank my literary agent, David Fugate, who has provided valuable feedback on each of my novels. The version you are reading today is much different than the manuscript I submitted, partly because of David's excellent feedback.

I also had a great group of beta readers that helped bring this story to life. You all know who you are. Thanks again for your assistance.

Trackers is more than just a post-apocalyptic thriller about the aftermath of an attack on American soil. It's meant to be a mystery as much as it is a thriller. There are a lot of EMP stories out there, but I wanted to write one that included new themes and incorporated elements of Cherokee and Sioux folk stories. I spent years researching and reading Native American history at the University of Iowa where I received a certificate in American Indian studies.

This story, like many works of fiction, will require some suspension of belief, but hopefully not as much as my other science fiction stories. Any errors in this book rest solely with me, as the author is always the gatekeeper of the work.

In an interview several years ago, I was asked why I write. My response was that while my stories are meant to entertain, they are also meant to be a warning. Trackers could be a true story, and I hope our government continues to prepare and protect us from such a threat.

Captain Eric Rose of the Estes Park Police Department told me that he wasn't sure he was ready for a post-apocalyptic Estes Park. I'm not either. Let's all hope this story remains fiction.

With that said, I hope you enjoy the read, and as always, feel free to reach out to me on social media if you have questions or comments.

Best wishes,
Nicholas Sansbury Smith

Foreword

Dr. Arthur Bradley

Author of

Disaster Preparedness for EMP Attacks and Solar Storms
and The Survivalist.

When used conventionally, a nuclear warhead could destroy a city and cover the surrounding region in deadly radiation. Horrible to be sure, but at least it would be localized. When detonated in the atmosphere at the right altitude, however, that same warhead could generate an electromagnetic pulse (EMP) that would cause almost unimaginable harm to our nation.

The most significant effect of such an attack would be damage to the nation's electrical grid. Due to the interdependency of systems, the loss of electricity would result in a cascade of failures promulgating through every major infrastructure, including telecommunications, financial, petroleum and natural gas, transportation, food, water, emergency services, space operations, and government. Businesses, including banks, grocery stores, restaurants, and gas stations, would all close. Critical services such as the distribution of water, fuel, and food would fail. Emergency services, including hospitals, police, and fire departments, would perhaps remain operable a little longer using generators and backup systems, but they too would collapse due to limited fuel distribution, as well as the loss of key personnel abandoning their posts.

In addition to the collapse of national infrastructures, an EMP could cause widespread damage to transportation systems, such as aircraft, automobiles, trucks, and boats, as well as supervisory control and data acquisition hardware used in telecommunications, fuel processing, and water purification systems. Such an attack could also damage in-space satellites and significantly hamper the government's ability to provide a unified emergency response or even maintain civil order. Finally, many personal electronics could also be damaged, including our beloved computers and cell phones, as well as important health monitoring devices.

With the collapse of infrastructures, loss of commerce, and widespread damage to property, an EMP attack would introduce terrible financial ruin on the nation. Consider that it is estimated that even a modest 1-2 megaton warhead detonated over the Eastern Seaboard could cause in excess of a trillion ($1,000,000,000,000) dollars in damage.

Testing done in the 1960s, such as Starfish Prime and the Soviet's Test 184, provided some idea of the potential damage, but weapons have become even more powerful and our world more technologically susceptible. No one really knows with certainty the extent of the damage that would be felt, but expert predictions range from catastrophic to apocalyptic. What is universally agreed upon is that the EMP attack allows for an almost unimaginable amount of damage to be done with nothing more than a single nuclear warhead and a missile capable of deploying it to the right altitude. Given that there are more than 128,000 such warheads and 10,000 such missiles in existence, it seems prudent to better understand and prepare for this very real and present danger.

What many do not know is that the U.S. has been

openly threatened with an EMP strike by Russia, Iran, and North Korea. Leaderships of these countries have come to appreciate the truly asymmetric nature of such an attack. Consider that an EMP strike would be largely independent of weather, result in long-lasting infrastructure damage, and inflict a damage-to-cost ratio far greater than any conventional weapon, including a nuclear "dirty bomb." Worse yet is that our enemies would not limit themselves to a single EMP strike. Rather, they would detonate several warheads, carefully timed and positioned across the nation to achieve maximum damage.

Author Nicholas Sansbury Smith understands how an attack could cripple the United States. I first spoke with him when he was working for Iowa Homeland Security and Emergency Management in the disaster preparedness field. He reached out when he was writing a science fiction story about solar storms with some questions about my book, Disaster Preparedness for EMP Attacks and Solar Storms. Since then, Nicholas has also spent a great deal of time researching EMPs.

Trackers is a work of fiction, but many of the places in the story are real. Utilizing his background in emergency management and disaster mitigation, Nicholas has done an excellent job of describing a realistic geopolitical crisis that sets the stage for an EMP attack. The following story is a terrifying scenario in which brave men and women must adapt to a challenging new world—a world that we could see ourselves being thrust into. Part of me wishes Nicholas had continued writing purely science fiction stories about aliens and government designed bio-weapons because Trackers is a novel that could become non-fiction.

— Prologue —

Secretary of Defense Charlize Montgomery marched with an entourage of heavily armed soldiers down a well-lit concrete hallway. Both Charlize and Albert Randall, her security agent and closest ally, carried a military-issued M4 and wore a ballistic vest. The snug armor seemed to compress her pounding heart. Each step she took, it got tighter.

"Execute," one of the soldiers said.

Two men slung their rifles over their backs, punched in codes on the security panel, and then stepped away from the door. The hydraulics clicked, the sound echoing in the narrow passage.

Albert moved in front of Charlize and raised his M4. Taking a step to her left, Charlize strained to see if the helicopter had already landed on the island. Albert matched every step she took. He was no longer her shadow; he now walked by her side wherever she went. The soldiers gave an all clear, and Albert motioned for Charlize to follow him out onto the grass.

A dark bowl dotted with stars hung over Cape Canaveral. She searched the darkness for any sign of the Sikorsky SH-60 Seahawk. The mid-September breeze, still humid, whipped the palm trees back and forth on the berms disguising the island. There was no sign of civilization in the distance, making it easy to spot a single red flashing dot on the horizon.

Charlize stepped forward to see if it was the Seahawk. Although she was surrounded by a dozen soldiers, she still felt uneasy. Just miles away, American citizens were killing one another for cans of SpaghettiOs. Reports were also trickling in of civilians taking potshots at military choppers across the country.

"Echo 1, incoming," announced a muscular sergeant named Collins.

Charlize watched the outline of the Seahawk approach with a breath held in her chest. The breeze rustled her short-cropped hair and stung her burned skin, but her eyes were clear. For the past twenty-four hours she'd sobbed and sobbed until she couldn't cry anymore. It had been so long since she'd held her son, Ty, but in a few more minutes, he'd be here.

Her joy was shadowed by guilt. This reunion had come at a staggering cost. Dozens of soldiers had died to save her son, including her own brother.

"Make way!" shouted Collins. He waved the other men back. The island, barely the size of two football fields, had no permanent tarmac. A few days earlier, Charlize had arrived by boat with a team of Navy SEALs from mainland Florida, but it was too dangerous to travel that route now. Anyone that saw the bird might follow them to the island and compromise the location of Constellation. It was imperative the new location for the recovery efforts in the United States and home of Central Command remain top-secret.

The Navy pilots touched down on the grass. Several Marines hopped out and turned with their hands extended. Flashlights flickered on from the soldiers surrounding Charlize, and the beams flitted toward the troop hold.

Charlize choked down a sob at the sight of Ty. He looked so small, so fragile.

"Go, go, go!" shouted Collins. His team ran to support the newcomers. Charlize stepped forward, but Albert held her back.

"Just hold on, ma'am," he said calmly. "They'll bring him to you."

A large Marine hopped onto the grass with Ty in his arms. Another Marine followed with Ty's wheelchair.

"Ty!" Charlize shouted. This time Albert didn't try to hold her back. She limped forward, into the gusting rotor drafts.

"Mom!" Ty yelled.

Despite the pain of her injuries, she ran to meet her son. The Marine carrying Ty held him while the other unfolded the wheelchair. Charlize almost tripped, but Albert steadied her.

Ty reached out for Charlize as the two Marines placed him gently in his chair. She bent down and hugged her son, gripping him as tightly as she dared.

"Mom," he said into her ear. "I didn't think I was ever going to see you again."

She pulled away and crouched in front of him, scanning his body for injuries in the glow of the flashlights.

"I'm fine," Ty said, his voice steady and strong. His eyes widened as he scanned Charlize. "You cut your hair and…you're hurt."

"I'm okay, and the hair will grow back." Charlize smiled warmly to reassure her son. Over Ty's head, she saw the Marines removing something else from the troop hold. It was a casket, wrapped with an American flag. Ty looked over his shoulder as the Marines carried it across the grass.

"I miss Uncle Nathan," he said. He sniffed loudly and wiped his eyes with his sleeve.

Charlize couldn't imagine what her boy had seen back in Colorado. The man calling himself General Dan Fenix had executed her brother right in front of Ty. The thought filled her with a mixture of rage and despair that almost made her knees buckle.

Albert had been hanging back with the soldiers, giving Charlize a moment with Ty, but he approached now.

"Hi, Mr. Albert," Ty said.

"Hey there, little man," Albert said with a quick flash of his white teeth. He reached for the back of Ty's wheelchair, but Charlize took his place.

"I've got him," she said. Her friend and bodyguard nodded, patted Ty on the shoulder with one massive hand, and then fell into step beside them.

"Let's move out!" Collins shouted.

The Seahawk lifted back into the sky, and the soldiers jogged back toward the blast doors. While Charlize wheeled Ty across the lawn, four Marines carried the casket containing her brother's remains.

I'm going to kill that Nazi-loving son of a bitch Fenix, Charlize thought. *No mercy, no quarters. Every single one of the Sons of Liberty soldiers will die.*

***

Ever since Secretary of Defense Charlize Montgomery left Estes Park, all Sam "Raven" Spears had been able to think about was ten million dollars in gold bars and revenge. It was one hell of a reward for catching General

Dan Fenix, and Raven was planning on collecting the money as soon as he fixed his Jeep Cherokee and fulfilled his promise to Lieutenant Jeff Dupree and the other dead Marines Fenix had ambushed on the road.

Days earlier, Raven had been forced to leave his most prized possession on Highway 7 about fifty miles south of town. He was heading there now, blazing down the highway on a 1970 Harley Davidson FLH.

Estes Park Police Chief Marcus Colton had tried to stop him. Raiders had been hitting the survivors hard, striking in broad daylight east of the mountains. But Raven was determined to get his Jeep back. Ultimately, it was the promise of adding the Jeep to the police department's fleet that had swayed Colton. There weren't many working vehicles around, and the current department vehicles consisted of a ragtag fleet of rusty dirt bikes, a 1952 Chevy pickup truck, and a VW van.

If Raven ran into trouble, help was just a few minutes away. Mechanic Nelson Purdue, who had quickly become one of the most valuable residents of the town, and Detective Lindsey Plymouth, the feisty redhead who somehow seemed immune to Raven's charms, were just two miles behind. Creek, his four-legged best friend, was riding in the van with them, no doubt with his head hanging out of the window to catch the breeze.

He twisted the throttle to give the engine some extra juice. The speedometer ticked up a few miles per hour, but at forty-five miles an hour, the bike was pretty much topped out. The fifty-year-old Harley struggled up the next hill, the engine rattling and the exhaust pipes coughing.

At the crest of the hill, he spotted his Jeep in the dead center of the highway. It was right where he left it—and so were the bodies of the Sons of Liberty soldiers. Dark blotches marked the road where the soldiers had taken their final breaths. Raven was responsible for several of the bodies, but he didn't feel any regret. The only thing he regretted from his encounters with the SOL was not being able to save Major Nathan Sardetti's life.

He twisted the throttle hard as he recalled General Dan Fenix firing a bullet point blank into the pilot's skull. He gritted his teeth and gave the engine more gas. The bike vibrated violently, but he didn't let up. Nathan wasn't the first soldier Raven hadn't been able to save. In North Korea, during the ill-fated raid that had been the catalyst for this whole mess, he had watched his friend Billy Franks torn apart by enemy fire.

He kept his eyes closed, adrenaline soaking his muscle fibers as he pushed the bike harder. Raven knew how reckless this was. Driving blind down a highway littered with abandoned cars wasn't much different than drinking himself stupid and playing Russian roulette.

For months, Raven had tried so hard to bury the past, to be a better man. But no matter what he did, he always ended up making things worse. If he'd been a little faster, maybe he could have saved Nathan. And if he'd been a little smarter, he wouldn't have made a deal with that snake, Mr. Redford, in the first place. Nile Redford's goons had raided Estes Park's supplies and burned down the Stanley, leaving hundreds of people homeless and hungry. Secretary Montgomery had replaced the supplies, but nothing would bring back the historic hotel.

I'm going to make it right, he promised. *No more stupid mistakes. No more wasting my chances. And no more driving blind, either.*

Raven snapped his eyes open just as the front tire was

about to veer onto the shoulder. He eased off the throttle and moved the handlebars back toward the center lane, careful not to overcorrect and tip the bike. His heart slowed with the speed of the motorcycle, but he could still feel the blood pulsing in his neck.

He parked the bike on the shoulder of the road and secured the kickstand. A black sea of burned forests surrounded him in all directions, save for the single green island where a red tent was pitched, flaps whipping in the wind.

Raven pulled off his helmet and flipped his long hair over his shoulders. Then he unhooked his Bushmaster AR-15 from the bike. He brought up the scope for a quick scan. Charcoaled vehicles lined the highway to the south, and he saw no signs of activity since he'd abandoned the Jeep.

There was only a flicker of motion in the sky where a bald eagle circled over the skeletal black trees. It was the first living thing he had seen since crossing into the dead zone outside of Estes Park. The air detonation had caused fires that had burned through much of the area, leaving behind a wide path of destruction.

The eagle swooped down to pluck something out of the graveyard of pine trees. Raven stopped to watch it soar away with a snake in its talons. As the raptor climbed, the reptile writhed and wiggled, fighting for survival. After a few seconds, it dropped the snake and flew east to search for a less difficult meal.

Raven always tried to find the meaning in Mother Nature, and this time the story seemed crystal clear. The eagle was Redford, and Raven was the snake. He would bite back when the time came.

Just stay frosty for now, Sam.

He stalked toward his Jeep. Most of the windows were shattered, and bullet holes peppered the panels on the passenger side and hood. He replayed the attack in his mind as he approached. Unlike many men who couldn't seem to remember what happened after bullets started flying, Raven remembered combat as vividly as if he were watching a movie.

Raven had climbed out of the ditch after one of the Sons of Liberty soldiers had taken his crossbow. Nathan had gone berserk as soon as they were in the open and had almost gotten both of them killed. Raven had saved Nathan's life by burying one of his hatchets in the chest of a soldier who was about to fire on the pilot. He could still hear the crunch of metal in bone. That blade was now sheathed across Raven's back, but his other hatchet was still lodged in Brown Feather's skull on Prospect Mountain. There hadn't been enough time between disasters to retrieve it.

He shouldered his rifle as he approached the side of the Jeep. Nothing stirred behind the shattered windows, but that didn't mean there wasn't someone or something hiding inside. Raven walked by the passenger side first, peeking in at the ruined leather seat. He had put those in himself, damn it. Most of his gear was gone, lost in the Humvee that Nathan had abandoned at the Sons of Liberty's compound.

But he didn't care about a few bags of gear. He was here for his Jeep. Raven needed a reliable vehicle to track down Redford and then Fenix, and his Jeep was the only ride he trusted.

Raven pulled out his walkie-talkie. "All clear," he reported.

"On our way," Lindsey replied. It was hard to tell over

the channel, but her voice seemed anxious. "Hold your position, Spears."

The putter of an engine sounded in the distance as Raven continued to prowl the area. He stepped over the corpse of a soldier lying on his back; something had already pecked the eyeballs out.

Raven continued to the front of the Jeep, where three bullets had punched into the hood and another two through the windshield. At least that was still intact. He opened the hood to check the damage, even though he already knew the radiator was hit.

The VW van emerged on the hill to the north. The local cops called it The Swag Wagon, and Raven didn't want to think about how many times it had lived up to its name over the years. Olive green and decked out with shag carpet and tie-dye curtains, the van looked like it had dropped out of time warp into modern-day Colorado. The cough of the ancient engine was worse than the old Harley's. Any raiders would have heard it coming from ten miles away. He scanned the southern road to make sure no one had snuck up on them. The way appeared clear, and he went back to checking under the hood of his Jeep.

The faster they got his baby fixed, the quicker he could get on with things. Plus, he'd promised Sandra and Allie he would be back for dinner.

Lindsey parked the van behind the Jeep and hopped out with a shotgun in hand. A short man with a gray mustache emerged from the passenger side. Nelson Purdue rolled up the sleeves of his coveralls, showing off the Navy tattoos on his burly forearms.

Raven let Creek out of the back of the van. The dog licked his hand and barked, his way of scolding Raven for leaving him behind. Then he trotted over and pissed on the side of the road.

"What the hell? You didn't say there were going to be dead guys out here," Nelson said in a stunned voice. He stared at the corpse to the left of the Jeep. Creek joined them and sniffed the body.

"Back," Raven ordered. The dog walked over to him and sat on his hind legs.

Nelson shifted his gaze from Raven to Lindsey. "Is it safe out here?"

"Just focus on the Jeep," Lindsey said. "Let us worry about security."

He spat on the ground. "I ain't no coward. I served in Korea, and I don't want to get my ass shot up again."

Raven smiled at Lindsey as she pumped a shell into her shotgun.

"No one's going to be shooting you," she said.

Nelson avoided looking at any more of the corpses as he grabbed his tool bag from the van. Death was new to most of the residents of Estes Park. Most of them had lived a quiet and peaceful life, sheltered from the world. Even veterans like Nelson were shaken by the aftermath of the North Korean attacks.

"You said it's the radiator?" Nelson asked.

"Yeah, take a look for yourself," Raven said. He stepped away from the propped hood and joined Lindsey on the side of the road. Creek, ears perked and alert, sniffed the air and then nudged up against Raven.

"Can't believe Colton sent me out here to babysit you," Lindsey muttered.

"Did you have something better to do?"

She twisted her lips to the side. "Only about a hundred things. And getting a drink with you isn't included in the list, if you were wondering."

"Is that the hundred and first thing on the list? Because that's not too bad. I can wait."

She pulled a water bottle from her cargo pocket, took a swig, and then offered it to Raven. "This is the only drink you will ever get with me."

"I promise not to tease you too much about being wrong," he said with a smirk.

"You don't give up, do you, Sam?"

"Never."

Lindsey rolled her eyes, but he could see she was trying not to smile. He wondered if she had anyone out there. She never spoke of her family or friends. She just did her job and kept to herself. Maybe she would open up to him eventually, but it wasn't going to be anytime soon. Raven liked the challenge, and there would be plenty of time to work her down until she finally accepted his offer.

For now, they guarded Nelson in silence, no more jokes or half-assed attempts at flirting. Raven and Lindsey both knew how dangerous it was out on the open road.

"Looks like you're right, Raven. The radiator was dinged and the serpentine belt is toast," Nelson reported as he looked up from the engine. "Can't fix it out here. We need a tow truck."

"Well, we don't have one, so do what you can and hurry up," Lindsey said. "I don't want to be out here all day."

She cradled her shotgun and walked away, leaving Raven and Nelson looking at one another.

"She always like that?" Nelson whispered.

Raven chuckled. "Sometimes she's worse."

Nelson walked back to the van to get supplies and Raven followed Lindsey to the shoulder of the road, where she stood looking at the red tent.

"Nathan and I saw that too. Gotta wonder who was camping out there and what happened to 'em."

"They're dead, like everyone else," she said coldly.

Raven didn't reply, but she was probably right. He slung his AR-15 over his back and crouched in front of Creek. "Stay here, buddy. I'll be right back."

Lindsey looked over her shoulder, brows arched. "Where you going?"

"To get my bike."

"You shouldn't have parked it so far away in the first place."

Raven shook his head again. *Damn.* He was used to attitude, but Lindsey was really in a bad mood today.

He burned some energy in the short jog to his bike. The bruises and cuts were finally starting to heal, but he ached like an old man. Still, things could be worse. If it weren't for his sister, the wounds would have probably become infected. She had made a point of cleaning them every day and pulled some strings at the hospital to ensure he had plenty of antibiotic ointment and clean bandages.

Creek's bark stopped Raven mid-stride a few feet from his motorcycle. He turned and brought his hand to shield his eyes from the sun. Lindsey was pointing her shotgun at two figures walking down the highway from the south.

Raven hopped on the bike and started the engine. These were the first people he'd seen out here in days, and his gut told him right away they were dangerous. Lindsey must have had the same thought. She directed Nelson to stay behind the Jeep. Creek stood his ground, snarling.

"Stay back!" Raven shouted as he zipped toward the newcomers.

"Raven, be careful!" Lindsey shouted after him.

He held back a grin—maybe she did care after all. He focused on the two figures that were making their way down the highway, a man and a woman from what he could tell, neither of them armed that he could see. That didn't mean they weren't hiding weapons in their coats. One hundred yards away, he eased off the gas and came to a stop.

"Stay where you are!" he shouted again, unslinging his rifle.

The people held up their hands and did as ordered. He dismounted his bike and put up the kickstand, and then slowly made his way toward the couple. They appeared to be in their mid-forties, although it was hard to tell with the dirt smeared across their faces. Both of them carried large backpacks over filthy coats and brown tactical pants with cargo pockets.

"Who are you, and where are you headed?" Raven demanded.

The man remained where he was and didn't lower his hands. Raven got the sense they had both had guns pointed at them before.

"Estes Park," the man said. "We heard they have food and medicine from an air drop a few days ago. My wife needs insulin."

Raven scrutinized them from his position. The man had a thick beard, cracked lips, and dirt smeared over his wrinkled forehead. His brown eyes were kind, though. Not the hardened eyes of a killer.

"How did you hear about the drop?" Raven asked.

The woman exchanged a glance with her husband. He

13

nodded and she said, "Someone reported it over a radio channel. Is it true?"

Raven bit back the urge to curse. If what she said was correct—and he had no reason to believe it wasn't—then Estes Park was going to see an influx of refugees very soon. He had to get back to town.

"Will you please let us pass?" the man asked.

Raven heaved a sigh. "I'm from Estes Park. If you have a useful skill, like anything with medicine or engineering, they might let you past the barriers."

"I'm an electrical engineer," the man said. He took a step forward, and Raven took a step back. What the hell were the odds the guy would be an engineer?

There was fear in the man's eyes now, and something else—desperation, maybe. Both were equally dangerous.

"What about you, ma'am?" Raven asked.

"I'm a...a nurse."

Raven heard footsteps behind him, but didn't take his eyes off the couple. Lindsey stepped up with her shotgun leveled to stand beside him. Creek was right behind her. He trotted over, not meeting Raven's eyes, knowing damn well he'd broken a command.

"*Sit,*" Raven hissed. The dog sat on his haunches.

"Where are you folks from?" Lindsey asked.

"Laramie," the man replied.

Raven chuckled wryly. "Yeah, right. You're from Wyoming?"

"Yes," the man said, his eyes narrowed. "We left Laramie a few days after the bombs went off."

Raven wiped the grin off his face. It made no sense; Wyoming was to the north. "Why are you coming from the south then?"

"We took 34 first but had to backtrack due to the

raiders," the man replied.

His wife nodded along as he spoke and then picked up the story. "We didn't think we were going to make it. We're the only ones left. The others…"

Raven directed his gaze at her. "Others?"

"They were killed yesterday in an ambush. We lost our dog and my cousin."

"I'm really sorry," Raven said, instinctively reaching down to pat Creek. "We've lost a lot of friends since the bombs, too."

The woman pointed at the road. "What happened to those men?"

"They were part of an Aryan Nation gang called the Sons of Liberty." Raven watched both the man and woman for a reaction, but the name didn't seem to resonate with either of them. He glanced over at Lindsey. "How long until Nelson's finished?"

"He's not sure."

Raven looked at the Jeep, then at Lindsey. "Take these people back to town, Detective, and tell Colton about the broadcast they heard. He needs to know we should expect company."

"Thank you, by God, thank you both!" the man said. The woman beamed and hugged her husband.

"Chief's not going to be happy," Lindsey said.

Raven put on his helmet and jumped back on his bike. Creek ran over, but Raven held up a hand and ignored the Akita's whining.

"I'll be an hour or so behind you, Lindsey," Raven said. "Take care of Creek for me. I've got some unfinished business."

"What? Where the hell are you going?" Lindsey called after him.

Raven put the bike in gear. He didn't have the patience to deal with Lindsey right now and she wouldn't understand where he was going anyway. He had another mission to complete—a promise he'd made Lieutenant Jeff Dupree and his men, who had perished in the ambush by the SOL soldiers. The Marines were all going to get a proper burial even if it took Raven back into harm's way.

— 1 —

Three weeks had passed since the North Korean attack, and winter was drawing close. Snowflakes fluttered down from the heavy clouds overhead. Police Chief Marcus Colton pulled on the reins of his stallion, Obsidian, directing him to the right as they rode up a windy road to the top of Prospect Mountain.

Colton caught a flake on his glove and watched it melt. It was mid-October, late for the first real snow, but he wasn't complaining. The warm fall weather helped keep the morale up among the residents of the quaint tourist town.

Since the North Korean attack, they had lost over one hundred people. Most had died from illness but a few from violence, including two of Colton's police officers. He still couldn't quite believe his best friend, Captain Jake Englewood, was gone. The days after the North Korean attack had been one disaster after another, and the supplies from Secretary Montgomery were already running out.

"Looks like we might get a few inches," said Raven. He was riding a beautiful ivory-colored mare named Willow with a mane the color of sand. Her hooves crunched over the snowy trail. Creek trotted between the two horses, looking up at his handler, then at Colton, and then back again to Raven.

"Good boy," Raven said. He patted the mare's neck

and said, "And you're a good girl, Willow Lady."

Colton looked up the winding trail. At the top of the mountain, newly-minted Estes Park police officer Dale Jackson stood watching over the town from the Crow's Nest. Raven was relieving him today, and Colton was along partly to make sure the two men didn't get in another fight. But that wasn't the only reason the police chief was making this journey.

"Keep your cool up here, Raven. I don't need any more problems today," Colton said.

"You don't trust me?" Raven frowned and glanced over his shoulder. "Dale's a classless asshole, but I got bigger fish to fry these days."

Colton grinned and looked up at the Crow's Nest. The metal fence surrounding the aerial tramway was just overhead. Dale stood behind the barrier with a Bushmaster AR-15. They had someone posted here at all times to watch for refugees and raiders trying to sneak into the town. One flare shot from the Crow's Nest meant trouble, and two flares meant to prepare for a skirmish, or worse—war.

The scent of death filled Colton's nostrils as they approached the rocky outcroppings where Mike Tankala, also known as Brown Feather, had been left to rot.

"Easy, girl," Raven said. He dismounted from his saddle and held up a hand to Colton. "I'll be right back, Chief. Need to grab something."

Raven navigated the rocks and trees underneath the tramway. The red carts still dangled high above, and Colton recalled all too clearly the battle to save Raven's sister and niece from the deranged kidnapper. That fight had cost Jake his life.

"Screw it." Colton swung his leg over the horse to

dismount. His boots crunched into the compact snow. It was coming down in sheets now, the powder sluicing like rain off his warm waterproof coat. He followed Raven through the maze of rocks, cautious not to slip. The corpse of the demon that had terrorized Estes Park was still where it had plummeted from the top of the tramway.

"Maybe we should have buried him after all," Raven said. He perched on a rock next to Brown Feather and reached for the hatchet still wedged in the man's skull.

Colton pulled his scarf up over his nose. The stench was awful. Raven was right—they should have buried or burned the body. Raven wiggled the hatchet from Brown Feather's skull. It snapped free, opening the gaping hole wide enough that Colton could see the maggots feeding on what was left of the dead man's brain.

"The ground's too hard now. I'd burn the bastard if it weren't snowing," Colton said.

Raven wiped the hatchet in the snowy grass. He sheathed the blade over his back and started back to the horses. They walked through the rock field in silence, nothing but the sounds of birds calling out in the distance and the snort of the horses in the chilly wind.

They moved quickly up the final stretch of the trail, winding around to the back of the Crow's Nest. Dale waited for them on the concrete landing, his back resting against the ledge.

"How's it going up here today?" Colton asked.

"Pretty quiet, Chief," Dale replied. He took off his cowboy hat and looked at Raven, but didn't say a word. Raven kept his mouth shut too—probably for the first time in his life, Colton thought.

"Let's hope it stays that way," Colton said. "I was

worried that radio broadcast would have refugees lined up outside Estes Park, but maybe the news didn't spread very far."

"Or maybe there just aren't that many people listening," Dale said with a shrug.

Raven gave a mirthless grin. "You guys should be more paranoid, like me."

Colton waited for Raven to speak his mind, but the tracker, back to his usual tricks, was waiting for someone to ask him about his theory. The man loved to have an audience.

"You got a problem, Sam?" Dale asked. He was a big man, with a beer belly and fat covering old muscle on his arms and chest. Stubble shadowed a jaw that was slowly losing the fight against gravity.

Raven stepped up to the railing. "The raiders out there know we're here. Once they finish hitting the cities to the east, they will come for us. First, they will test our defenses. Probably several times, to see which route into the town is the easiest. We need to add more lookouts and send out scouts to watch all the roads."

Colton followed Raven's gaze out over the Rocky Mountains. The jagged peaks stretched across the horizon like the maw of a shark. It was a natural barrier, but they needed more security.

"I've thought about it," Colton said after a pause. "But I've already got as many men as we can afford stationed at each roadblock—"

"They won't stand a chance if Redford's posse comes back. Or Fenix. He escaped with a small army. He would steamroll his way right into Estes Park, killing everyone that stood in his way. The only way we survive is if we get advance warning."

Colton reached into his coat and pulled out a toothpick, wedging it in his mouth. It was the closest thing to a cigarette he could find now that those were all gone. At least his wife was happy he'd finally quit.

Raven was right again. Estes Park was at risk, and this time nobody was going to fly in to help them. Nathan was gone, and his sister had bigger problems than their little mountain town to worry about. A few roadblocks weren't going to stop the coming storm. He looked out toward Rocky Mountain National Park. Twenty-five years prior, the dam at Lawn Lake had broken and washed away part of the valley. The natural disaster had given him an idea last night when he'd lain in bed awake.

"I haven't run this by Mayor Andrews yet, so keep this between us," Colton said. "I'm not as worried about Trail Ridge Road now that the snow is falling, and I think we can defend the town to the south. I'm more worried about highways 34 and 36."

Raven immediately shook his head. "Don't tell me you're thinking about blowing the dam at Lake Estes."

"We may not have a choice."

"Before we do anything drastic, I think we should send out scouts," Raven said. "Those raiders are coming, Chief, and you know it."

"I got your back," Dale said. He jammed his hat back on his head and pulled the brim down. "Even though you left me on the road that night of the attack…"

Raven laughed. "Brother, you deserved it."

Colton chomped on his toothpick. "A lot has changed since that night. We're all in this together now. Right?"

"I ain't got nothin' against you, Sam," Dale said. "And I'm sorry if I pissed off your sister that night. I wasn't thinkin' right."

Colton almost breathed a sigh of relief. For a moment Raven stood there, glaring at Dale. Then he reached out with a hand and said, "Water under the bridge, my man."

Dale took Raven's hand and shook it. "Yes, sir, it is."

"Great, now that's all cleared up, why don't you go back to town, Dale? Get some rest."

"I'll grab a few hours, then head to the roadblock Don's assigned me to."

Colton offered a smile at the veteran as he mounted his horse. Dale seemed to be enjoying his new duties with the Estes Park Police Department.

"I still don't understand why we're not seeing more refugees," Raven said.

Turning back to the railing, Colton scanned the valley again. So far they had only seen a couple dozen refugees since the attack a month ago. Something—or someone— was stopping them from getting to the isolated mountain town.

He knew it wasn't radiation. Most of the south was safe. It had been dangerous days after the attack, but since there wasn't any fallout—only something called "fission products," he still didn't fully understand—the threat had dissipated quickly. The only other explanation was that someone was killing refugees before they got to Estes Park.

The idea should have made Colton angry, but instead he just felt tired. The signs of violence were etched into the concrete platform, where bullets had chipped the ground and walls three weeks earlier. Jake had lost his life a few feet from where Colton stood now.

He realized that this was the exact spot where he and Raven had shaken hands after the showdown with Brown Feather. So much had happened since then, but one thing was certain—Colton was proud to have Raven on his team.

Raven hefted his crossbow up and glassed the valley to the west while Colton studied the town, which looked like a miniature Christmas village below. He pulled his scarf up around his throat to keep the wind off his neck. The air carried the scent of cedar and burning firewood. Fingers of smoke rose from hundreds of chimneys.

"I can put together a team of scouts," Raven said. "I'd suggest sending some up Trail Ridge Road. We can't write off that side of the town just because of the snow. If Redford decides to come back, I bet that's the way he would come, probably in some old trucks with plows."

Creek trotted over to them, showing his muzzle for the first time since they'd gotten up on the mountain. He clamped down on a dead chipmunk in his mouth.

"Resourceful little guy," Colton said.

Raven chuckled. "He knows the only way he'll get a snack is if he hunts it himself. Some folks down there could learn a thing or two from him."

"No shit." Colton thought of the town administrator, Tom Feagen. The arrogant bastard didn't seem to understand rations, or that food had a shelf life. That was another thing on Colton's to-do list, but having a come-to-Jesus meeting with Mayor Andrews and Administrator Feagen was something he wasn't looking forward to.

"Speaking of Redford, have you given up—"

Raven cut Colton off. "Nope. I'm going after him when the time is right. Then I'm going to find Fenix."

"We've been through this, Raven. You need to let the military take care of Fenix."

Raven glared at Colton, his nostrils flaring with rage. "That Nazi prick is still out there, Chief. He murdered

Nathan, ambushed American soldiers, and killed refugees in cold blood."

"I know."

"So you also know we have to stop him."

"I know we have to protect Estes Park," Colton said. "If Fenix shows up here, I will kill him myself, but I'm not going to hunt him down. That's Secretary Montgomery's job, not mine—and not yours."

Raven lifted both brows. "Have we even heard from her?"

"Not for a week."

Snorting, Raven turned to look back out over the town. "You didn't see what Fenix is capable of."

"I'm sorry," Colton said.

Raven gripped the cold railing and clenched his jaw, closing his eyes clearly to bury the memory of what he'd seen at the Sons of Liberty compound. Raven hadn't spoken much about it, so Colton didn't know the details of what had happened that night. He figured the time would come when Raven would tell him.

Raven loosened his grip, unslung his crossbow, and walked away with Creek on his tail. That was Colton's cue to leave him alone.

"You need anything?" Colton called out after Raven.

"Don't worry about me, Chief. I got everything I need for the night."

"Just watch your back," Colton said.

"I always do." Raven stopped and turned around to face Colton. "Maybe I should be watching Estes Park instead of the roads. Half the town still wants my head on a pike for what Redford did."

"People tend to have short memories when disaster strikes. Sure, you're a scapegoat, but I hardly think any of them are going to come after you. Just look at Dale. You guys are cool, now."

"Yeah, but what about Don? I've seen the way he looks at me."

Colton spat out his toothpick. "I've got Don under control. Only reason he's still on the force is because we need the manpower. Nobody's gonna follow him again if he tries to start anything."

"Well, what about Sandra and Allie?" Raven said. "I've seen the way people look at them, too."

"I won't let anything happen to them," Colton promised. "I should get back. You sure you're good up here?"

"Yeah."

"All right. I'll see you in a few days then," Colton said.

"Days?" Raven scrunched his black brows together. "You planning a trip?"

"You're right, Raven. We can't hold back a major attack. Scouts may give us warning, but what we need are allies."

"What are you suggesting?"

"There's a FEMA camp near Loveland. I'm going to take Detective Plymouth with me to see if we can get some help, maybe contact the sheriff and anybody else who's still out there. If we work together, I believe Estes Park and surrounding communities can stop the raiders before it's too late."

Raven set his crossbow against the railing. "I thought you didn't like politics?"

"I don't."

"Well then, maybe you should let Lindsey do the talking."

Colton cracked a grin. "Maybe. I'm also thinking I

should send someone up to Storm Mountain and try and reach some sort of a deal with John Kirkus and his men."

Raven looked at the ground, trying to hide a scowl.

"I know you don't like 'em, but we may need their help," Colton said.

"Those preppers aren't going to come out of their bunkers up there to help us. You crazy, Chief? They're probably all hunkered down and waiting in the brush with sniper rifles. I sure as hell ain't going up there to ask that cowboy for help. It's way too dangerous."

Colton snorted. "Since when are you scared of danger, Sam? Besides, John Kirkus is a good man, and so are most of the folks that live up there. They just want to be left alone to live out their lives."

"Precisely," Raven said, eyes wide. "They want to be left *alone*."

Colton shrugged slightly. "Maybe you're right about Kirkus being dangerous, but these are desperate times. I think we can work together against a mutual enemy."

This time Raven shrugged.

"Watch over Estes Park while I'm gone, okay?"

"You got it, Chief."

They shook hands firmly, holding each other's gaze for a moment before Colton returned to his horse. He stroked the black mane of the stallion and then climbed into the saddle. Obsidian snorted and set off down the dirt path into town. It would take him almost an hour to get back to the police station. Colton drew in a breath of crisp air and tried to enjoy the quiet afternoon. There was no doubt in his mind it wouldn't last for long.

He looked out over Prospect Mountain, wondering what was happening beyond the peaks. The analog radio transmissions painted a dreary picture. Many of the surrounding cities had fallen into anarchy, including Loveland and Fort Collins. FEMA and the National Guard had set up a camp, and Colton had a hunch that refugees had been heading there instead of Estes Park. That still didn't explain why so few had shown up. Even if most folks ended up in Loveland, they should have seen more than the handful of refugees that had arrived.

Halfway back to town, Obsidian's ears suddenly perked, and the horse halted on the rocky path. Colton reached for the Colt Single Action Army revolver just as a flare shot up toward the clouds. The red light scudded through the falling snow and burst in the clouds, blooming over the Estes Park lake.

Colton twisted in his saddle toward the aerial tramway, his heart pounding. Letting out a breath of icy air, he waited anxiously. One flare was bad, but two...

A second flare never came, and Colton relaxed in the saddle. Whatever Raven had seen up there had only warranted the single shot.

"Let's go, boy," Colton said. He gave Obsidian a nudge. The quiet afternoon had been shattered even sooner than he'd expected. His town might not be facing a full-out attack just yet, but he knew it was only a matter of time before the storm hit.

— 2 —

Secretary of Defense Charlize Montgomery arrived on the outskirts of Charlotte, North Carolina, shortly after noon. She hated leaving Ty behind, but it was too dangerous for him to leave Constellation. Surprisingly, her son had been okay with the trip. He trusted her word that she would be back.

But Charlize was already questioning her decision. The flight from Cape Canaveral had revealed a nation in chaos. Charlotte, like every other city, had been devastated by the events that had followed the North Korean attack. Without electricity, transportation, or communications, most people were starving and scared. Some of them had seized the opportunity. Looters had picked the cities clean. Gangs were thriving in the lawless streets. And everywhere Charlize looked, fires raged. There was no one left to put them out.

Charlize couldn't hear the crack of gunfire over the rotors, but she knew that every few seconds someone, somewhere below, was firing at their former co-workers, neighbors, friends, and perhaps even their own families. The country was tearing itself apart, pitting good people against one another in an effort to survive. And with a pre-attack population of over eight hundred thousand, the survivors in Charlotte would be growing more desperate by the day.

The last food delivery had been a month ago, and the

onset of cool fall weather was helping fuel the fear of what was to come. Charlotte was a Southern city, but the nights would still get cold enough to kill this winter. She recalled a FEMA report about food and water shortages. The report had said that three days after the attack, food shortages would escalate. A week after the attack, hospitals would exhaust their oxygen and medical supplies. Two weeks after the attack, clean water would start to run dry.

They were almost at the month mark now. Without access to drinking water, people would start dying very quickly. Disease would spread like wildfire through the camps and the ravaged cities. Another report—one of the hundreds she'd read since stepping into the role of Secretary of Defense—had stated that only one percent of the population had been prepared for a disaster. Those people had stores of clean water, canned food, and other emergency supplies. Most of them also had enough weapons to protect themselves.

The average American had run out of supplies mere days into the crisis. Fifty million Americans were expected to starve by winter, and another twenty-five million were expected to die from disease and violence.

For the survivors, the only choice was to flee to one of the FEMA camps, but even that was no guarantee of safety. The survival centers, or SCs, couldn't keep up with the demand for food, water, and shelter. It was Charlize's job to fix that problem, but looking out over Charlotte, she had no idea where to start.

We can't save everyone, Charlize. That's what President Diego had said to her before she left for this trip. She realized now more than ever that it was true.

Charlize tightened her restraints as the Sikorsky SH-60

Seahawk dipped. The pilots were flying like they were heading for a combat zone.

Then again, the city did look like a war zone. Burning cars on the street. People smashing storefronts with baseball bats. Families pushing shopping carts stuffed with their belongings down highways.

There was something else that gave Charlize pause—a train with hundreds of train cars backed up on the tracks in the distance.

What if we can get them running again? she thought to herself. It was the same way the American West was built and won. If they could do it again, they might have a chance at moving supplies, and people.

"Almost there," Albert said, snapping her from her thoughts.

They were nearing the airport, and Charlize could see the concourses and air traffic control tower. Not far from one of the tarmacs, the wreckage of a 747 lay where the plane had crashed after losing power. Both wings, sheared off, stuck out of the dirt like arrows.

A patchwork of bright colors covered the grounds beyond the tarmacs like a quilt. Thousands of tents were pitched across the terrain. Charlize unbuckled her harness and moved over to one of the windows. On one side of a fence made from concrete and barbed wire were hundreds of soldiers dressed in green. Trapped on the other side were tens of thousands of civilians. Maybe even a hundred thousand. It looked like a gigantic music festival from this height.

"Good Lord," Albert said. He gestured for Charlize to move back. "Stay away from the windows."

"The sight of a working helicopter might draw more than just eyes, ma'am," said a young corporal named

Marko. "This bird's got a big target on her side."

Charlize sank back into her seat and buckled the harness. More than one transport had been ambushed en route to a survival center. People were furious at the government's failure to protect them.

Albert didn't take his own advice. He lingered near the window, gazing out over the crowds. She knew he was searching for one face in particular. Yesterday, he'd gotten word that his twin sister, Jacqueline, had been entered into the system FEMA was using to track people. She was here in Charlotte, or had at least passed through here a few days ago. After losing Nathan, Charlize was more than willing to help reunite Albert with his sister. Although the big man rarely showed emotion, she knew he'd been going through hell as he waited for some word of his family.

"We've got gunfire at two o'clock," reported one of the pilots. "Everyone hold on."

The bird banked hard to the right. Charlize jerked forward, the straps tightening across her burned skin. Albert moved away from the window to shield her body with his own.

"Take it easy up there!" he yelled.

Charlize tried to look beyond his massive torso. The bird continued to turn sharply, away from the airport.

"I'm getting us the hell out of here," said one of the pilots.

"No, you're not. Turn around," she said over the comms. They had made it this far; she wasn't going to retreat now. Besides, the Seahawk needed a drink, and the nearest safe refueling site was too far to risk it.

The pilot took his time responding. "Your call, ma'am."

"Damn right it is. Take us down."

Albert looked at her. "You're sure about this?"

She dipped her head. "I just wish I was the one flying."

Below, a sea of bodies surged toward the checkpoints around the airport. The North Carolina Department of Emergency Management, the local police, and the National Guard hadn't been anywhere near prepared for an event of this magnitude, and the airport was the best option for a survival center. It wasn't a terrible choice. From the sky, it appeared to be fairly easy to defend, with lots of open space for shelters, including the hangars and concourses.

"Ma'am, we're going to be exposed no matter where we try to cross," said one of the pilots over the headset.

Charlize took a moment to think, and then gestured to the crew chief sitting across the troop hold. "Get on that M240," she said.

The soldier didn't hesitate like the pilots had. He stood and opened the door. Wind rushed into the open space as the man grabbed the big gun.

"Don't shoot anyone unless we're shot at first," Charlize ordered. She was banking on the sight of the gun deterring anyone from taking another shot at the bird.

"Yes, ma'am," said the crew chief.

Albert continued shielding Charlize with his body as the pilots prepared to come in for another pass. Every head seemed to turn in their direction from the fields below. She could picture what they were seeing—a big gray helicopter packed full of soldiers, the perfect target for any asshole that felt the government was responsible for their predicament. It had only taken a few weeks for ordinary, patriotic, tax-paying citizens to turn on their country.

The crew chief raked the barrel of the M240 back across the crowds as the Seahawk flew over the fields and tarmacs, but he didn't fire. The din of angry shouts rose over the thump of the rotors.

"You think she's down there?" Albert asked her.

Charlize reached up and patted his muscular arm. "She is, Big Al, and we're going to find her."

"Thank you, ma'am," he said.

That was Albert—always the southern gentleman, even when people were taking shots at them. God, she was glad to have the big man by her side. Kind-hearted and strong, he was the most loyal person she had ever known, and the closest friend she had left in this world after losing Nathan.

She drew in a shaky breath as a wave of grief crashed over her. This wasn't the time to mourn her brother. Motion snapped her from her thoughts. The door gunner had swiveled the big gun to the right and leaned into the butt like he was preparing to fire. Trusting the instincts she'd honed as a fighter pilot, Charlize ducked just as a bullet punched into the metal side of the chopper.

Albert curled around her. "Protect Secretary Montgomery!"

Soldiers closed in, forming a phalanx of bodies to shield her flesh with their own. Charlize brought her hands up and covered her ears, but it didn't seem to make a difference. The bark of the M240 rang out, the *GAGAGA* echoing through the troop hold. Charlize counted the seconds, calculating the number of rounds the crew chief had just fired into the crowd.

"I think we're clear," he said over the comms. "I think

I got the bastard that shot at us."

You think? Charlize had lost sight of the crowd, but she knew fifty 7.62 mm rounds would have inflicted major damage—especially from this height, where it would be almost impossible to get a clear shot. The other soldiers remained clustered around her as the helicopter wheeled over the camp once more.

"Prepare for landing," one of the pilots said.

Charlize pulled off her headset with a shaky hand and glanced up at Albert. His eyes met hers, his chest heaving like he couldn't breathe.

"It's going to be okay, Al," she said, so quietly that only he could hear her. "I'm fine, and we're going to find Jacqueline."

After a long moment, Albert nodded and straightened up. The other soldiers fell back, revealing the crew chief still gripping the gun. A month ago, the man would have earned himself a court martial for firing into a crowd of civilians, but the country was under martial law now. His only punishment would be living with the guilt of killing innocent civilians in his attempt to hit a single shooter.

The Seahawk landed on the tarmac with a jerk a moment later.

"We're going to find your sister," Charlize repeated to Albert as she stood.

The soldiers jumped out and fanned away from the bird to set up a perimeter on the tarmac. Albert nudged past the crew chief, giving him a furious look before turning and helping Charlize out onto the pavement.

She looked at the crew chief one last time before taking Albert's hand. His glassy, downward gaze told her that he was already regretting his actions.

Once her feet were on the ground, Charlize and Albert

moved quickly toward a group of National Guard soldiers on the tarmac. The sound of the rotors waned in the background, the draft mixing with the cool afternoon breeze at her back. There was only one other helicopter parked here. Most of the military assets that had been hardened against an EMP attack were being kept in secure locations, and this wasn't one of them.

An Army captain stood out front of the dozen soldiers. He came to attention as Charlize approached. Recently shaved and boots polished, the man had clearly prepared for her visit.

"Secretary Montgomery, I'm Captain Zach Harris. Welcome to Survival Center Charlotte." He met her gaze with cool blue eyes behind black-rimmed glasses.

She sized him up quickly, from his neat appearance to the keen intelligence in those eyes, and what she saw tracked with the briefing she'd received that morning. SC Charlotte was overcrowded and undersupplied like many of the survival centers, but from what she had been told, Harris was one of the more prepared and competent captains in charge.

"I'm sorry about the…excitement," Harris continued. "I beefed up security, but it's hard to keep guns out of those crowds. Another reason I told Command it would have been safer to approach at night."

Charlize acknowledged his apology with a curt nod. "We're here now, so let's get to work."

"Absolutely. If you'd follow us, please."

Charlize walked alongside Harris, talking as they moved. Albert fell into step just behind her.

"I'm told you have experience with setting up camps like this one," she said.

"Yes, ma'am, I helped establish civilian centers that

fed and protected tens of thousands of local refugees in both Iraq and Afghanistan."

"Sounds like you're the perfect man for the job. I wish we had soldiers of your caliber for all of the SCs."

Harris smiled with appreciation. "Thank you, ma'am. We're doing the best we can, but no matter how many shipments come in from abroad, there are always more mouths to feed. Security is also a major problem."

A single gunshot cracked in the distance to punctuate his words, but the noise didn't even seem to faze Harris or his soldiers. They continued walking across the tarmac like nothing had happened.

Charlize eyed the guard towers rigged with industrial lights around the perimeter of the tarmac. Soldiers manned M240 machine guns on the towers, protecting the two choppers, but no one fired. Harris's men were disciplined.

The captain led the group toward a dozen warehouses. A Humvee raced by, a soldier in the turret swiveling in their direction as the truck rounded a corner and vanished. Another gunshot sounded. Then three more. The flurry of shots hinted at a battle rather than a random shooting.

"Like I said, violence is a major problem here. I estimate one person is killed every few hours somewhere in the city. Sometimes it's much worse, but it's never better. Outside these walls it's a goddamn warzone with the Latin Kings, MS-13, and other gangs wreaking havoc."

Charlize shook her head. She'd read it all in Harris's reports, of course, but seeing the SC in person was much different from reading about it from the safety of Constellation.

Harris pointed at the hangars. "That's where we're storing our food and supplies. I've got this area on lockdown, and we only fly in at night. That way the locals don't riot. Most of the time, that is."

Charlize examined the massive hangars, previously used to house 747s and other airplanes. Now they were full of life-saving food, medicine, and supplies. Harris indicated a particular hangar ahead with open doors.

"Welcome to the EOC," Harris said as they approached.

She did a quick scan of the emergency operations center. Metal tables were set up inside the open space, and a swarm of people were moving about. A wall of soldiers stood sentry behind a machine gun nest. Laptops in metal cases were spread out over tables, along with maps and stacks of reports. Civilians and military worked side by side on recovery efforts, but Charlize could tell just by looking that the SC was understaffed. If this was one of the better-run centers, then the rest must be in terrible shape.

"How are you selecting who gets in these walls?" she asked Harris.

"We've been screening mostly by occupation. Doctors, scientists, engineers, and soldiers are high priorities."

"And if you don't have any skills?" Albert asked.

"You're shit out of luck," Harris said dryly, his gaze sweeping over Albert.

Charlize had forgotten the two men hadn't been introduced. "This is Capitol Police Officer Albert Randall," she said. Harris shook Albert's hand. "He's looking for his sister. Apparently she was logged into the FEMA system here."

"When was that?" Harris asked.

"Thirty-six hours ago," Albert replied. "She signed up for housing and medicine."

Harris pointed at a group of people near a workstation. "Those people can help you locate her. But I'll warn you, lots of people check in and then move on. If she left the area, it's going to be hard to find her."

"Jacqueline is smart, but she doesn't have any of the skills you mentioned earlier," Albert said.

Harris frowned. "Then chances are we turned her away." He paused, held Albert's gaze, and added, "I'm sorry."

"Let's at least figure out if she's here before we start worrying," Charlize said.

"And if she's not here, I need to know where she went," Albert said.

"I'd consider it a personal favor," Charlize added.

Harris hesitated for a moment. He probably got requests like this all the time from civilians, but if he was upset about Charlize using her position to lean on him, he sure didn't show it.

"If your sister is still in Charlotte, I'll help you find her," he said. "Officer Randall, I'd advise checking in with the FEMA staff first. In the meantime, Secretary Montgomery, why don't you follow me so I can show you more of our facility?"

Albert didn't budge, but Charlize gave him a nod. "I'll be fine. Go see what you can find out about your sister."

"Yes, ma'am, thank you."

Albert hurried away while Charlize followed Harris out of the hangar. While they walked, Harris said, "This is confidential, but we're about to shut the gates. We're bursting at the seams with civilians that we can't take care of. I'm planning to place the entire SC on lockdown."

Charlize saw what he meant by bursting at the seams. The next hangar was packed full of civilians. A thousand cots filled the massive space. The air was thick with the smell of unwashed bodies and despair. Coughing rang out in all directions, and hungry, filthy faces stared at Charlize.

She swallowed hard, trying her best not to stare. But her eyes betrayed her, and she found herself looking at a woman clutching a baby to her breast, trying her best to feed the crying boy to no avail.

"We're almost out of water again," Harris said quietly.

"This is worse than I thought," Charlize said. She looked back to the woman and her child, noting the red blotches on the boy's head. The baby was sick, and as Charlize looked around the room, she saw nurses and doctors dabbing the fevered foreheads of other sick people.

Charlize realized that this wasn't merely civilian housing as she'd originally thought. "This isn't the barracks, is it?"

"No, this is our medical wing," Harris replied. "I thought I'd show you the worst place first."

A young nurse hurried past them, her eyes glassy and hard as though she'd seen too many horrors to process. Someone nearby was vomiting, and the sound of it nearly made Charlize retch.

"This is…dear God. I had no idea things were this bad."

Harris clasped his hands behind his back and jerked his head at the other soldiers. They began to work their way back toward the first hangar, where Albert was checking with the FEMA staff.

"Frankly, I'm just glad you had the guts to come out

here and see for yourself. Most politicians would be hiding in their bunkers instead of—"

Before he could finish his sentence, an air raid siren wailed. Unlike the gunfire earlier, the siren got Harris's attention. His eyes flitted to the balding lieutenant that had been shadowing them.

"Get me a SITREP, Washington," Harris said.

The lieutenant took off running for the hangar just as Albert jogged over with a hand on the grip of his holstered pistol. "What's going on?" he shouted.

"Not sure," Harris said. "But my team won't sound the alarm unless it's a level 2 threat or higher. My guess is someone made it through the barricades or cut through a fence. They won't get far."

The captain led them back to the EOC, standing in the open doorway to look out over the room. The staff and soldiers were scrambling. Lieutenant Washington conferred with a woman wearing a headset, and then ran back over to them a moment later. Charlize felt the tingle of adrenaline, wondering if she had made a major mistake coming here and leaving Ty.

"Sir, we have a riot at gates nineteen and twenty," Washington said. "This one looks coordinated."

Harris cursed. "Stay here, Secretary Montgomery. I'm going to have a look from the rooftop."

"I don't think so," Charlize replied. "I'm coming with you."

Albert snorted, but the man knew better to argue with her.

"Suit yourself," Harris said.

Albert and Charlize followed Harris toward a door across the room. Harris opened it and began jogging up a spiral staircase to the top of the building. Several snipers were already set up, their eyes pressed to their scopes and their barrels angled out over the survival center. Smoke from multiple fires rose across the Charlotte skyline.

"You wanted to see things firsthand," Harris said. He pulled out a pair of binoculars and handed them to Charlize. "Welcome to the front lines of the second Civil War, ma'am."

**

General Dan Fenix slammed down his empty beer can. They were down to their last case, but at least the snow kept it cold. There wasn't much more that he hated in life than a warm brew. Well, besides that bitch Montgomery and the redskin that had murdered a dozen of his men at the Castle.

"Carson, get me another one," Fenix snapped. He tossed the can at the soldier's boots, frustrated, tired, and bored.

Carson put on a stocking cap over his shaved head and then opened the door of the small cabin, letting in a flood of light and chilled air. Fenix squinted and raised a hand to shield his eyes.

The Sons of Liberty, or what was left of them, were camped out on the border of Rocky Mountain National Park. The abandoned cabins were in good shape, considering their age. The Civilian Conservation Corps had built them ninety years ago. Fenix appreciated the craftsmanship those men had put into their work. Once his army was back on their feet, he'd follow in President Roosevelt's footsteps and put together his own New Deal to rebuild Colorado. It was part of his long-term plan—a plan that was currently derailed because of a damn redskin asshole.

Son of a bitch. I still can't believe that fucker killed so many of my men.

Fenix rose up from his chair and walked across the creaky floorboards to the window. Pulling back the curtain, he looked out over the camp. Several soldiers stood guard in white coats, disguised against the snowy landscape. A single pickup truck was parked under a metal shed along with several motorcycles. They'd lost most of the heavy vehicles during the assault.

The camp was isolated, easily defended, and remote. The nearby pines provided plenty of cover from the sky. It was the perfect fallback point for the Sons of Liberty to regroup and plan their next move. For now, Fenix was lying low and waiting for his scouts to come back with intel. For their sakes, they'd better get back with good news before the beer ran out.

Montgomery would come for him, and when she did, he would be ready. Anger seethed just below his skin. The attack on the Castle had set him back considerably. They'd lost two-thirds of their working vehicles, half of their supplies, and fifty men. They were running out of food, and they couldn't risk fires for fear of giving their location away.

Fortunately, Fenix had other camps throughout Colorado and allies across state lines that would come to his aid. That was the benefit of being part of a brotherhood of like-minded patriots. As long as his heart continued to pump blood through his veins, he would fight for the America he believed in—one that aligned with the values of the Aryan Nation.

First, he needed a win—a major victory for morale. His men were hungry and cold. If they sat around here much longer, they might start getting ideas. The worst thing was when men had too much time to think. They needed something to do—something fun—while they waited for the scouts to return.

The door to the cabin opened, and Carson ducked inside with the cold beer. He held it out, but Fenix shook his head.

"Save it for later," he said reluctantly. He ran a hand through his thick hair and then put on his baseball cap. He squeezed past Carson and walked out into the crisp mountain air. Every soldier turned to look at him.

Spreading his arms wide, Fenix yelled, "You boys ready for a hunt?"

"Yes sir!" chanted his men.

A grin spread across Fenix's face. "Whoever brings me the Injun Spears gets all the beer they can drink!"

— 3 —

Raven pushed the binoculars to his eyes. A tide of refugees slowly advanced toward the barricades on Mary's Lake Road. Colton had arrived on his black horse, and several other newly-minted officers were running toward the refugees, including Dale Jackson.

"That's a lot of mouths to feed," Raven muttered. He counted two dozen people on his first pass, and another group was rounding the corner near the junkyard on the southern edge of town.

How the hell did they get past the roadblocks on Highway 7?

Raven answered his own question with a quick glance. The roadblocks were meant to stop vehicles, not foot traffic. It also explained why it had taken them so long to get here. He moved positions on the concrete landing to look for more refugees. For several days the town had been waiting in anticipation for these people, but now that they were at the doorsteps of Estes Park, Raven found himself surprisingly calm. Zooming in with his binos, he watched from above.

"Scouts would have caught these people," Raven grumbled. "Guess I got to do everything myself."

He cursed when he saw another small group emerge to the south. Colton didn't have enough spotters to keep everyone from getting through the security net, and this time an entire crowd had slipped through. At least the

Crow's Nest had an aerial view of most of the valley. If Raven hadn't seen them and sent up a flare, these people would have walked right into town.

He centered his binoculars on the throng of civilians, zooming in on their weapons. Some of the men had rifles slung over their shoulders, while others carried pistols. There were children and women in the group, which told him these weren't raiders. Still, he kept the flare gun at his side, just in case.

Creek looked up and licked a snowflake off his black muzzle. He wagged his tail, anxious to know what was going on.

"Stay put, boy," Raven whispered.

Colton walked over to talk to the group as the rest of the Estes Park police directed their rifles at the newcomers. The refugees kept their weapons lowered or holstered. Raven could imagine what was being said below. These people would have to be vetted, and most of them would be turned away and told to go to the FEMA camp outside of Loveland. Colton had already planned to send armed and mounted escorts down Highway 34 with any refugees they turned away.

It was a good plan, but most of these people weren't going to like it. Chances were they'd already been to the FEMA camp, especially if they were coming from the south like the couple Raven and Lindsey had met on Highway 7 last week.

He lowered his binos. Colton appeared to have the situation under control. Creek followed him toward the railing overlooking Lake Estes and the eastern edge of town. Highways 34 and 36 ran parallel to the lake. There were roadblocks set up in multiple locations along both of them, but Raven could only see the one on the southern side of Lake Estes. Several officers and volunteers manned the post. The rest had all taken off to meet the refugees on Mary's Lake Road.

A single vehicle was chugging along the street. He zoomed in on The Swag Wagon. Behind the wheel of the VW van sat Don Aragon, everyone's favorite police officer. Raven still wasn't sure why Colton hadn't stripped the man of his badge. He was a liability—and an asshole.

Strength in numbers, Raven reminded himself. Still, something felt off. Don suddenly slowed and parked the van. Someone else jumped inside, and Don pushed back down on the gas. Raven couldn't see who Don had picked up, but he could see they weren't in any race to get to the refugees. The van drove slowly, like Don wasn't in any hurry, or was perhaps trying to kill time...but why?

Raven began to cross back to the landing overlooking the south when a distant gunshot halted him mid-stride. He whirled back to the eastern railing. The echo quickly faded away as Raven searched the terrain for any sign of the shooter. He looked toward Lake Estes and glimpsed motion on Highway 36. Bringing his binos back up, he focused on a Toyota pickup truck racing toward the barrier Don had abandoned ten minutes earlier.

A man in the bed of the truck directed a rifle at the roadblock. Raven zoomed in just as the gun cracked to life. Bullets lanced into the car and RV positioned behind the concrete blocks set up at the barrier. Raven flinched as an Estes Park officer was caught in the fire, a round punching through his neck. The man slumped to the ground, dead.

He reached for the strap of his own rifle, but stopped. There was no way he could get a shot from this far out. Instead, he could only watch in horror as the man in the back of the pickup truck continued firing on the roadblock.

A second Estes Park officer popped up to fire. His body slumped a moment later. The third defender fired a shotgun blast that hit the grill of the pickup truck. The driver stopped, but the shooter in the back kept firing. The bullets hit the third Estes Park police officer in the arm, spinning him around. He crashed to the ground and crawled to safety just as another volley of bullets punched into the concrete.

The refugees had been a distraction, Raven realized, just like the burning of the Stanley Hotel. He had to get down there and help fight the raiders.

He put the binos back in their pouch and whistled at Creek. He couldn't just stand by and watch as officers and volunteers were gunned down. After firing off two flares into the sky, Raven grabbed his gear and ran toward his horse. He quickly untied the tether, jumped on the saddle, and gave Willow a nudge.

"Time to fly, girl," he said.

***

Colton craned his neck to the east. The blood pulsing through his veins seemed to ice at the sound of gunshots. He unclipped the walkie-talkie on his ballistic vest and brought it to his lips.

"Margaret, this is Marcus, do you copy, over."

A scratchy response came from the speakers. "Roger, Chief."

"I've got gunfire coming from somewhere near Lake Estes," he replied as calmly as possible. "You hear anything about what's going on out there?"

"Negative, sir, but I'll check. Stand by."

"Where the hell is Don? He should be here by now," Colton said.

"On his way, should be to your location shortly."

Colton looked at the refugees waiting on the other side of the roadblock. There were fourteen of them, dressed in filthy clothing, faces smudged with dirt and ash. Kids, adults, even a couple of elderly folks. None of them said a word. Their hopeful eyes were all focused on Colton.

Detective Lindsey Plymouth looked over at him, waiting for orders. There were a dozen other officers and volunteers already here, including Dale, all of them with their guns pointed at the refugees. A single flinch could start a firefight neither side could afford. Quick decisions were the only thing that was going to keep the people of Estes Park alive now.

"Drop your weapons, all of you," Colton said to the refugees. He nodded at Plymouth. "No one leaves. I'm heading east to see what the hell is going on."

He slung his AR-15 over his back and jogged away from the barricade toward the approaching Volkswagen van. Lindsey disarmed the men and women on the other side of the roadblock with Dale's help. The other volunteer Estes Park officers kept their rifles shouldered.

Colton waved at the van, and Don brought the ancient rust bucket to a stop, sticking his head out the open driver's window. Officer Sam Hines and Detective Tim Ryburn were in the back of the van, their hands resting on their weapons.

"Where you going in such a hurry, Marcus?"

Colton pointed toward Lake Estes. "You didn't hear the gunfire?"

"Gunfire?" Don looked over his shoulder as Colton

jumped into the passenger seat.

"There's some sort of an attack on the east side of town," Colton said. "Punch it!"

Don twisted the wheel to perform a U-turn.

The van screeched back to the north and Colton turned back to the front. Townsfolk were already running down the streets, away from the gunfire.

"We're not ready for this," Colton said. All he could think was how stupid he'd been. He should have listened to Raven and sent out scouts. At least they would have had a warning.

Colton could only pray this wasn't a coordinated attack from the raiders who'd been hitting towns along the foothills of the Rocky Mountains. He would know in a few minutes. In the meantime he pulled out his Colt .45 and thumbed back the hammer. He already knew the weapon was loaded. The AR-15 next to him was also charged with a full magazine of 5.56 mm rounds. If it came down to it, he would use his bare hands to protect his wife and daughter.

"Chief, you got any idea what's going on?" asked Hines.

"Are we under attack?" Ryburn asked.

Colton spat out the open window and then said, "Get ready for a fight." He looked up at the Crow's Nest as they passed Prospect Mountain. Raven was nowhere in sight—another bad sign. If he'd abandoned his post, then they were really in trouble.

"Don, who'd you leave on 36?" Colton asked.

The patrol sergeant stroked his mustache nervously. "John Palmer, Mike Evans, and Alex Stokes." He put his other hand back on the wheel. "You think those refugees on Mary's Lake Road were a distraction to get us to take men off that barricade?"

"My gut says yes." Colton dragged his sleeve across his mouth.

Hines palmed a magazine into his rifle. "That barricade is the last defense before town."

Don's eyes flitted from the road to the rear review mirror, sweat dripping down his forehead.

"You told me to pull everyone else and send 'em to Mary's Lake Road," Don said. After a beat, he added, "Just like you said to send everyone to the Stanley when it was on fire."

Colton could feel Hines and Ryburn looking at him from the back seat, but he didn't reply. Despite counting to ten in his head, and employing every other trick to remain calm, Colton felt like his heart was going to break through his ribcage.

Had he been tricked again?

He cursed under his breath as the van sped through town toward Lake Estes. Another flurry of gunshots rang out in the distance.

"That's automatic fire," Don said.

Rayburn pumped a shell into his shotgun. "Holy shit. Who the hell has automatic weapons?"

Colton waved out the window at a group of civilians standing on the streets, looking east.

"Get inside!" he shouted.

They passed several more groups of people clustered in the middle of Elkhorn Avenue. A crowd had formed in Bond Park, where Mayor Gail Andrews had set up a soup kitchen. She was standing outside town hall with Tom Feagen, both of them looking toward the lake.

Colton grabbed his AR-15 as they sped toward St. Vrain Avenue on the south side of Lake Estes. The roadblock was just ahead. Colton spotted a hand, palm up, lying beyond the barricade. There were casualties, but he couldn't tell yet if it was his men or the raiders.

"Get the medical pack ready," he said. As they rounded the barricade, his heart sank. Evans, Stokes, and Palmer were all sprawled on the road, none of them moving, a river of blood flowing freely from their bullet-riddled bodies.

Colton brought his rifle up and scanned the roads and terrain for any sign of the raiders, but they were long gone. Don eased off the gas and rolled to a stop behind the barriers. The police officers all jumped out and bolted for the fallen officers.

"Oh shit, oh God, oh…" Don was muttering as he knelt beside Evans. Ryburn and Hines rolled Stokes over, revealing four red spots on his chest. A few feet away, Palmer lay on his stomach halfway under one of the cars making up the barricade. The volunteer firefighter jerked as Colton approached.

"Palmer's alive!" Colton shouted. He set his rifle down and helped move the firefighter onto his back to assess his injuries. Both of his arms had been hit, but Colton didn't see any wounds to his chest or head. If they could stop the bleeding, they might be able to save him.

"You're going to be okay," Colton said calmly.

Palmer, eyes wide, coughed. His lips parted, trying to speak. "Headed toward town… Gotta stop 'em, Chief. Don't let 'em hurt my family."

Colton looked over his shoulder. "Don and Ryburn, you hold security. Hines, help me."

The radio on Colton's vest crackled, but he kept his hands on Palmer's right arm, applying pressure to stop the gushing wound. If an artery had been clipped, they wouldn't have long.

"You're going to be okay. Stay calm and breathe," Colton said.

Palmer tried to look down at his body, but he could barely raise his head. "I'm hit bad, aren't I?"

"Just hang on," Colton said. "Hines, where are you with those supplies?"

Hines opened the medical pack and pulled out combat dressings. "Here, Chief."

"You see anyone out there, Don?" Colton asked. His radio squawked again, but his hands were covered in blood.

"Negative," Don said.

"No more gunshots either," Ryburn added. He was panting heavily behind them. "Maybe these guys just did a hit and run."

Another flurry of automatic gunfire sounded in the distance. "Or maybe not," Colton said.

He moved to look in the direction of the gunfire, but Palmer grabbed his arm, gripping it tightly. "My family," he gasped. "Please."

"Watch out," Hines said, nudging next to Colton. He pulled his hands away from one of the bullet holes and allowed Hines to make a tourniquet. Palmer gritted his teeth against the pain, and as soon as they tightened the second tourniquet, Colton and Hines picked him up as gently as possible and carried him to the Volkswagen. Don jumped into the front seat, and Colton piled into the back with the other officers.

Palmer groaned as the van jerked into gear.

"You're going to be just fine," Colton said. "Just stay calm and breathe, man."

Hines and Rayburn continued to apply bandages to

stop the bleeding. Colton wiped his gloves on his tactical pants, smearing blood down the front. He moved between the front and passenger seats for a view of the road.

"You see anything?" Colton asked.

Don shook his head. Scanning the roads, Colton searched for the men responsible, but all he saw were civilians. Men, women, even kids. All terrified. Raiders running wild in Colorado seemed like something out of a graphic novel, not reality. How had it come to this?

Several men on horses emerged on a side street to the right. He recognized two of them as volunteer officers. They were galloping south, probably toward the Mary's Lake Road barrier.

Don took a left, heading for the Estes Park Medical Center. A Volkswagen bug squealed onto the road ahead of them. Margaret was behind the wheel. When she saw Colton, she waved and leaned on the horn.

"Let me out," Colton said. Don slammed on the brakes, and as soon as Colton shut the door, he squealed away. Margaret waved Colton toward the Volkswagen Beetle.

"Get in, Chief. I know where these bastards are."

— 4 —

Raven galloped down the side of Prospect Mountain along a trail that had been used by a construction company. Creek struggled to keep up with the mare, but he was quickly falling behind.

"Faster, girl, faster!" Raven said to Willow, trusting Creek to catch up with them later.

The raiders in the Toyota pickup were driving down Stanley Avenue, firing randomly at civilians, but they didn't seem to be headed toward any of the town's supply caches. Was their plan just to kill as many people as possible?

Raven gripped the reins tighter as he urged the horse to hurry. He lost sight of the truck a moment later. Sitting up in the saddle, he searched for the vehicle. A gunshot rang out, followed by a scream. Raven glimpsed the truck turning back onto Stanley Avenue, leaving behind a body in the middle of the street. It was Doug Moore, a local hunter, his rifle still gripped tightly in his limp hand.

If the truck stayed on Stanley, he would intercept them at Prospect Avenue. Bobbing up and down in the saddle, he strained for a better view of the road. The familiar sight of the Estes Park Medical Center rose in the distance, and Raven's heart clenched.

Now the route the raiders were taking made sense. They weren't after food; they were headed to the hospital. His sister was on the tail end of a double shift. Allie was there, too, hanging out with Teddy.

"Hell no, you don't," Raven said.

He let go of the reins and leaned down to grip Willow around the neck, making himself as aerodynamic as possible. Sucking in the cold wind, he prepared for battle. His ancient ancestors would have done the same thing, riding low against their horses and visualizing victory against their enemies.

Willow finally reached the bottom of Prospect Mountain and galloped out on Landers Street. Instead of taking the road, Raven directed the horse straight through the backyards of several houses. If she ran fast enough, they would come out at Prospect Avenue right before the Toyota pickup truck.

"Faster, faster!" he shouted.

Willow galloped over the fresh powder, icy breaths coming out in poofs as Raven worked her hard. Far behind them, Creek howled. Several civilians were standing in their front yards, looking toward Prospect Avenue.

"Get back inside!" Raven yelled at them.

Halfway down the street, he tucked his boots tightly into the stirrups, sat up, and unslung his AR-15. The rattle of an old engine grew louder as Willow's hooves thundered through the fresh snow. They were almost there.

Reins in one hand and rifle in the other, he nudged Willow's sides. She made a final dash for Prospect Avenue. He was only going to get one chance to stop them. Here he would make his stand. He pulled up on the reins, and Willow slowed to a stop.

Raven quickly dismounted and slapped the horse on her flank. She took off while he ran toward the end of the street where he took a knee behind a boulder, waiting for the perfect shot.

The Toyota screeched around the corner of Stanley Avenue and pulled onto Prospect Avenue. Raven held a breath in his chest and flicked the safety off. From his vantage point, he could see that the driver and passenger both had pistols in their hands. Raven readied his rifle, preparing to fire.

Steady, Sam. Steady...

A man standing in the back of the pickup bed gripped what looked like a mounted M249 SAW. An armored plate surrounded the gun, providing a shield. They all wore bandanas and stocking caps, more like bank robbers than soldiers despite their military hardware.

Raven lined a shot up on the front tire, intending to disable the truck first. He cursed when he saw the armored rim around the tires. He pulled the trigger anyway, firing three rounds into the wheel-well before turning the barrel toward the driver. Several squeezes of the trigger peppered the side of the vehicle and shattered the glass, but the driver powered through the spray, pushing down on the pedal instead of letting up.

"Shit," Raven muttered. He aimed for the man in the bed of the truck next, but the shots streaked into the sky as the raider ducked down. Before Raven could fire again, a barrage of gunfire lanced into the boulder.

The driver finally squealed to a stop, allowing the gunner to fire on Raven. Rounds kicked up the dirt as he bolted for new cover. He nearly lost his footing, but kept upright and slid behind a tree just as rounds lanced into the bark on the other side. Taking in a deep breath, he made a run for another tree.

Several shouts followed.

"There, over there!"

More gunfire riddled the tree Raven had just left, and the driver pushed back down on the gas. Keeping his back against the bark, Raven once again waited for a chance. Down the other end of the street, he glimpsed a flash of white and gray fur.

Creek…stay back…

Raven had to end this—and end it right now. He moved his finger back to the trigger, sucked in a breath, and darted around the tree, firing a round as soon as the sights were lined up on the gunner in the truck.

His aim was true, and the round hit the man in the top of the shoulder, jerking him backward. The next shot hit the M249 and knocked the man over the side of the pickup.

The driver sped away, leaving the injured man in the ditch. Raven strode forward, firing several more shots after the vehicle. The rounds shattered the unprotected back window, glass raining down. The passenger broke away the shards with a pistol and then returned fire at Raven.

He rolled for cover and watched from his belly as the truck tore around Fir Avenue and onto Moccasin Circle Drive. The driver made no effort to slow down. A few seconds later, the truck passed the medical center and kept going.

Relief flooded Raven. Sandra and Allie were safe—at least for now. He pushed himself up, panting, and moved toward the ditch. He expected to find a corpse, but instead stepped up to the side of the road and saw the man standing with a pistol raised.

The bullets slammed into Raven's chest before he could even flinch. The air exploded from his lungs, and

57

he staggered backward a step before crashing onto his butt, losing his rifle in the process.

Gasping for air, he tried to reach over his shoulder for his hatchets, but raising his arms hurt so badly he couldn't bring his hands up. The shooter climbed out of the ditch, blood dripping down the front of his chest. He aimed the pistol in a shaky hand and narrowed his blue eyes at Raven.

"Why?" Raven asked. The pain had overloaded his body, and he felt strangely calm. "Why kill civilians?"

The man pulled his bandana away from his face, revealing a silver goatee and a crooked nose. He kept the gun pointed at Raven and shrugged. "They got in our way."

The rattle of an engine drew his gaze toward the street just as a Volkswagen Beetle turned the corner. Raven could vaguely make out Margaret and Colton behind the windshield.

"Time's up," the man said. He aimed his gun at Raven's head and pulled the trigger. A sharp pain raced through his skull, but the bullet didn't hurt as bad as he thought it would; more of a sting than anything. The impact his skull made with the concrete was worse. It jolted on the hard surface, blinding him momentarily. He blinked and looked up at the fluttering snowflakes, his vision fading in and out as the VW screeched to a stop.

There was another gunshot, and then a shout.

"Raven!"

Red and black swirled across his vision as he began to slip away. The last thing he heard was the ferocious barking of an Akita.

***

Charlize stood in the air traffic control tower overlooking Charlotte Douglas International Airport. One of the windows was completely shattered, allowing in a cool breeze. Visibility was ideal from the tower, with a three-hundred-sixty-degree view of the city, and what she saw chilled her to the core.

There were over two hundred thousand people surrounding the airport. Many of them had come for safety—others had simply come for a meal. But everyone on the other side of the fence was a potential threat. The violence beyond the walls surrounding the survival center was spreading like a wildfire, with desperate civilians fighting to get through the twenty-five gates around the perimeter.

Charlize couldn't help but feel somewhat responsible. Her flyover seemed to have lit the match that set the fire off. Now the entire zone had broken into chaos. Captain Harris was barking orders into a handheld two-way radio. At the edge of the rooftops below, snipers were set up along with their spotters.

"They don't have enough bullets to keep the civilians back if those gates fall, do they?" she asked.

"I've ordered them to only shoot if fired upon, and to retreat if the gates fall and the masses flood in. Our job is to help these people, not kill them."

Honorable, Charlize thought to herself, but she also had to ask the inevitable. "And what happens to the supplies and generators if the gates fall? I've been given strict orders to protect them at all costs."

Harris stroked his jaw. "You'd have me slaughter people to protect these supplies?"

A tense moment followed. She wasn't used to making decisions like this. Dropping bombs and firing missiles at enemies was one thing, but killing American citizens was entirely different. Even if they were shooting at her.

"For now, we have to do everything to ensure the integrity of the perimeter," Charlize said.

"I'm trying, ma'am, but more and more people are coming in from the city by the minute. I've ordered the gates closed, which means they are going to be even more pissed off."

Charlize raised her binoculars at the hangar that had been turned into a makeshift medical center. Fans were set up in the open doorway, blowing air on the civilians. Soldiers had moved into position outside, holding sentry.

"Gang members have been trying to sneak in," Harris said. "If any of them get inside, they could sabotage the gates and open them for their buddies. Then it would really be a bloodbath."

He looked back out the broken window and shook his head. "It would only take one mistake or a rusted pickup truck packed full of explosives to take down those gates. I saw that happen in Afghanistan."

Albert cleared his throat. "Ma'am, I think we should get you back inside the EOC."

"And do what?" Charlize asked. "We're just as safe up here."

Charlize raised her binoculars back toward gates nineteen and twenty. They were just three blocks away from the fences. Close enough that she could hear the civilians on the other side of the fence chanting *We want food! We want food!*

Harris wagged his head and looked over at Charlize. "Everyone's riled up because of the chopper," he said. "I've got to do something, and soon."

"I'm truly sorry," Charlize said. She wasn't sure if she

was completely responsible for the riots, but the flyover had definitely made things worse.

"I'm sorry too, because there's no way in hell I can authorize a mission outside the gates now, sir. I've already lost a lot of good men out there," Harris said to Albert.

"I'll go by myself," Albert replied.

Charlize brought her binos back up and zoomed in on gate nineteen. Two guard towers rose above the fences, and the soldiers inside had angled their machine guns down at the crowd. The civilians pounded against the metal gate, beating it like a drum with fists and feet, chanting and screaming at the top of their lungs.

A gunshot rang out, and the soldier in the turret to the right ducked down. The other guard opened fire on the crowd.

"God damn it," Harris snarled. He brought his radio back to his lips. "Eagle 2, I said no shooting!"

"They were fired upon, sir," came the response.

Harris exhaled a breath and said, "For now tell everyone to hold their fire. We do not want to piss off that hornet's nest."

"Little too late for that," Albert said.

Across the airfield, the crowd surged, slamming into the walls and fences in anger.

Albert stood so close to Charlize that his arm touched her side. "Ma'am," he whispered, "this is madness. I have to find my sister and get her out of here. She's...sick."

Charlize lowered the binos and pivoted away from the ledge. The snipers positioned on the rooftop all kept their barrels angled at the crowd. Albert hadn't told her much about Jacqueline. She'd tried to picture a female version of Big Al and failed.

"What's wrong with her?" she asked.

Before he could answer, another shot rang out in the distance and the roar of the crowd surged into a deafening blast.

The civilians who had made it inside the SC stood on the tarmac below, watching the gates. Many of them had their own weapons. Even if Harris ordered his men to stand down and retreat, it was possible those civilians might put up a fight. One way or another, a major battle seemed inevitable.

If the situation here was indicative of what was happening in the other survival centers, Charlize wasn't sure America had a chance of recovering.

Insanity is doing the same thing over and over and getting the same results, she thought.

"Captain Harris, how did you handle situations like this in Afghanistan?

"Once, we were forced to kill civilians to get a crowd back. It only made things worse. The next day we were hit by two suicide bombers. That's why I'm trying to keep my men from stirring the pot."

Charlize looked down at the hangars. She didn't know how much food was stored there, but it wasn't going to do any good just sitting there. If it meant getting them out of this mess without bloodshed, it'd be worth it.

She looked back out over the city. She couldn't see the railways or the idle trains, but she knew they were out there.

"You know anything about the rail systems in this area?" she asked Harris.

The captain shook his head. "Not really, ma'am. We get most of our supplies from truck convoys. It's dangerous and slow moving, but that's all we have. Why?"

"Curiosity. If we could get the rails running again, we would have a form of transportation that could move a lot of supplies and people without fear of attack. Unlike the highways."

"True, but right now I'm more worried about protecting what we have. Got any ideas?"

She nodded, returning her attention to the hangars below.

"I'm all ears, Secretary Montgomery."

"We need to get the word out that at nightfall we're going to bring a container of food outside the gates to be distributed fairly," Charlize said.

Harris smirked. "One container to feed two hundred thousand people? Ma'am, all due respect but we've hardly got enough for the twenty thousand already inside the gates."

"We have enough for this," Charlize said, keeping her tone polite. "It will buy us time to bring in more supplies—and give us a distraction."

Harris stroked his jaw again. "A distraction?"

"Yes, so Albert and a small team can escape the walls and go look for his sister."

Albert's hopeful gaze flitted to Harris, then back to Charlize. "But what about you, ma'am?" he asked.

"I'll stay here and help Harris get things under control. I want to make sure no one dies for a can of beans."

The radio crackled, and Harris held it up so they could all hear.

"Sir, gate nineteen isn't going to hold much longer."

Harris sighed and pushed the radio to his lips. "Washington, I want you to pull a shipping container of MREs and get it ready to drive out through the gates for distribution. Announce it over the loud speakers. At 1900 hours, we'll use a flatbed to take it outside the gates."

He ended the transmission and shook his head. "I sure hope this is going to work, Madam Secretary."

"Me too," she replied. "Me too."

***

The doors to the emergency room exploded open, and Sergeant Don Aragon and Officer Sam Hines pushed a gurney inside. Sandra Spears recognized the patient immediately by his bushy beard. It was volunteer firefighter John Palmer, one of the nicest and most genuine men in Estes Park. Blood dripped off the edge of the gurney, splattering the floor.

"We've got a gunshot victim!" yelled Doctor Duffy.

"He's been shot four times," Hines announced. "Twice in the left arm and twice in the right."

Palmer, still conscious, groaned as they wheeled him into the emergency room. He tried to raise his head, but Doctor Duffy eased it back down.

"Don't move," Duffy said calmly.

Don and Hines were anything but calm. Both men, pale and covered in blood, were breathing heavily.

"He's lost a lot of blood," Don wheezed. "I tried to stop it. How the hell did those assholes slip past Colton? Damn it, we lost two men today! When Gail hears about this—"

"Now's not the time," Duffy said.

The doctor made a cursory inspection of the wounds, but even from a few paces away, Sandra could tell it was bad. The blanket covering Palmer was soaked.

"We need to get him into surgery," Duffy said. He waved the team into the other room and, working together, the three men helped move Palmer onto the operating table.

Sandra and Jen, the only two nurses on duty, were already dressed in their operating gowns. Gloves and facemasks were in short supply, but with this much blood, Sandra decided to tap into their supplies.

"We've got to get back out there, Doctor," Don said. "The town is under attack."

Hines and Don turned to leave, but Duffy called out after them. "What kind of attack?"

Don paused in the open doorway. Keeping his voice low, he said, "Raiders, Doc. They hit one of our checkpoints. Alex Stokes and Mike Evans are dead, and we saw other bodies on the drive here."

"Better get ready for more injured," Hines said. "This is what happens when we don't have strong leadership."

Duffy looked to Jen. "We need Doctor Newton back here. Go get the word out and then get back here."

She nodded and took off after Hines and Don, while Sandra stepped up to the table with Duffy.

"Just you and me, Spears," he said. She could hear the weary smile in his voice even if she couldn't see it behind his mask.

She worked fast to get a catheter in Palmer's external jugular vein and connect the IV while Duffy grabbed his instruments. By the time she had finished Palmer was losing consciousness, which was probably for the best. The last thing they needed was to have their patient flopping around on the table. She exposed his chest and quickly placed ECG electrodes to monitor his heart rhythm.

"My family," he whispered to Sandra. The veins in Palmer's neck bulged.

"Your family is fine," she replied. She infused a liter of normal saline, talking as she worked. "Please, don't move. Just try to stay calm, okay?"

Palmer's eyelids slowly closed and Duffy cut away Palmer's shirt to expose his wounds. The officers had already applied a tourniquet on both arms, which had probably saved his life, but the work had been done hastily, and Sandra had a feeling Duffy would want new ones.

"Ulnar artery was clipped. I need to resect it, but first let's use the BP cuffs to cut off the blood flow," Duffy said.

She helped remove the old tourniquets. Blood gushed out of the wounds, and Palmer's chest heaved with a ragged breath. Working together, Duffy and Sandra quickly used blood pressure cuffs on both arms, inflating them to cut off the flow almost instantly.

"Does he have a femoral pulse?" Duffy said. He went to work on stitching up the torn artery while Sandra tried to stabilize Palmer. Her gloved fingers, slippery with blood, searched for the pulse in Palmer's femoral artery. Weak, but still palpable at the same rate as the heart monitor's rapid beeping. She tried not to let her thoughts distract her, but she couldn't help picturing Palmer's wife and kids waiting for him to come home.

She knew that feeling all too well these days.

Allie was safe inside the medical center, hanging out as usual in Teddy's room, but Raven was out there in the thick of things. She had a feeling he was hunting down whoever shot Palmer.

Her damn fool brother was always trying to play the hero while she worked to save the innocent people caught in the crossfire. One of these days, he was going to be the one on the table. She had pulled so many double shifts at the hospital she barely had a chance to talk to him about the guilt he was carrying like a millstone around his neck. It was going to get him killed.

She switched to Palmer's right leg and finally found the femoral pulse. It was weak, but it was there. Palmer was a strong man, but even the strongest of men would have a hard time surviving his wounds. If he made it through the surgery, he would still have an uphill battle against infection. She relayed her findings to Duffy as he continued working.

"Looks like his right humerus is shattered, and so is his left radius," Duffy said. "Damn, they really did a number on…"

Duffy's words trailed off as he focused on the task at hand. They worked together methodically, Sandra passing instruments, hanging more IV fluids and monitoring vitals while Duffy repaired the shredded artery and removed a bullet that had lodged in Palmer's bicep. Ten minutes after Palmer had been dropped off, shouts rang out in the hospital lobby. Doctor Newton pushed open the doors to the emergency room, panting as he jogged at the head of a gurney.

"We've got more gunshot victims," he said.

Duffy looked up. "How many?"

"Five." Newton met Sandra's gaze. "One of them is your brother."

"General, we've got company!" Carson shouted, jolting Fenix out of his uneasy doze.

Fenix jumped out of his chair and grabbed for his M4, accidentally knocking the gun over. It clanked on the floor. He threw on his coat, laced his boots, and then plucked the carbine off the ground.

Nearly stumbling in the darkness, he hurried outside the cabin into the chilled night. Carson and a dozen other Sons of Liberty soldiers had been hanging out around a small campfire, but it had been doused recently. The men fanned out across the snow in the waning glow of the dying embers.

Fenix scanned the horizon above the pine trees towering over the buildings, but he didn't see any suspicious lights in the starry sky.

"Where?" he shouted to Carson.

"On the road! It's one of ours!"

Fenix charged across the camp, still emerging from the fog of sleep. They weren't under attack from above, as he'd feared, but a vehicle was making its way down the road. He followed his men toward the checkpoint they'd established at the southern edge of the camp. A dozen soldiers were already there with their rifles raised at a pickup truck rattling down the road. Fenix stopped a few feet behind them, sucking in icy breaths. He was out of shape, and it was getting too damn cold up in these mountains. He needed to step his game up and set an example for his men.

"Is it Butzen?" Fenix asked when he'd caught his breath.

Carson shrugged. "Not sure. Can't see."

The truck puttered down the pass and stopped about one hundred feet from the barriers. Flashlight beams painted the pickup, and Fenix saw two men sitting inside. A dozen rifles followed the rays of light while the soldiers waited for the driver and passenger to identify themselves.

"I thought each team was sent out with three men?" Fenix said, turning to Carson.

"They were, sir. Something must have happened to the third."

A large man dressed in a camo green coat and black stocking cap hopped out of the cab, leaving the engine running. Flashlight beams illuminated the rough face of Aaron Butzen, one of Fenix's most loyal soldiers.

"I sure hope you got Raven's corpse in the bed of that truck," Fenix called out. He stepped around his men and made his way to the checkpoint.

The other soldiers all lowered their weapons and several moved the barrier out of the way. The others returned to finish off their supper, leaving Carson and Fenix with Butzen and his passenger—a man named Rich Blake, if Fenix remembered correctly.

"Where's your other comrade?" Fenix asked.

"Shot," Butzen replied. He hocked spit onto the snow and wiped his mustache with a sleeve.

"And left behind?" Carson said.

Butzen nodded. "Didn't have a choice."

"You better have a good goddamn story and an excuse

for not bringing me Raven Spears," Fenix said. He zipped his collar up to his chin to keep out the chill.

"The roads east of the Rocky Mountains are pretty well blocked off, and Estes Park is dug in with multiple defenses," Butzen said. "We also scoped out that FEMA camp near Loveland and then proceeded to Fort Collins. It was there that Maxon took a sniper bullet to the forehead. Blew his fucking brains out all over the road, man. It was nasty."

"Never saw the shooter," Rich added. He snorted out an icy breath.

"Damn shame," Fenix said a bit too quickly. His mind was already on other matters. "That FEMA camp. How well guarded is it?"

Rich shrugged. "About fifty National Guard soldiers and some wannabe cops. I think we could take 'em. Thing is, that sniper wasn't part of the camp. There are vigilantes in that area. Makes things even more dangerous."

"Estes Park is probably a better target," Butzen said. "We intercepted a few refugees who claimed the town got a government supply drop."

Fenix narrowed his eyes. "That's where Raven Spears lives, isn't it?"

"Yes, sir," Carson replied.

The intel seemed too good to be true. Raven Spears was number one on Fenix's hit list, and if the town had supplies, then it made Estes Park a plum target. He considered putting together a platoon of men to take the town, but before that happened, they needed more information.

Motion in the sky distracted Fenix. He squinted at a light crossing the horizon to the east of the mountains.

Looked like an aircraft, which meant trouble.

"Shit," Fenix muttered. He turned to his men. "Get everyone to their stations!"

***

Static crackled over the radio with a chilling message from the FEMA camp outside Loveland.

"We're under attack by an unknown number of hostiles," reported the operator. "To anyone listening, please stay where you are and do not attempt to approach the gates until we've given the all-clear."

Colton shook his head and leaned over a table covered in maps, sweat beading his forehead despite the chilly room. A drop plopped over the marker for the Lawn Lake trailhead, spreading out like a miniature lake over the paper. That was where this madness had started back in September, when Raven and Colton had set off on the trailhead to find Melissa Stone.

So much had happened in the past month, and Colton feared that society would only continue to crumble. Desperation brought out the worst of humanity. Once again there was a killer loose in Estes Park, the police were down two more officers, and three civilians were dead. To top of it off, Palmer was in critical condition and Raven was unconscious in the hospital. But his people weren't the only ones facing violence. The FEMA camp sounded like it had even bigger problems.

Hurried footfalls rang out in the hallway, and Colton looked up as Lindsey entered the room, Don right behind her.

"Those new refugees are all rounded up and waiting for us to talk to them in Bond Park," Lindsey said.

Don pulled off his cowboy hat. "We got two guards on them. None of them are going anywhere until we figure out what's going on. But you already know my opinion…"

"Mayor Andrews and Administrator Feagen are on their way," Margaret said. She was waiting in the hallway, mascara bleeding down her cheeks from sobbing. Mike Evans had been her brother-in-law.

Colton brought his hands up from the war table and folded his arms across his chest. He was even more convinced now they were going to need allies. People like John Kirkus of Storm Mountain, or Sheriff Gerrard. They were all facing the same enemies these days, and the only way he could see to survive was to join forces.

He exhaled and prepared himself for the conversation with the mayor and her second in command. Things were going to get heated, and Colton was thankful there weren't more officers in the room. Tension and emotions were already running high. Colton had sent almost everyone to guard the roads or look for the raider Raven had injured. At least Raven had taken his advice about wearing a vest; he'd taken three rounds to the chest that afternoon, and bruised ribs were a hell of a lot better than bullet holes.

"Where are we at in our search for the shooter?" Colton asked.

"Last sighting of our suspect was here." Don pointed at the map, and Colton drew a red line from Riverside Drive to Trout Haven Fishing Pond. He dropped his pen and balled his hand in anger.

"How the hell has this guy slipped through our nets?" he growled in a voice that would have given Jake a run for his money. "This bastard's managed to get from the east side of Prospect Mountain all the way to the west."

No one else spoke, and Colton took that as a cue to continue. "We've lost five people today. *Five.* With another five injured."

Margaret hovered in the doorway, wringing her hands, and Lindsey brushed a strand of red hair over an ear without meeting Colton's eyes. Don simply stared at the map. His left hand, still covered in Palmer's blood, was shaking by his side. Colton closed his eyes for a second and then snapped them open. Now was not the time to take out his frustration on anyone else. They were all in this together.

"I'm sorry," Colton said. "I'm just…"

"It's okay, Chief, we're all shaken up. But we will find this guy," Lindsey said. "Just a matter of time."

Colton reached for a toothpick from his chest pocket. "I want him alive. Get the word out to everyone on the search. We need to know who this guy's working with."

Margaret moved away from the doorway as Mayor Andrews and Tom Feagen walked into the room.

"I've got the situation under control," Colton said, trying to cut off the interrogation before it began.

"We've lost three civilians and two officers," Feagen said. "Tell me how you have the situation under control."

Don remained quiet, his eyes flicking from face to face as everyone waited for Colton to answer.

"I told you raiders were coming, Tom. I told everyone. We're lucky they didn't hit us harder. So before you decide to throw me under the bus again, remember that this is just the beginning." He turned on the radio for everyone to listen to the messages coming from the FEMA camp.

"We're not the only ones that are dealing with

violence," Colton said. "We all need to remain calm and united."

Lindsey, hands on her hips, cleared her throat. "He's right. This attack was just the first salvo. They were testing us and trying to strike terror into everyone that lives here. My guess is that the raiders that hit us are also the ones testing the defenses at that FEMA camp. These guys were organized and smart. They're not just some random gang."

Colton nodded, impressed, and then scrutinized the map for a moment, looking at all the arteries leading into and out of the heart of the town.

"We're going to need help protecting Estes Park," Colton said. "That's why I'm heading to the FEMA camp once they give the all clear. If Lindsey is correct, then maybe the soldiers there will see this as an opportunity to join forces and fight against a common enemy. I'm also looking into other allies, like John Kirkus and his group on Storm Mountain."

Gail took off her green-rimmed glasses and rubbed her eyes before putting them back on. "You know I'm not a huge fan of Kirkus, but I'm not opposed to reaching out to him. What I am unsure of is you leaving Estes Park. Sounds dangerous if you ask me, Chief."

"What choice do we have? Those raiders are going to come back, and we're going to need allies to help repel them. If we're careful with our supplies, we will get through the winter. But not if we're attacked again, and especially not if we continue to fight amongst ourselves," Colton said. "I'm going to talk to those refugees, and then I'm going to hunt down the shooter myself. By this time tomorrow, I hope to be on the road to Loveland."

Gail and Feagen both nodded in agreement, to

Colton's surprise. He tapped his knuckles on the desk and walked away from the table before they could question him on anything else.

He motioned for Lindsey and Margaret to follow him out the door, leaving Don behind with the administrators. Colton knew it was dangerous leaving the trio together, but he had a dozen other things to worry about right now besides them stabbing him in the back. Don had been acting shifty all morning, and Colton still intended to confront him about what happened at the roadblock. But not in front of an audience. Stepping through the doorway, he paused in the hallway and turned slightly.

"You're welcome to come with me to the FEMA camp, Mayor Andrews. To see with your own eyes what we're up against this winter," Colton said.

"I'm not sure…" she said.

"Sleep on it, ma'am," he said as he continued into the hallway.

Lindsey and Margaret followed him away from the conference room. Colton handed over his walkie-talkie to Margaret and then stopped outside the door to the police station. She stuck her hands inside her Estes Park Police Department sweatshirt. The hood was over her dark hair, casting a shadow over her features. Colton could see the purple bags under her bloodshot eyes.

"I'm sorry about Mike," he said.

She smiled and pulled the hood down. "I'll be here throughout the night, monitoring things. Be careful out there, Marcus."

"I will. Thanks."

Colton didn't like leaving her to pull a night shift, but they needed her now more than ever. Margaret was the only person that could help Colton communicate with his other officers. She had become the heart of the department.

"Let's go talk to these people," Colton said to Lindsey.

They left town hall and set off across the parking lot to Bond Park, where the refugees sat huddled around two fires burning inside rusted barrels from the junkyard. Colton motioned to the two men guarding them to lower their weapons. He wanted the refugees to feel comfortable while he talked to them. They'd be more likely to tell the truth that way. He was still reeling over the refugee from Laramie that claimed she was a nurse. Turned out she was a receptionist at a car dealership.

"As many of you know, there was a shooting today about the same time you all rolled into town," Colton said, not wasting any time. "Now I'd call that one hell of a coincidence."

The group's apparent leader, a tall woman with the build of a long distance runner, took a few steps forward with her hands in her tight fitting jacket. She was about Mayor Andrews' age, with crow's feet around her eyes and streaks of gray in her hair.

"Sir, I can assure you we had nothing to do with the shootings. We came here for help. The FEMA camp is hell, and we heard you had supplies," she said. "Please, please help us."

The desperation in her voice tugged at Colton's heart, but he'd gotten used to hearing stories like hers from people trying to seek refuge within Estes Park. These people would do almost anything to get in. He'd even had a woman offer her body if Colton would shelter her and her son.

"What's your name?" Colton asked.

"Jennie Song, sir. I'm begging you. Please do not send

us away. We will work. We will do whatever's asked of us. We may not be doctors or engineers, but we can contribute."

She took another step forward and pointed to the man on her left. "Wilbur Smith here is an expert locksmith, and his brother Brett Gilmore knows how to can food."

Colton raised a hand to stop her, but Jennie kept talking. She pointed to a couple standing behind her. "This is Todd and Susan Sanders. Todd is former military and Susan is a police officer. They can both help protect the town."

"I'm a good hunter with a bow and a rifle," Todd said.

Susan nodded firmly. "I'll stand guard all night if I have to. Please, just give us a chance."

Colton could feel Lindsey looking at him from the side, but he kept his focus on Jennie. There was something about her that seemed sincere. He felt the same way about Susan and Todd. He could really use the help securing the borders if they were who they said they were, and while his gut told him these people weren't responsible for the attack, he had no way of being sure. It was too risky.

"Look, I get that you're all capable of helping out, but we hardly have enough resources to get through the winter," Colton said. He pulled his leather gloves out of his pocket and put them on, looking north for a moment at the area the Stanley Hotel had once stood. "I'm sorry, but you can't stay."

A girl no older than ten made her way up next to Jennie. "We can fight," she said. "We can help you get the bad people that shot your friends today."

Jennie put her arm around the young girl, who reminded Colton of his daughter, Risa. Her voice, her innocent yet feisty demeanor, even her frizzled hair in untidy braids under a colorful stocking cap.

"This is Sarah," Jennie said. "She's quite the little firebrand."

Sarah smiled at Colton despite the fact he'd just told her they had to leave Estes Park.

"Her parents were both killed by raiders outside of Loveland. Maybe even the same raiders that killed your folks here," Jennie continued. "Sir, we didn't have anything to do with what happened today—and we can help you stop it from happening again."

Colton kept his eyes on Sarah, picturing his daughter standing there instead. Could he really send her back out there to face the same fate as her parents? Jesus, how had it come to this? His position of power frightened the hell out of him. What if Risa were in this girl's place, and a man like Don stood in Colton's shoes?

He let out a long sigh and flexed his fingers in his gloves. "I need to think about this. In the meantime, you can all stay here for the night. We have fires to keep you warm, and I'll have someone bring you soup."

"Thank you," Jennie said. "You're a good man, Chief Colton."

Colton turned with Lindsey, who greeted his gaze with a smile.

"There's nothing to be happy about, kiddo," he said as they walked away. Pulling out his Colt .45 from the holster, he said, "We have another killer to catch."

***

Raven dreamed of the Cherokee spirit world.

Six small humanoid nature spirits called the Yunwi

Tsunsdi' danced around him under the glow of the moon. Normally the creatures were invisible, but these had decided to show themselves. They were squawking and clicking their tongues at him. Dressed in colorful outfits with necklaces made from bone and beads, the dwarf-like spirits were trying to tell him something. They shook ceremonial turtle shell rattles, the clicking sound echoing through the quiet night.

In his dream, he was sitting cross-legged in a field of prairie grass that seemed to go on and on. The blades whipped back and forth in the breeze under a full moon. The heat of a raging fire warmed his face, the crackle of burning wood joining the din.

Creek sat on his haunches a few feet away, grinning at the Yunwi Tsunsdi'. Willow was there too, but the horse didn't seem interested in the dancing or the camp fire. She kept her head down, chomping on grass near an oak tree.

This wasn't Colorado, but wherever his dream was taking place, he didn't recognize it.

"Where am I?" Raven asked. "What do you want?"

Something furry brushed against Raven's left hand, and he looked over to see a rabbit looking up at him, an all-too-human grin on its face. Not a real rabbit, then, but the trickster Jistu. Raven jerked his hand away. He looked back to the six humanoids with the bodies of children and the faces of adults, still circling around the campfire with their haunted eyes on Raven.

Thunder boomed in the distance, and the clear sky transformed as bulging clouds suddenly rolled across the skyline, bellies swollen with lightning and rain. The largest of the masses began to sculpt itself into a towering figure, and Raven's eyes widened at the sight of a Thunderer, a storm spirit.

The Yunwi Tsunsdi' halted and lowered their turtle shell rattles to stare at the sky. The rabbit trickster followed their gazes, grin folding away and leaving behind two buck teeth.

Raven looked up as the Thunderer took the shape of an ancient Cherokee warrior dressed in a leather loincloth with a plate of bone chainmail over broad chest muscles. Braided hair with feathers intertwined blew in the wind behind the man's stony face. A quiver of arrows and an intricately decorated bow shaft were slung over his wide, muscular shoulders.

"Raven," the warrior boomed, "You must let go of your guilt."

Emerald lightning flashed through the clouds, and thunder answered. A brilliant strike sizzled through the sky and speared into the fields.

Willow looked up from her meal, and Creek nudged up against Raven.

The warrior raised the battle-axe in the sky and yelled, "Your guilt consumes you like a snake consumes a mouse. Inevitably, it will swallow you whole. You must move on to have any hope of surviving the coming storm!"

Apparitions of Billy Franks, Nathan Sardetti, Melissa Stone, Jake Englewood, and the dead officers at the checkpoint near Lake Estes joined the Thunderer in the cloudscape. The raid in North Korea that started it all played out in shades of gray and black, each bullet punctuated by lightning. Raven flinched and looked away, but the faces of the people he'd failed to save still haunted his mind. The warrior in the sky was right—the guilt was eating him alive.

"I can't," Raven finally said. "I don't know how."

The Thunderer reared back, his long hair flowing behind his head like a waterfall. He let out a bellow that shook the clouds. Rain surged, pounding the earth. Jistu and Creek both huddled next to Raven, and the Yunwi Tsunsdi' wiped the water from their wrinkled faces.

"You can't control the destiny of others," the warrior said. "It was their time."

"Why them?" Raven asked. "Why not me? Why do I always survive when better people die?"

Another network of lightning surged across the skyline, and the boom of thunder rattled the muddy ground. The chill rain came down in sheets, pecking his skin like tiny ice needles.

After the thunder faded, the warrior said, "The chain of events on Earth is set in motion by the Creator, and the Creator only. If a life is lost, it is not your fault. If you continue to dwell on the past, you won't survive the future, and the future needs you like a flower needs water."

Raven had learned this lesson long ago, but for some reason it was always hard to accept. He always wanted to control things, to fix them. His blood was a mixture of Sioux and Cherokee, and the Sioux side compelled him to try and change destiny.

But it was time to start listening to the Cherokee side. It was the only way he was going to survive and keep his family safe.

"I hear you, Thunderer," Raven shouted. He pushed himself up, feet squishing in the mud. He looked up and raised his hands into the sky. "The past is the past, and the future is the future. All I can do is continue fighting without guilt, without regret."

"There will be things you can't change, Raven, and before the storm passes you will lose more that you hold dear to your beating heart, but a warrior never gives up fighting. A warrior doesn't look over their back at the bodies they've left behind."

The Thunderer suddenly turned away, and the rain ceased. The clouds melted into a clear, jeweled sky. When Raven looked back to the smoldering fire, the Yunwi Tsunsdi' had vanished. Jistu was gone, too, leaving Raven alone with Creek and Willow.

A distant voice called out in the quiet night. For a moment Raven thought it was the Thunderer again, but this voice was kind and familiar. A woman, calling his name.

The fields and sky vanished, replaced by a bright bank of recessed lights in the ceiling. Raven blinked and then reached down to feel his chest. It hurt to breathe, but he couldn't remember why.

"You're okay, Sam," said the same kind voice.

He tilted his head and found his sister standing next to him. He focused on Sandra's freckled nose as she talked. A tear streaked down her face, and she used her shoulder to brush it away.

"Why do you always have to be so brave?" she asked. "Why do you always have to be the one to get hurt?"

"I'm fine," he muttered, trying to look down at his chest.

"You're lucky as hell, Sam. The ballistic vest stopped the rounds, but you have a bruised rib, a mild concussion, and you lost a hunk of your ear from the bullet that was meant for your brain."

Raven didn't feel any pain when he touched the bandage covering his right ear. That seemed like a small blessing, given the circumstances.

"Did Colton find the guy?" he asked, wincing as he tried to sit up. "That hurt."

Sandra reached out to stop him from moving. "Sit still. You're going to be here for a few days while the swelling goes down."

"Did you find the shooter?"

"Not yet."

Raven sat up farther, gritting his teeth against the pain. "How long have I been out?"

"Ten hours, maybe a bit more," Sandra said.

Memories continued to flood his mind. He recalled the sting of the bullet, the chase on horseback, and Creek's frantic barking. His heart kicked. Raven searched the room for Creek, but the Akita was nowhere in sight.

"Where's my damn dog?"

"Creek is with Allie. You need to rest, Sam." She heaved a long sigh. "You've about used up all of your lives, I think. No more adventures for a few days. You need to heal."

Raven swung his legs over the side of the bed and ripped the IV catheter out of his arm.

"Sam, what are you doing?" Sandra shouted.

"I've already wasted enough time. I have to track this son of a bitch down before he can kill anyone else."

Sandra grabbed Raven's arm, but he pulled away. "Sis, you can't keep trying to turn me into someone I'm not. If there's a fight out there, I need to help. I can't rest. I can't stop."

They locked eyes, and Raven saw the sadness in his sister's gaze. Sandra was a healer at heart, and she didn't want him to get hurt. But this was the reality of the world they were living in now, and it needed people like him.

Fighters. Killers. His dream had shown him the truth, and helped him realize he had to stop harboring the guilt of the past or it would get him killed.

The Thunderer had also said he would lose another loved one.

He had to prove the warrior spirit wrong.

— 6 —

Charlize watched from the observation tower as the gates were sealed all around the survival center. The public address system continued playing the message about a food delivery, keeping the masses at bay for now.

She watched as the final gate was closed three blocks away. A second metal gate was moved into place, creating an additional barrier just in case someone got any bright ideas about driving a pickup truck packed full of explosives forward.

"It's done," Harris said. "Now let's see if your plan works."

They made their way back down into the EOC hangar, where Albert began final preparations for his trip outside the walls. Decked out in matte black body armor, a helmet to match, and night vision goggles, he looked like he was about to raid a terrorist compound. He palmed a magazine into a suppressed M4 and looked through the scope.

Charlize thought about going out there with him, but Albert would never agree to it. Besides, she had Ty waiting for her back at Constellation. She'd promised her boy she would be back within a day or two, max, and she needed to return to Command to report on the state of SC Charlotte. Her job was to keep SCs like this one running. The future of America depended on places like this.

Two Army Rangers, outfitted with same armor as Albert plus additional Beretta M9s, joined them, followed shortly by Captain Harris.

"You ready to rock 'n roll, boss?" one of the men said.

Albert dipped his helmet politely. "When you are, brother."

"Two men isn't much, but it's all I can spare," Harris said. "Make no mistake, though, Corporal Van Dyke and Sergeant Flint are two of my best."

"I appreciate their help," Albert said.

Charlize took a second to scrutinize both men. They were both in their mid-thirties and muscular. Van Dyke sported a mustache, but Flint was clean shaven. They had the confident, capable look of career soldiers. She hoped they were as good as Harris promised.

"Captain Harris!" a voice shouted from across the room.

Lieutenant Washington, the second in command at the SC, hurried over from a table of radio equipment and cleared his throat.

"Tell me you don't have more bad news," Harris said.

Washington stopped and straightened his back. "President Diego is on the horn and wants to speak to Secretary Montgomery."

Charlize frowned. She already knew what the president was going to say, and she really didn't have time for a scolding. A young female officer stood at the radio equipment, holding a receiver. Charlize took it from her and brought it to her lips.

"Hello, Mr. President, this is Charlize."

"I sure hope you have a good explanation for the stunt you pulled this morning. I'm told you created quite the ruckus on your flight in," Diego said.

Charlize glanced over at Albert, who was watching her.

"I'm sorry, sir. We didn't realize things were so bad here, which is another reason I'm glad I came. You put me in charge of the survival centers, and seeing this one up close and personal has been a very sobering experience. I hope that I can use what I've learned here to ensure the other SCs run more smoothly."

"Remind me why you're in North Carolina again? There were other, closer, SCs to tour." His tone sounded frustrated, and although he didn't come straight out and say it, Charlize had a feeling Diego knew she had picked Charlotte for another reason.

Albert continued to hold her gaze. He trusted her, and she wouldn't throw him under the bus.

"I wanted to see with my own eyes how the SCs are doing so I can adapt our strategy," she said firmly. "I heard that Harris was the best, so I came here."

If Diego did know about Albert's sister, he didn't say anything. He simply let out a sigh and said, "Well, I hope you've seen enough, because I need you back at Constellation. We've got a situation."

Situation, Charlize knew, was a codeword for *classified*, so she didn't bother asking for details.

"I'll get in the air as soon as it's safe, sir," Charlize said.

The connection severed, and Charlize walked back to Harris and the other men. Although she was anxious to go home to Ty, she really didn't want to leave Albert behind.

"I've got to return to Command," she said. "Let's get started."

Harris nodded and gestured to Washington, who had returned to another table. Throughout the space, officers, civilians, and foreign aid workers were sitting at their desks and stations. They would be at it through the night, fighting to keep the people here alive for another day.

Charlize had toured much of the SC earlier, and had seen how the civilians lucky enough to make it inside were living. The concourses were set up as mass housing units, and the hangars were too, with heat coming from the generators brought up from southern Florida. Food and water was distributed twice a day, but supplies were running out, and new supplies were difficult to move. The more she thought about it, the more she was convinced that the railways were the way to jumpstart the recovery efforts. They were faster, safer, and more efficient.

Seeing these people living like rats was heartbreaking, and now she was headed back to Constellation where food, water, and everyday comforts like a warm shower were still the norm. But at least she was heading back there with an idea to help these people.

"Ma'am, is everything okay?" Albert asked. "Do you want me to put this mission on hold and return with you to Command?"

She shook her head. "Absolutely not. After you find your sister, I'll send a bird to get you both."

That got Harris's attention. He glared at them, showing his disapproval. "I hope you're not planning another daylight flyby," Harris said.

"I'll have the bird packed full of medical supplies," Charlize said. "Get me a list of what you need the most, and I'll have it delivered for you. Under cover of night, of course."

Harris nodded, but he still didn't seem mollified.

"Do we have a problem?" she asked, one eyebrow raised.

"Permission to speak freely, ma'am?"

Charlize hesitated before granting it with a jerk of her chin.

"I heard about Lieutenant Dupree and his men," Harris began. "Word gets around, even now. I'm a father myself, so I understand why you sent those men to their deaths in the search for your son."

She opened her mouth to interrupt, to somehow justify Dupree's sacrifice, but she couldn't find the words. Harris was right, and the guilt continued to eat at her conscience.

"I'm not happy about sending my boys into a warzone to find a single civilian," Harris continued. "No disrespect meant, Officer Randall, but a lot of people have families out there. We've all lost people, and we'll all lose more."

Albert looked down at his boots, his eyes gleaming with emotion. He'd finally given up wearing his charred and tattered Air Jordans. "Sir, I don't—"

"The trailer is ready to move," Washington announced, interrupting at the perfect moment.

Harris brought his fingers to his lips and let out an impressive whistle that got everyone's attention. Fifty faces roved in his direction.

"All right, everyone, the next few hours are going to be intense, and I want everyone on their A-game. I'm sending out the trailer and armed escorts. Food will be distributed quickly and fairly. I don't want *any* civilians killed. Do I make myself clear?"

Charlize knew that order would be difficult to follow, but fifty voices all echoed in sync. "Yes, sir!"

"Get it done, people," Harris said. He turned back to

Charlize. "Once that trailer is on the move, you'll be back in the air and Albert will sneak out with Van Dyke and Flint. My reservations have been noted, but I respect the chain of command."

"It takes balls to say what you just did. I have a feeling that's why you're so good at your job, Captain. I appreciate your support," Charlize said. "I won't forget what you're doing for us."

"Like I said, I'm a father, I understand why you did what you did using your position." He gestured back toward the open hangar doors.

Charlize nodded and followed the teams. When they got outside, Albert halted. He clenched his jaw and flared his nostrils. "Thank you, ma'am, for helping me with this," he said once his emotions were under control.

She put a hand on his shoulder pad. "You just get back safely, or I'll hunt you down myself."

That got a chuckle from Albert. "Will do, ma'am. Tell Ty I'll be ready for my Star Wars monopoly rematch when I get back."

This time Charlize was the one to laugh. "You always let him win," she said.

"Time to move out, sir," Flint said, jerking his chin.

Albert nodded one more time at Charlize, and then reached out to shake her hand. She embraced him with a hug instead.

"Be careful," she whispered.

"You too."

As soon as they pulled apart, Albert took off running to the south with Van Dyke and Flint. She watched them for a few minutes before Harris directed her to the east, where her chopper was waiting.

"Thank you for the hospitality, Captain," she said as

they walked. "I'll make sure you get all the support we can manage. Continue to hold the SC until then."

"I'll give it my all, ma'am," Harris said. "Good luck."

She caught a hint of anger in his voice, but she understood the source now and she didn't blame him. Her trip hadn't gone as planned, but it had taught her how terrible things were outside. She would return to Constellation with a new appreciation for the work they had ahead of them, and with some ideas on how to strengthen the other SCs across the country. They were going to rebuild their country the same way they built it in the first place—using the railways.

A few minutes later, she was inside the Seahawk and climbing into the sky. The soldiers that had accompanied her from Constellation held their weapons at the ready, ready to give their lives for her own. Charlize rested her head on the bulkhead as they climbed.

"There's the transport," one of the soldiers in the troop hold said.

Charlize twisted to look out the window. A semi with a shipping container on the bed drove toward the gates on the west side of the airport. The majority of the crowd had clustered in front of those fences. Albert and his comrades were moving across the SC in the opposite direction.

Flying dark, the pilots pulled away from the SC. Charlize lost sight of Albert. She looked for him again as they banked over the airport, but it was too dark. It didn't feel right to leave him behind, not when he'd been by her side every step of the way since the night the bombs fell. She pressed a palm against the window and prayed he would find his sister soon.

***

Albert Randall never would have said so out loud, but he felt relieved that Charlize was heading back to Constellation. He never balked at his duty, but protecting her had come at a high cost. Most of his family had perished in the nuclear explosion in D.C., but as much as he blamed himself for leaving them to protect Charlize, he knew that nothing he could have done would have saved them even if he had tried. He would have ended up dead along with them.

Fate was a weird thing. Albert found himself thinking about it more and more as the pain of his loss cut deeper. Duty before self was something he'd learned a long time ago, but it was hard to stomach when your family was at risk.

That's why he was here in Charlotte, on a mission to find his twin sister. A woman he hadn't spoken to in almost a year. Or was it longer than that? Before the North Korean attack, Albert had been consumed with work. When he'd been home, he had tried to be a good husband and father, but now he would never have the chance to make up for all those missed dinners and skipped recitals. It was just him and Jackie now.

His relationship with Jacqueline had always been strained. Albert had chosen the high road: sports, academics, and duty to country and family. His sister, on the other hand...well, he hoped that the end of the world had finally put the fear of God into her, or the fear of something, at least. He didn't really care what it was as long as she believed in something, especially herself.

Albert was determined to save the only family he had left—whether she liked it or not.

He shook his mind clear and followed Flint and Van Dyke to gate ten. The world had taken on an eerie green glow. The night vision optics had taken some time to get used to, but it was better than nothing. From the sounds of it, the goggles were hard to come by, most of them having been fried when the grid went down. The pair on his helmet were French, delivered in a shipment a few days earlier.

Glancing up, he saw a carpet of clouds rolling across the sky, blocking out the moon and stars. That was good. As soon as they left the safety of the center, they would have targets on their backs. He focused on the barbed wire fences that separated the airport from the fields beyond. Where there had been thousands of people earlier that day, there was now only trash and a sea of empty tents. The sound of the civilians was distant, the masses drawn away by the promise of a food drop a mile to the west.

So far, Charlize's plan was working. Her Seahawk was already gone, the distant thump of the rotors hardly audible over the shouts of hundreds of thousands of civilians. Albert could feel them moving toward the food like a stampede of starving animals. Nothing good happened when starving humans armed with high-powered rifles were squeezed into a small area. Humans, in his mind, were good by nature, but even a good dog would bite when starved. And while he was glad Captain Harris had ordered his soldiers to only fire if absolutely necessary, he had his doubts the food drop was going to be peaceful.

Heck, Albert wasn't sure anything they could do at this point would ensure peace. People were desperate, resorting to actions they would never have dreamed of months before. That's what life had come to in the cities—good people doing bad things to survive in extraordinarily difficult times. He could only pray his sister was still alive.

I'm coming, Jackie. I'm going to find you and get you out of this mess.

Albert paced as they waited in front of the gates. The snipers in the towers flanking the gate did a final scan of the area. From his vantage point, Albert didn't see anything moving out there. He thought back to the map they'd memorized, and tried to orient himself with the terrain.

The Carolinas Aviation Museum stood on the other side of the tarmac, and beyond that was a small forest they would have to cross before gaining access to a residential area. Whole blocks of houses were already burned to the ground, leaving behind charred buildings and rafters. Downtown was another two miles beyond that, approximately, and it was in even worse shape, apparently. There were thousands of threats standing between him and the apartment building his sister called home.

"All clear," Flint said in a gruff voice. "I'll take point. Officer Randall, you stay behind me. Van Dyke, you got rear guard."

The chain-link fence creaked open on wheels that crunched over the concrete, revealing a second gate, this one made of pure metal. It towered fifteen feet and took five men to push open. The soldiers put their shoulders into the steel and pushed it open manually to reveal the dark terrain beyond.

Van Dyke shouldered his carbine and tilted his helmet at Albert, a cue to start walking. Albert followed Flint through the open gate and across the tarmac separating them from the fields. Setting off on foot seemed like a terrible idea, but zipping out of here in a Humvee or helicopter would have been even worse. They wouldn't have made it far before gunshots took them down. The three men bolted across the tarmac, moving quickly toward the grassy fields. Albert slowed when he saw the outline of a civilian lying in the grass, unmoving. He gestured toward the fallen man, but Flint shook his head and flashed a signal to the tree line.

Van Dyke put a hand on Albert's back and whispered, "Nothing we can do for that guy. Hopefully he's just drunk."

Albert had moved another few steps and was close enough to see the guy wasn't intoxicated. Someone had bashed the left side of his skull in, and the grass was matted red.

They continued moving, and within minutes they had crossed the tarmac and were moving into the fields. Trash, feces, and discarded belongings littered the grass where the desperate civilians had camped out just hours earlier. Flint kept to the east side, cautious to stay out of sight. Anyone might be hiding here, and one wrong move could end with them all dead.

These men were risking their lives to accompany Albert, and he didn't even know their first names.

A voice stopped Albert mid-stride. "Hey, who's there?"

Flint balled his hand and crouched down, Albert following suit. Van Dyke took a knee right behind him and pointed to a tent ahead. The noise of a zipper opening sounded, and a face peered out from the tent. The moon emerged overhead, spreading a faint glow over the encampment. Albert could see the ghostly shape of a thin man with curly hair. He didn't appear to be armed, and Flint waved the small team onward.

"Is someone out there?" The man coughed into a sleeve. "Gloria, is that you?"

The man crawled through the opening into the grass, coughing louder. Flint stood and began to move before he could spot their position.

"Hey, I can hear you!" he called out to them. "Wait up. I need help!"

Albert ran after Flint, and Van Dyke kept pace behind. They raced around the edge of the encampment. They had almost cleared the final tent when a new voice called out.

"Soldiers! There are soldiers coming!"

Albert risked a glance over his shoulder as more tents were unzipped. Several figures appeared, and in the green hue of his optics, he saw one of them had a rifle.

"Don't let them get away!" yelled another man.

Albert ran as fast as he could, but he wasn't in nearly as good a shape as when he'd played college football. Flint and Van Dyke were much faster, and within a few moments Albert was starting to fall behind. Looking over his shoulder didn't help. He nearly tripped over a bag abandoned in the grass. When he looked to the forested area ahead, both of the soldiers were already slipping into the safety of the trees.

A shotgun blast boomed behind them, and the spray peppered the trees.

"Move it, Randall!" Van Dyke yelled.

The corporal knelt next to a tree and brought the scope of his carbine to his NVGs while Albert jumped over a fallen tree.

Pop. Pop. Pop.

The suppressed fire whizzed past him, away from the woods. A scream rang out, followed by the sound of a body hitting the dirt. A female voice began shouting profanities.

"Hostile down," Van Dyke said quietly. He brought up his rifle and stood, scanning the encampment one more time before following Albert into the forest.

And just like that, the first blood of the night soaked into the soil. Shock gripped Albert, freezing him in place. They had only left the camp a few minutes ago, and a life had already been taken.

"You bastards!" the woman screeched. "You're supposed to help us!"

The words stung Albert like a bee. She was right, and it was all beginning to sink in, right now, right here in the woods. He was a firm believer the government had a duty to protect its citizens, but the combination of the EMP and nuclear attack had crippled the United States beyond repair. People tended to forget he was there listening, despite his massive bulk, and they said things he wasn't supposed to hear. He'd heard plenty while Charlize was being briefed. There was no coming back from this; there was only surviving by any means possible.

"Let's move, Randall," Van Dyke said.

Albert pushed onward through the underbrush, more determined than ever to find his sister. He'd drag Jacqueline kicking and screaming from this madness if he had to.

He picked up his pace as he followed the two soldiers into the inky green darkness, doing his best not to make any noise. Through the fence of limbs and branches, he glimpsed the residential area. They were almost there.

A shot rang out in the distance, but Albert couldn't tell where it was coming from. Van Dyke and Flint halted at the edge of the forest, crouching down and waiting. He leaned against a tree when he got to them, chest heaving, sweat dripping down his forehead.

The sporadic gunfire evened into a steady flurry of different calibers.

"That's coming from the other side of the camp," Albert said, still trying to catch his breath.

"Goddamn," Flint said. He drew up and walked a step back into the forest as if a magnet were pulling him toward the airport.

"The food shipment must have been hit," Van Dyke said. "Maybe we should go back and help."

Albert hesitated. They were almost a quarter of the way to the city, and he needed these soldiers to help him get the rest of the way there. Flint and Van Dyke exchanged a few hushed words while Albert stood guard, his heart beating in sync with the gun battle.

"Harris gave us orders," Flint said.

"Shit don't work the same way it used to, Sarge," Van Dyke replied.

Flint moved over closer to Van Dyke and said something that Albert couldn't make out. Van Dyke seemed to slouch at whatever Flint had said, the fight gone out of him.

"Come on, let's keep moving," Flint said.

Van Dyke glared up at Albert for a long second before squeezing past.

— 7 —

"Got room for a third?" came a familiar voice.

The words sent a chill up Colton's spine. He shut the lift gate to the 1952 Chevy pickup truck and turned to see if it was really Raven.

It was.

Standing in the moonlight, a hand on his side, Raven flashed a wide pearly grin. Creek came trotting around the side of town hall, right behind his handler, ears and tail up.

"Uh, aren't you supposed to be in the hospital?" Lindsey asked. She dropped her backpack into the bed of the truck and joined Colton with her arms folded across her chest.

"The guy I shot should be in the hospital—or six feet under—but he's not, and I'm not lying around waiting for him to get caught," Raven said.

His wide smile didn't deceive Colton—he was injured, and injured bad. A man didn't take three bullets to a vest, have part of an ear blown off, and get knocked unconscious, and then expect to be walking less than half a day later.

Most men, anyway, Colton thought. Then again, Raven had proven to be one tough son of a bitch. He'd been stabbed, beaten, and shot in the past month. Colton wasn't sure whether to be impressed or worried.

"What did the doc *really* say about you getting out of

bed?" Colton asked, knowing he wasn't going to get a straight answer.

"Said I'm good to go and that I should be out here tracking this asshole down," Raven said. "I just need my gear. What'd you do with it?"

Colton could see by the determined look in Raven's dark eyes that there was no arguing with the man. Lindsey, however, wasn't done with her interrogation yet.

"And what about your sister?" she asked. "Did she say it was okay to come out here with us?"

"No." Raven's voice was firm and a little cold.

"You lost the top of your ear, for God's sake," Colton said, examining the side of Raven's head.

Raven turned away and touched the bandage. "I said I'm good, man."

"Okay, Sam, whatever you say," Colton said. He picked another backpack up and slung it into the truck. "But you're still not coming with. You need to sit this one out. We can find this guy on our own."

Raven's grin vanished in an instant. He staggered forward, his hand falling away from his tactical vest. "Bullshit. You haven't caught him yet. You need my help before he kills anyone else. You're dealing with a pro, Marcus."

Lindsey and Colton exchanged a glance.

"You think this guy is a professional?" Lindsey asked.

Colton heaved a long and deep sigh. He'd hoped their chase was just lucky, but Raven was probably right. The man had managed to avoid every officer and volunteer looking for him in Estes Park, despite being wounded.

"Fine, Sam. Grab your gear and meet me back here in five minutes. It's in your locker inside the station," Colton said.

A hint of a smile returned on Raven's face as he hurried off toward the back entrance of the police station. Creek stayed put, watching Lindsey and Colton finish packing the truck while Raven retrieved his weapons.

"He better not slow us down," Colton said.

Lindsey shrugged. "We're talking about Raven, Chief."

Colton started the pickup truck. The back door to the police station swung open and Raven walked out wearing a black coat, leather gloves, boots, and a stocking cap over his long hair. Instead of a rifle, he held his crossbow, and a pistol was holstered at his side.

Lindsey jumped into the passenger seat, and Raven climbed into the back with Creek. The truck rolled out of the parking lot, engine rattling and rusted underbody scraping the cement. The noise attracted the attention of the refugees in Bond Park. Most of the people were huddling around the fires in the old barrels from the junkyard. A few them shared bowls of soup provided by volunteers working in coordination with his officers. Jennie and the orphan girl, Sarah both stood and watched the truck drive past.

For now, these people were safe, but he still wasn't sure what he was going to do with them. He glanced in the rearview mirror at Raven, who sat with his back to the cab, stroking Creek's head. It was just after nine o'clock and the temperature had dropped into the forties. The ground would freeze tonight. The refugees would need shelter from the cold.

Lindsey loaded her weapons while Colton drove down the empty streets. Most of the residents were inside their houses, keeping warm, but everyone that knew how to use a weapon had been assigned a roadblock or critical facility to protect. After today's attack, Colton wasn't taking any chances. Until he managed to find some allies, he had conscripted every able man, woman, and kid old enough to fire a gun into service.

They were coming up on one of those roadblocks now. The first person Colton saw was Dale Jackson, and to his right was Heath Minor, the eighteen-year-old star quarterback of the high school football team. Colton knew Heath's dad and had even gone hunting with them a few times. He eased off the gas and held a hand up as he passed. Dale nodded, but Heath simply stared at the truck, a dumbfounded look in his eyes—the look of a boy thrown into war when he should have been off chasing girls and drinking beer.

After steering through the gap in the concrete barriers, Colton pushed down on the gas and sped out toward the Rocky Mountains. Behind them, Dale and Heath shoved the concrete barriers back into place and resumed their positions.

Lindsey finished her gear check and looked over. "Have you thought any more about those refugees, Chief?"

"I haven't decided yet," he replied. "Let's focus on finding this guy first."

She fidgeted uneasily in the old seat. He could tell she had something to say, but she remained silent, waiting for him to ask.

"Let's hear it, kiddo."

"I don't like it when you call me that, Chief. Detective Plymouth. Or Lindz, if you want. That's what my friends call me."

"I'm sorry, sometimes I just think of you as a…"

"Kid?" Lindsey shrugged. "Yeah, I get it, but hopefully I've proved that I can take care of myself by now." She shook her head and looked out the window.

"You have, but I don't want to see anything happen to you. I'm not sure I could forgive myself."

"Like I said, I can take care of myself."

Colton didn't reply. Lindsey didn't often talk about friends or family back home. Her life before arriving in Estes Park was a closed book, but he hoped that one day she would open up. *If we live that long*, he thought wryly.

Colton pulled out a toothpick from his vest and wedged it into the side of his mouth. They were coming up on the entrance to the park. The headlights hit the ranger station a moment later. As the truck climbed up toward Trail Ridge Road, the drab landscape became a white winter wonderland. Pine trees were coated with snow, their branches weighed down. The road turned to reveal a view of the Rocky Mountains, their snow-brushed peaks glowing under the light of the moon.

"Over there," Lindsey said, pointing at a Volkswagen Beetle.

Colton steered to the right and parked behind the car in the lot behind Beaver Meadows. A herd of elk were grazing nearby. As Colton and Lindsey approached, they all looked up, ears perking.

Colton flipped on his flashlight and pulled out his map. He flattened it on the hood of the truck.

"Officer Hines and Tim Beedie are on this trail to the northeast. There are other patrols combing the resort area just in case our suspect went that way," Colton said, pointing. "We'll take this trail to the southwest."

Raven nodded and whistled at Creek. "Time's wasting, Chief," he said. "Let's go."

Lindsey followed Raven across the gravel road and into the snowy field. Colton grabbed his gear and then jogged to catch up, gripped by a moment of déjà vu. A month ago, the night everything had gone to hell, they'd set off to find Melissa Stone. Brown Feather had been watching them then, and Colton felt that same sensation of eyes on his back now. He turned, raking his beam over the area, but all he saw was skeletal trees and snow.

***

Charlize arrived at Constellation shortly before midnight. She hurried through the hallways of the underwater bunker, guided by the pair of armed guards that had accompanied her on the flight. It felt odd not having Albert with her.

"I won't be long," she said to the two soldiers. "Please tell General Thor I'm on my way."

They nodded and continued walking down the white hallway, boots clicking on the tiled floor. She unlocked the door to her quarters and walked into the carpeted living space furnished with a small dining room table and love seat. A kitchenette with a sink, stove, and dorm-sized fridge took up the western corner of the room.

This was home now, and would be for the foreseeable future. It sure as hell beat the conditions back at the airport in Charlotte. Many of those people would have literally killed for a place like this.

She crossed the room and opened the door to the only bedroom. To her surprise, Ty was wide awake, sitting in his wheelchair between the two twin beds. He was reading a book called *Gates of Fire* by Stephen Pressfield so intently that he didn't notice her presence at first. She knew President Diego was waiting on her, but she hadn't seen her son this peaceful for a very long time, and took a moment to watch him.

He finally looked up and said, "Mom! When did you get back?"

"You're supposed to be in bed, mister," Charlize said. She stepped into the room and walked over to Ty.

He closed his book and smiled, his cheeks dimpling. "I wanted to stay up until you got home. An officer came by earlier saying you were on your way."

"I'm sorry I was gone for so long, but Albert and I had an important mission."

"It's okay." Ty shrugged and placed his book on his lap. "It's just…every time I fall asleep, I think I'm back there. With *him*."

She sat on the bed in front of him and took his hands. They felt so small in hers.

"You're safe now, and I'm never going to let anyone hurt you again," she said soothingly. "He will pay for what he's done." She didn't like saying the so-called general's name out loud, but they both knew who she was talking about.

Ty bowed his head, shaggy hair falling over his forehead. "When do I get to see Emma and Micah? Are they okay?"

Charlize didn't know how to answer the question. The kids that had been rescued from the Castle had been taken to various locations, and she wasn't even sure where Ty's friends had ended up.

"I'll find out where they are, okay?" she said.

Ty nodded and looked up. "I really miss Uncle Nathan."

"Me, too. And I promise we're going to punish the man that took him from us."

Sniffling, Ty reached up and wiped his nose. "You

better, Mom. I told General Fenix you would come for him. I told him he would be sorry."

"We don't call him that," Charlize said. "He doesn't deserve the respect of a title. And he will be, soon." She helped Ty into bed and pulled the sheets up over his thin legs. He tugged them up over his chest and smiled.

"I missed you."

"I missed you too. Now go to sleep, sweetie."

"Aren't you going to bed?"

"I've got some more work to do, but I promise I won't be gone too long."

Ty's lips moved, twisting into a frown, but he didn't reply.

Feeling guilty, she said, "I'll stay with you until you're asleep."

Charlize ran her hand through his hair. His breathing slowed and his eyelids fluttered until they were closed. Within a couple of minutes, Ty was fast asleep. She tucked the sheets in tightly and then left the room, slowly shutting the door behind her.

By the time she arrived at Central Command, the cabinet meeting was already underway. She paused in the main chamber, unsure which conference room she needed to find. The multilevel room was set up like an auditorium. Officers and staff were working on each level and at every station to monitor events across the country and the world.

Colonel Mark Raymond stood at the bottom of the stairs dividing the two levels of operations. The tall officer with a bulbous nose and thick brown hair was one of her favorites at Constellation.

"Follow me please, ma'am," Raymond said. He led her across the bottom floor, around several workstations, and past the war table set up in the center of the space. He opened the door to one of the conference rooms and gestured politely for her to go inside.

"Colonel, will you get me a map showing the rail system in the United States?" she asked.

"Certainly."

"Thank you." She walked inside the room and did a quick scan. Secretary of State Lane Hudgins, a forty-five-year-old former tech CEO, sat at the end of the table next to Secretary of Health and Human Services Doctor Ellen Price, a stern-faced woman with shoulder-length brown hair. Price's presence told Charlize something was up at the survival centers.

"Ah, Secretary Montgomery, welcome home," President Diego said as she entered. He stood and pointed toward the seat next to General Thor.

She took a seat between General Thor and the new National Security Advisor, Duane Ibsen. The advisor looked up from his briefing to acknowledge her.

"Good to see you safely returned from Charlotte. I presume you will have a full report shortly," Diego said.

"Yes, sir, I do. But don't let me interrupt." She wanted to wait for the maps before she gave her briefing.

"Please turn to page nineteen, Secretary Montgomery," Thor said.

Charlize opened the folder marked *Classified* in front of her. The usual charts of resources and memos about the survival centers filled the pages. There were death estimates put together by actuarial scientists that had previously worked for insurance companies and were now crunching the numbers of how many people would die by year's end. She found page nineteen, opening it to see aerial images of North Korea.

Thor cleared his throat and continued the briefing. "Our allies in the Pacific are on high alert for other North Korean submarines. Japan, South Korea, even our friends down under, are sending out warships. But so far the seas remain calm, with no indication the North Koreans have other subs out there."

"And no indication they were working with the Chinese?" Diego asked, a brow raised.

Thor nodded firmly. "That's correct, Mr. President. The Chinese have also been one of our biggest allies when it comes to aid shipments. If they wanted this to happen, they sure aren't showing it."

Charlize remembered trailers back at the SC in Charlotte marked up in Chinese. Thor was right; the Chinese had gone above and beyond what any of them had expected, which seemed fishy to her.

"The North Korean leadership still hasn't emerged from their bunkers, but we've got constant surveillance in the area," Thor added. "If any of those bastards survived, we will take them down eventually."

"What about casualties in South Korea?" Charlize asked.

"Page twenty," Thor said.

Everyone in the room turned the page. This was the first time Charlize had seen any hard numbers. Her fears were confirmed when she saw the data. Their forces in the demilitarized zone had been decimated, but the civilian death toll was unimaginable.

Colonel Raymond returned with a folder containing the rail system maps.

"Thank you," she said.

"I'll turn it over to Ibsen for a report on Korea," Thor said.

The National Security Advisory waited for Raymond to sit, and then continued the briefing.

"The South Koreans are still evacuating survivors from Seoul, but we're finally seeing numbers of casualties." Ibsen paused, and then continued solemnly. "Hundreds of thousands of civilians were killed in artillery fire from the North Korean military. They were dug in pretty well, and a good number seem to have survived our initial nuclear attack."

Thor nodded and took over. "Our forces only had twenty minutes to retreat from the demilitarized zone after we launched our nuclear arsenal. Thousands of our soldiers were killed in the North Korean bombardment of Seoul."

Ibsen's icy glare swept over Charlize and then Diego. "Mr. President, I'm afraid the radiation from our nuclear warheads has affected the survivors in South Korea. Many more will die."

Diego maneuvered the folder on his table, a nervous habit. Perhaps he was right to be nervous. If the United States ever managed to rebound, people would be very critical of every move Diego had made. After all, he had ordered the nuclear attack that had resulted in the artillery bombardment of Seoul. Thousands of Americans and hundreds of thousands of innocent South Korean civilians had died. Now the radiation was killing millions more.

"We're all disturbed by these reports," Diego said. "Our prayers are with everyone lost abroad. However, we did what we had to do to cripple the North Korean regime. With that threat and the threat of their submarines eradicated, our job now is to focus on the violence spreading across our country."

He looked at Charlize, and she sat up a little straighter.

"That's why I asked you to come back to Command, Secretary Montgomery. We aren't just dealing with violence, starvation, and dehydration at the SCs. I'll let Dr. Price explain."

Price tucked her hair behind her ears and nodded. "Thank you, Mr. President. We've been working with the CDC and supporting agencies to get ahead of the outbreak, but the close quarters and lack of clean water at many of the SCs has provided the perfect outlet for the spread of cholera. As noted in your folder, the worst hit is the SC outside Houston, Texas. We've lost control of the situation, and we'll be evacuating all personnel and assets from that center over the next twenty-four hours."

"Just personnel?" Charlize asked. "What about everyone living there?"

"We're abandoning this SC and moving our resources to others that are in better shape," Price said. "It's a matter of resources. Cholera is extremely contagious, and we simply don't have the ability to stop the spread."

"You're just going to leave all of those people to die?" Charlize asked. She thought of Captain Harris and the orders to his men about respecting all innocent lives.

"It's a lose-lose situation." Diego rubbed his forehead and sighed. "We all know the reality. We all can see the numbers. We have to focus on saving the people we can."

Charlize stared at him, aghast. "We're talking about hundreds of thousands of lives. We can't abandon that many people and leave them to die."

"We have no choice," Price said. She paused to look Charlize in the eye. "Have you seen what cholera can do, Secretary Montgomery? Have you ever held a starving, dying child in your arms?"

A memory of the woman clutching the sick child to her breast in the medical wing of SC Charlotte surfaced in Charlize's mind, quickly replaced by Ty shortly after his accident.

Price didn't give her a chance to respond. "I have, Secretary Montgomery. I worked in third world countries for the first ten years of my career."

"And I've fought in them," Charlize said. "Do not lecture me. I just spent the day in Charlotte witnessing exactly what you've just described. They may not be afflicted with cholera, but they have other problems that are just as bad."

Price hesitated. She looked to Diego for his opinion. General Thor tapped his pen on his folder, and Colonel Raymond folded his arms across his chest, both of them clearly preparing for a battle between the two cabinet officials. President Diego apparently had the same idea.

"Everyone, take a break. Secretary Montgomery, a word," he said.

Price held Charlize's gaze for a moment before getting up and leaving. Charlize felt adrenaline flood her system as the room cleared. As soon as the last person left and the door clicked shut, Diego stood and palmed the table.

"First off, don't you ever pull a stunt like the one in Charlotte again," he said sternly. "I didn't make you Secretary of Defense so you could go on personally motivated rescue missions and put yourself in the line of fire. I need you to help now more than ever to get our SCs under control." He let out a breath. "Hell, Charlize, you saw firsthand what we're up against. I need your support."

Charlize stiffened in her chair. "I'm sorry, sir, it's just…"

"I know you've been through a lot after losing your brother, but I won't put up with insubordination again. I also won't have you questioning me in front of my cabinet and staff. When you were off playing tourist, the decision was made to start the evacuation in Houston. I'm sorry, but Dr. Price is correct. There is simply nothing further we can do there given the supplies and manpower we have at our disposal. If it comes down to it, I'll cut the country in half to save those that we can. It's the burden of leadership in these troubled times, and you share that burden with me now, Charlize."

He paused and looked at the ceiling, then back at her. "We're fighting for the very future of our children, and I need to know you're on board. Diseases aren't the only problem. Gangs are infiltrating the SCs. Gangs like MS-13. The Sons of Liberty aren't the only domestic terrorists out there."

Charlize stood to face the president. "I know, sir, and *that's* why I went to Charlotte. While Dr. Price looks at numbers in the safety of this bunker, people are dying out there in terrible ways. She may have been in the field when she was younger, but I've been in the muck most of my life, and today I saw the horror with my own two eyes. It's hell out there."

She tried to keep her voice measured, but her response grew in pitch and volume until she was nearly shouting, causing Diego to rear back.

"I'm more determined than ever to help those people and save our country, sir," Charlize finished, reigning in her temper. "I'm sorry."

Diego stroked the scruff on his jaw and scrutinized her for a moment. Then he nodded and said, "That's all I wanted to hear."

"I don't suppose you want to hear my idea on how we can start moving supplies more efficiently, do you?"

"I'm all ears," Diego replied.

She picked the folder off the table and pulled out a map showing the network of train tracks across the United States.

"On the flight to Charlotte, I saw trains stranded on the tracks in multiple locations. So far we've focused our recovery efforts on moving supplies using the highways, but that's just slowed us down."

"Go on," Diego said.

"I was reminded that we had the same logistical issues of moving supplies and people when we were settling the American West as we do now. If we can get the rails working again, we can start moving more supplies as they come in from foreign nations. It's safer, and more efficient. We won't need as many soldiers to guard the transports either."

Diego studied the map, then looked at her. He cracked a half smile. "Let's run it by the rest of the team. I don't know the slightest thing about the rail system, but perhaps there is a way. I'm sure Doctor Lundy will have some insight."

A knock sounded on the door and Thor opened it slightly.

"Sorry to interrupt, Mr. President, but I have some news both you and Secretary Montgomery will want to hear."

Charlize waited patiently, lacing her fingers together to keep from tapping the table.

"We think we may have found Dan Fenix," Thor said. "I have a team moving in on his location right now."

— 8 —

Dan Fenix awoke to a hand gripping his shoulder. He swung at the air, and his fist connected with something that felt like bone.

"Son of a…" someone grumbled.

In the glow of a candle, Fenix saw a figure staggering away from his bed. Still in the grips of a deep sleep—and a bit hungover—he grabbed the Desert Eagle he kept under his pillow and directed it at the figure.

"Sir, don't shoot! It's me, Carson!"

Fenix slowly lowered the gun and blinked until his eyes adjusted to the light. His skull pounded from a beer-induced headache, and his tired body groaned.

Carson pulled the ratty drape back from the window and ducked down to look at the sky. "We have to get out of here, sir."

"What the fuck do you mean?" Fenix asked. He swung his legs over the bed. As soon as his feet hit the floor, he heard the faint chop of a helo in the distance.

Carson looked away from the window. "They found us, sir. We have to leave, now!"

Fenix had slept in his boots just in case something like this happened. He grabbed his rucksack while Carson palmed a magazine into an M4. He tossed the charged gun to Fenix and then grabbed an M4 of his own.

They left the cabin and stepped out into the chilly night. A second after the freezing air stung his exposed skin, an M240 lit up the skies, sending green tracer rounds into the camp at six hundred rounds per minute. The finger-sized spray punched into the fresh snow, kicking up dirt and pine needles as it carved through the center of the camp.

Sons of Liberty soldiers bolted for cover, but for one it was too late. Lance Hawkings screamed in pain, both of his muscular arms now nothing more than stumps. His rifle hit the snow, hands and riven stumps still attached where the 7.62 mm rounds had severed muscle and bone.

Stunned, Fenix stood staring at the silhouette of a Black Hawk descending on his hideout. All around him, soldiers ran out of their cabins. The chopper's crew chief, clearly an expert on the big gun, cut them down with automatic fire, shredding flesh and painting the fresh snow red.

It took the spray of bullets slamming the dirt in front of Fenix to snap him into action. He hopped behind a tree just as a dozen rounds bit into the ground where he'd been standing a second earlier. Carson hit the dirt beside him, rolled, and fired his M4 at the bird.

"Follow me to the trucks!" he yelled.

Fenix raised his M4 and peered around the tree to aim at the door gunner. Soldiers were already fast-roping from the troop hold as he pulled the trigger. The crew chief cried out as Fenix's bullets found their mark, and the bark of the M240 went silent. The gunner slumped and fell out of the open door, plummeting past the men on ropes, taking one of them with him. They crashed into the snow, a tangled mess.

"Fuck you!" Fenix yelled.

A dozen government soldiers hit the ground a few beats later, night vision goggles snapped into position.

Beams from Sons of Liberty flashlights flickered across the camp, trying to track the men.

The government soldiers strode forward like machines, rifles shouldered, firing with calculated precision. The SOL men, lacking the night vision optics, fell beneath the onslaught.

Fenix popped off another three shots and took one of the Special Ops soldiers down before Carson yanked on his arm.

"We have to move, General," he said.

The chopper pulled away, but Fenix knew it would be back. The men it had dropped were fanning across the camp, hunting down SOL soldiers.

Fenix looked over his shoulder as he ran after Carson toward the south side of the camp, where they kept their pickup trucks. The vehicles were all stocked with gear and supplies, ready to move at a moment's notice. They rounded a cabin and dove into the dirt as one of the four trucks exploded. A tire whizzed overhead and smashed into the side of the cabin they just passed. The two SOL soldiers guarding the trucks followed, their smoldering bodies landing in the snow a few feet from Fenix.

The main storage shed collapsed in a ball of fire. Fenix shielded his face from the wave of heat. Carson pointed at another shed where two more trucks sat idle. He helped Fenix to his feet. He could barely hear or see from the combination of his hangover and the explosions, and he had to lean on Carson as they ran toward the vehicles.

The battle raged in all directions, but Fenix knew his loyal men stood no chance in these conditions against the better-trained and equipped Special Ops soldiers. Automatic gunfire, explosions, and shouting filled the early morning hours as his men were slaughtered.

Fenix used to love the din of war, but not when he was losing the battle. He fought against the ringing in his ears and wobbling in his legs as he made a final push to the trucks. They were fifteen, maybe twenty, feet away when Carson yelled, "Get down!"

Carson tackled him to the ground and shielded Fenix's body with his own. From the ground, Fenix saw a grenade sail through the air and into the open door of a cabin. He buried his head in the snowy dirt just before the explosion. Shards of wood and hunks of a foundation blew through the air, and the ground rattled Fenix.

"Get off me," Fenix tried to say. His ears were ringing so bad he couldn't even hear his own voice. He yelled again and then pushed Carson off when the man didn't respond. The soldier's body crumpled to the ground next to Fenix, blood flowing from his lips, eyes wide and dead. Two dozen shards of wood stuck out of his back like arrows.

A damn noble act—and one that surprised Fenix. The Sons of Liberty talked a lot about loyalty, but Carson had proven himself to be a true patriot and martyr to the cause. His sacrifice would not be forgotten. He patted his old friend on the arm and then stumbled away into the darkness, head pounding and vision fading. He almost lost his balance from a wave of dizziness. There was no time to get to the trucks; the soldiers were already on his trail. His only chance of escape was the woods.

Two other SOL soldiers came running around another cabin.

"General!" one of them yelled.

In the flickering glow of light, Fenix saw the features of Aaron Butzen and Rich Blake.

"This way!" Butzen yelled.

Fenix took off running for them, thrilled to see two of his best soldiers were still alive. They were bolting for the forest.

Rich suddenly jerked and his legs gave out. Looking to the right, Fenix saw a salvo of bullets tear into the fallen soldier. Butzen turned to fire off a shot.

"Run, sir!" he shouted.

Fenix sprinted past Butzen just as a bullet hit the man in the center of his forehead. He crumpled to the ground in a fetal position.

Rounds whizzed past Fenix, but he somehow made it into the forest unscathed. The crack of suppressed rifles followed him into the trees, cutting into the bark and branches all around him. He tripped on a log, hit the dirt, and fumbled for his rifle. He couldn't find the damn thing.

Pulling out his Desert Eagle instead, he aimed at the shapes of the government bloodhounds moving into the woods. Three men hunted his trail. He'd have to make every shot count, but this wasn't the place he would stand his ground. He needed to get farther away first.

Fenix continued onward, pushing past the pain that came with every step. The gunfire seemed to fade behind him, or maybe that was just his hearing. There weren't many of his men still fighting out there, judging by the sounds.

"That bitch," he raged as he moved, thinking of Secretary Montgomery and how sweet it would be when he finally got his revenge. Although that revenge seemed less and less likely as he made his way deeper into the cold darkness of the woods.

He stopped to catch his breath, and flinched at a voice.

"Fenix."

He whirled with his gun up to see a man looking at him from behind a pine tree. It was too dark to see who it was. Fenix raised his pistol and prepared to blow the guy's face off. Better safe than sorry.

"It's me, General. Doc Rollins." The man stepped around the trunk of the tree with a shotgun in his hands.

"Doc," Fenix said, letting out a huff of cold air. He gestured for the gun, and Rollins handed it over.

"We have to get out of here." He turned to run in the other direction, but Fenix halted and looked back to the burning camp. Carson's body was still back there, and his men were being gunned down like dogs.

"Those traitor fucks are killing my men," he snarled. "I'm not runnin' no more."

Fenix pumped a shell into the shotgun and began to jog toward the camp, using the flames to guide him through the forest. He placed the butt of the shotgun in the sweet spot and aimed the barrel at a shadow making its way toward him, pulling the trigger as soon as he saw the soldier was wearing a helmet topped with NVGs. His boys didn't have fancy optics.

The boom was louder than Fenix had expected, and the recoil kicked against his shoulder. He quickly roved the barrel toward another shape and fired, just as a spray of bullets punched into the tree to his right.

Taking a knee, Fenix squeezed off a third shot toward where the muzzle flash had come from. He was rewarded with a wail of pain from the injured soldier he'd just shot.

Fenix made his way around and crouched down next to the two soldiers. Both were dead. The one on the left was missing part of his face, and the guy on the right had taken the brunt of the blast into a vest that hadn't saved him.

"Assholes," Fenix said. He snatched the night vision goggles off the dead man's helmet, put them on, and then grabbed one of their M16s. The sporadic crack of automatic gunfire told him a few of his men were still in this fight.

"I'm coming," he said quietly.

Armed with the M16 and renewed determination, he set off in a hunch through the forest, ducking under branches and navigating the trip-me logs. He was three steps from the edge of the forest when a stern voice stopped him.

"Freeze and put your weapon down."

Fenix's hand twitched toward the trigger, and a suppressed shot cracked behind him, the round hitting the tree to his left.

"*Now!*" the soldier shouted.

Fenix dropped the rifle when he felt a barrel stick him in the back.

"Put your hands on your head and start walking, you piece of shit," his captor said.

Judging by his voice, the man was young, maybe twenty years old. Fenix knew the type. He'd be anxious to make a name for himself. Twenty-five years ago, Fenix had been in the same position. He'd earned his reputation by gutting three soldiers in the Colombian jungle on a mission not that different from this one.

"Take it easy," Fenix said. He raised his hands and put them on his head, then began the march back to camp as a prisoner, watching the ground carefully so as to not trip and earn himself a bullet to the back of his head.

As he walked, he plotted his escape, calculating his

chances of taking this guy down before they got back. He put it at forty percent. He could definitely kill the guy, but he would probably get shot in the process, and Doctor Rollins wasn't around to save him now.

The Sons of Liberty would survive Fenix, but that was cold comfort. This hideout was just one of many. Several hundred more of his soldiers were spread out across central and southern Colorado. Communication was slow, however, and no one was going to come and help him now. Fenix was on his own.

A cabin collapsed in the center of camp, sending a mushroom cloud of sparks into the sky. He needed another distraction like that to take his captor down. He slowed his pace even more and waited.

Two hundred yards from the camp, his boots hit a root and he stumbled. He froze, not daring to move again in case the eager young soldier fired.

Guttural coughing sounded from behind Fenix. Then a thump, like a body hitting the ground.

What the hell?

Fenix slowly turned to see a man towering over the dead soldier that had been leading him back to camp.

"Got 'em," came the familiar voice of Doctor Rollins. He held a blade dripping with blood. It gleamed in the light of the raging fires.

"I'll be damned, you're not a coward after all," Fenix said with a grin. "Nice work, Doc."

***

Sandra Spears was running on pure adrenaline. Since coffee was in short supply, she had taken an Adderall to keep her working through the night. It wasn't ideal—nor was it especially safe—but she needed the energy to help Duffy and Newton keep the medical center running.

For now, the pill was doing the trick. Her mind felt focused, and she was able to provide care for all of her patients without keeping them waiting for long periods of time. Things were going as smoothly as could be expected in her domain. The main problem tonight was what was happening outside of the medical center.

Raven had once again defied her. Against both medical advice and her heartfelt pleas, he had left several hours ago to track down the man that had gone on a shooting spree and blown off the top of Raven's ear. This wasn't the first time she'd had to work while her brother was hunting someone down. It had become the norm over the past month, and judging from the recent uptick in violence, she had a feeling it wasn't going to end anytime soon.

There was nothing she could do for Raven now, but she could at least check on her patients again. She stopped by Teddy's room first, stopping outside the door to listen to Allie and Teddy. The kids had taken a liking to one another.

"When do I get to see Creek again?" Teddy said.

Allie shrugged from the chair next to his bed. "I think he's out with Uncle Raven."

"Doing what?"

Allie shrugged again.

"Someday I want to go out on a hunt with them. Maybe I'll catch the bad guy," Teddy said. His grin faltered. "A lot of people got hurt today. I saw them bringing in the stretchers."

"I think some of those people died," Allie said.

"I hope your uncle gets those bad men," Teddy replied.

Sandra pulled open the door and stepped inside the room before the conversation went any further.

"What are you guys talking about?" she asked.

Teddy didn't bother to lie. "The bad men." He raised his stump and rubbed the bandaged end with his hand. "Is what Allie said true? Did those people who got brought to the hospital today die?"

Sandra knew she was supposed to be checking on her patients, but she also had a responsibility as a mother to talk to these kids about death. There was no way to shield them from the harsh reality of the world they lived in now, but she could at least help them understand it a little better.

She moved up to the side of Teddy's bed. "I'm sorry, but we couldn't save everyone. Sometimes people are too sick or hurt for medicine to fix them."

"But Mr. Raven is going to hurt the bad guys, right?"

Sandra sighed. "He's going to bring them to justice."

"Why doesn't he just kill them?" Allie asked.

The question made Sandra flinch. Her daughter had changed so much in the past month. Sandra could barely recognize her as the little girl who used to play with ponies and sing pop songs. Allie was quieter now, her big, dark eyes ever watchful. Brown Feather had stolen some of Allie's innocence, and for a moment Sandra felt a surge of satisfaction in knowing that Raven had split the bastard's head open with a hatchet.

She took a deep breath, closed her eyes briefly, and then exhaled.

"When someone does something bad—really bad— sometimes you want to do something bad to them in return," she said slowly, searching for the right words. "For now, you two should focus on healing so that maybe someday you can be police officers or doctors and help people instead."

Teddy shook his head. "I don't want to be a police officer. I want to be a hunter like Mr. Raven. I want a dog like Creek, and I want to go out and track the bad people down and hurt them so they can't hurt anyone else. Besides, Chief Colton said he was gonna shoot the guys who hurt Mr. Raven and all those other people."

"What? When did you hear that?"

Teddy lowered his stump next to his side and hesitated before replying, "I overheard the doctors talking with Chief Colton, and he was saying he was going to kill the people responsible for the shootings. Doctor Duffy said that was good."

Sandra rubbed her forehead and sighed. A lot of things had changed so drastically since the bombs dropped.

Everything had changed.

"What about those people who were hanged in Bond Park?" Allie asked. "Those people deserved to die, right?"

"I...it..." Sandra's words trailed off. "Raven and Colton don't *want* to kill anyone. They only do it if they are forced to in self-defense, or to save someone else."

Teddy squinted at Sandra like he was trying to understand and finally said, "Okay, Miss Sandra."

Allie moved over to the bed to stand next to Sandra, holding her tattered stuffed pony.

"Nurse Spears," called a voice.

In the doorway stood Doctor Duffy. He gestured for her to join him in the hall. She smiled at the kids.

"I'll come check on you two later. Be good, okay?" Sandra said.

Allie and Teddy both nodded. Sandra kissed Allie on the cheek and then walked out into the hallway.

"What's wrong now?" she asked Doctor Duffy.

"What's not wrong? The generators are running low on fuel already. Doctor Newton thinks we're going to have to amputate John Palmer's right arm and part of his left. We've lost six patients today, and another six are critically injured."

"God," Sandra breathed.

"I sure hope Colton can find the bastard responsible, because we're all tapped out here. We can't take on another patient."

Sandra thought back to what Teddy had overheard earlier. "You really need to watch what you say around the kids, Doctor."

"Excuse me?" Duffy raised a brow.

"About how you hoped Colton kills the shooter. Teddy overheard you say that."

Duffy scratched the stubble on his chin, and then shook his head. "Did you not just hear me list all the problems we have, Sandra? And you're lecturing me about what I should say around Teddy?" He let out a huff.

"I'm sorry, it's just…"

"I have a lot to do, and so do you, so let's get to it," Duffy said, turning and walking away.

Sandra drew in a breath and followed Duffy. She stopped at the open door to their current morgue. Bloody blankets covered the victims of the attack. Six more souls lost. And there would be more bloodshed. Her heart sank at the thought of Raven laid out under a blanket. It seemed like just a matter of time.

Duffy continued on, but Sandra paused, her heart heavy. The evil that had killed these people wasn't going to stop, but she couldn't let Allie and Teddy grow up thinking it was okay to fight evil with evil.

And how can you tell them that when you're glad Brown Feather is dead?

She shook her head and kept walking.

— 9 —

A distant cracking sound rattled Raven's bones. His first instinct was to look up for Thunderer, but this wasn't his dream, and the sound wasn't thunder—it was a gunshot.

The herd of elk heard it too. They bolted across the meadow toward the woods, away from the gunfire, while Raven led Colton and Lindsey in the opposite direction. The single shot faded into the night, leaving only the crunch of boots on hardened snow. Creek emerged between a pair of Douglas firs on the trail ahead with his tail between his legs.

"I sure hope Hines or Beedie fired that shot," Colton said.

Raven slowly pivoted in the snow to find the source, but it was impossible to determine the direction from the echo, and he hadn't seen a muzzle flash. He waved the group down the trail meandering through the meadows, letting Creek take point. The Rocky Mountains towered all around them, the jagged peaks reaching toward the moon. Each step brought them deeper into the park, which made no sense to Raven. Whenever he began a hunt, he would transport himself into the mind of the creature or person he was tracking, trying to plot out their moves. But he couldn't figure out why their chase would have headed into the wilderness. Why not head south or take refuge in a house in the town? Why come all the way out here?

The farther Raven trekked, the more he struggled to understand the shooter. In his mind's eye, he pictured the man pulling down his bandana to reveal a silver goatee and crooked nose. Those cold blue eyes had stared into Raven's, but when Raven had stared back, he had seen nothing but hatred. Their chase was like Brown Feather and his brother, Turtle: psychotic.

Raven halted to check on Creek. The dog had stopped to sniff the snow. Crouching down sent a flash of excruciating pain across Raven's ribs. Stars danced before his vision. He sucked in an icy breath and waited for the pain to pass.

You're as light as a feather. Light as a feather, he repeated in his mind. It was the motto that had helped him in the past when darkness or pain threatened to send him over the edge.

After his vision cleared, he directed his flashlight at a cluster of red spots in the snow. Something or somebody had bled here. Creek took off running into the forest with the scent fresh on his muzzle.

Colton and Lindsey caught up to Raven a moment later. Another gunshot rang out before anyone could say a word. This one was closer than the first, and there was no doubt of the direction this time. Raven could tell it was coming from the northeast. Colton looked that way and flashed an advance signal.

They silently stepped off the trail and cut through the woods. Raven's shredded ear throbbed from the cold. He was really hurting now. Maybe Colton had been right back in the station parking lot. Hell, maybe he should have listened to Sandra just this once.

No. You have to fight.

The words from Thunderer in his dream replayed in

his mind, and he brought his crossbow up with new determination. They had to find this guy and take him alive. It was the only way to figure out who these raiders were and what they were after.

For the next thirty minutes, they moved toward the direction of the second gunshot. The wind had died down, but the temperature continued to drop. It was going to be freezing soon, and while Raven at least had the proper clothing, his injuries were starting to slow him down.

He knew this area well, fortunately. They weren't far from the place where he'd found a missing girl that had wandered away from her family into the park. That seemed like a lifetime ago.

As they moved deeper into the woods, Raven found himself once again contemplating why the hell their chase would come all the way out here. Unless the man had somehow managed to patch up his injury and get some warmer clothes, he wouldn't last long in the frigid temperatures without shelter.

A chilling thought rushed through Raven as they worked their way through the trees. Was it possible this guy was a former soldier himself, maybe a Special Ops type that was trying to lure the officers out into the woods to even the playing field? He recalled the heartless words the man had said when asked why the raiders had killed innocents. *They got in our way…*

Raven halted in the snow and searched the trees with his flashlight, cursing under his cold breath. What if he was leading his friends into an ambush? What if this guy was trying to inflict the most possible damage for no other reason than that he liked killing?

He suddenly had a bad feeling Hines and Beedie had

already walked into a trap.

"Why are we stopping?" Colton asked quietly.

Gusting wind rushed through the spindly branches overhead, loosening the compact snow. Chunks plopped down and crumpled on the hard ground. The howl of the wind ebbed and flowed like the forest was trying to speak to them—a warning, perhaps.

Colton and Lindsey raked the woods with their flashlight beams. Lindsey's captured Creek's white fur. He was almost camouflaged in the backdrop of snow. The dog wagged his tail and then took off running down a narrow trail they had previously overlooked.

Raven whistled after the dog, his heart pounding at the thought of his best friend bolting into a trap. Despite the pain, Raven ran after Creek. Colton and Lindsey fell into line behind them. The trail Hines and Beedie had taken wound up through the Rockies, where it would intersect with Trail Ridge Road. They were already at nine thousand feet above sea level, and Raven was having difficulty breathing from his bruised ribs. It was only going to get worse from here.

He kept moving, pushing past the ache of his burning lungs. Colton and Lindsey were by his side now, jogging with their weapons raised.

They moved for another ten minutes until Raven had to stop and rest. He raised a hand, gasping for air. Colton directed Lindsey to hold security and then walked over.

"You okay, Sam?"

Raven nodded. "I'm good, just need a second to catch my breath."

A flash of white darted across the trail, and Lindsey swiveled toward the movement. Colton raised his AR-15 and then lowered the barrel.

"Don't shoot," he said.

Creek had reemerged on the trail with something in his maw.

"I told you to get back here," Raven said sternly. He signaled for Lindsey to watch their rear and for Colton to take point while Creek trotted over. The Akita dropped a stocking cap on the snow in front of Raven's boots. He shone his light on the Estes Park Police Department logo stitched to the wool.

"Shit," Colton muttered.

Raven bent down and picked up the hat. "I think we got ourselves a real Rambo."

"Great," Colton said, spitting his toothpick out. "That's just fan-fucking-tastic."

Lindsey, shivering, looked away from her shotgun's sights to study the ridgeline. "There are some cabins and a ranch just over this hill, right?"

Raven knew the place she was talking about, but it still didn't make sense for the shooter to come all the way out here to take refuge. He motioned for Creek to get behind them. This time Raven took point with his crossbow aimed up the trail. Dizzy but relentless, he stalked his chase. They were getting close now—but Raven still had no idea what he would find at the end of this hunt.

"Stay sharp," Colton said, directing them onward.

The forest became a two-dimensional canvas, and Raven divided the terrain horizontally into thirds. His eyes moved with his flashlight beam, roving from left to right and back again in a systematic scan for movement. He was completely in tune with his surroundings, at one with nature, which helped keep his mind off the pain of his injuries. Flakes fluttered away from branches in the wind, falling to the rocky ground, but Raven paid them no heed.

Halfway up the trail, he slowed his pace and squinted at what looked like smoke rising from a chimney. They were right on the border of the park now. There were several people living out here. Some of them had been grandfathered in by the federal government, which allowed them to keep family property in the park, while others had built on the border.

Raven placed the butt of his crossbow against his shoulder and continued up the hill, his lungs rattling. He could see part of the valley beyond now. At the crest of the ridgeline, he stopped and shut off his flashlight, motioning for the others to do the same. Darkness flooded the forest, closing in like a blanket tossed overhead. Blinking, he waited for his eyes to adjust to the glow of moonlight. The wind howled and brought a voice that seemed to be coming from everywhere and nowhere.

"Help!"

Raven turned toward the silhouettes of Colton and Lindsey. For a split second, he hesitated, unsure if this was part of the shooter's ambush. "Lights," he whispered.

One by one, their flashlights flickered on and illuminated a crumpled body at the bottom of the hill about two hundred feet away. The bearded man reached up toward the lights with a hand covered in blood.

"That's Beedie," Colton whispered. He scanned the area for several seconds. "Where the hell is Hines?"

Lindsey took a step forward, but Raven held her back. "Wait."

"I'll check it out," Colton said. "You guys cover me."

He set off down the hill, and Raven and Lindsey took up positions to cover him. Creek had vanished again, but

Raven didn't call him back this time. He needed the dog in this fight even if it was a risk.

Colton cautiously made his way down the steep incline and stopped behind a tree about ten feet from Beedie. Raven could hear them talking quietly, but he couldn't make out the words.

Then a shout rose out above their hushed voices. "Over here!"

Lindsey waved at Raven and said, "That sounds like Hines."

She moved before Raven could stop her. For a moment his mind froze like the air around him. This didn't make sense. Why would Hines leave Beedie?

Gunfire whizzed through the forest, shattering his worried thoughts.

Raven dove for cover as bullets punched into the bark above his head. Return fire rang out at the bottom of the hill, lancing east toward the ridgeline. Flashlight beams crisscrossed the forest and sky like beacons. He shut off his beam and crawled in the pitch-blackness for safety.

For a moment everything was quiet, nothing but the rustle of the wind in the trees.

Then came the voices.

"Colton, where are you?" It was Lindsey.

"Stay where you are," Colton said back.

Raven pushed himself up, grabbed his crossbow, and set off at a hunch. Somebody was going to get shot if they carried on like this. Another flurry of gunshots flashed to the west and hit into the snow at the bottom of the hill.

Lindsey cried out in pain.

Light as a feather. Light as a feather, Raven repeated as he bolted for a tree. He stopped and whistled for Creek. He couldn't see the dog but knew he was out there, flanking the shooter. Raven was doing the same thing. He moved around the outcropping of rocks and halted to look down the valley. Lindsey was crouched behind a tree, and Colton was about two hundred feet away. Hines was still nowhere in sight, and Beedie was still in the snow, unmoving now.

The shooter was positioned in a fort of rocks to the west, dug in from the looks of it. Raven kept his beam off and moved in the darkness, using his other senses to guide him. He scrambled across the snow, keeping low. If Raven couldn't see much, then neither could their chase.

Colton fired, speckling the terrain with bullets. Return fire flashed, and Raven used the opportunity to move behind the fortress of rocks. Creek darted through the woods to his right and disappeared a moment later.

We got you right where we want you now, Raven thought.

He raised his bow as he ran up a track to the top of the rock formation. It was narrow and gave Raven little room to maneuver. Halfway there, he crouched and waited for Colton to distract the shooter, trusting him to understand the situation and back his play. The cracks came a moment later. Raven bounded around the final outcropping of rocks and fired a bolt at the sniper positioned against the north side.

A scream of agony echoed through the valley. The man slowly turned toward Raven, who had dropped his bow and un-holstered his Glock. He prepared to shoot again, but then he realized something that made him draw in a sharp breath. The man was unarmed.

So where was the rifle they'd heard?

The man he'd shot staggered into the moonlight, and Raven glimpsed his face. Instead of a silver goatee and blue eyes, he saw the pained features of Officer Sam Hines. The tip of the bolt Raven had fired into his back stuck all the way out of his upper chest.

What happened next seemed to unfold in slow motion. His gut dropped as the hammer of a revolver clicked and a cold barrel touched his cheek. In his peripheral vision, Raven saw the man with the silver goatee, now dressed in a heavy winter coat and holding a Colt .45 revolver.

"I thought I killed you already," the man said. "Guess I gots to kill you again."

Hines collapsed to his knees a few feet away, groaning in pain.

Raven suddenly understood what had happened and how devious the trap had been. The shooter had ambushed Beedie and Hines, taken Hines hostage, and used him as bait. It was smart, really smart.

"Any last words, injun?" the man said.

"What were you, Delta Force, SEAL? Green Beret?"

"Don't matter now. All that matters is this gun to your head."

Raven had to keep the guy talking to give Creek a chance.

"You said on the road you killed those people because they got in your way," he said.

"That's right, and since this is the second time you've gotten in my way, I'm going to make sure you feel it."

A growl came from above, and the man jerked the gun away to look for the source of the noise. Raven wasted no time turning and slamming into the guy. He glimpsed Creek standing on top of the rocks, teeth bared and saliva dripping from his mouth.

Raven wrestled the man to the ground, and Creek

leapt on top of the pile. The shooter screamed in pain from the dog's ferocious bites. While his dog worked on subduing their chase, Raven worked on getting the gun. He finally pulled it from the man's grip and stood, pointing the gun down.

Relentless, Creek continued to tear at the guy's neck. Raven let his dog have a few extra seconds before calling him off.

The question about the toughest, smartest, most lethal dogs had always been a matter of heated debate when Raven was in the Marines. Some people preferred German Shepherds, while others were partial to Rottweilers, Dobermans, or the Belgian Malinois. But for Raven's money, there was nothing more fearsome than a pissed off fully grown Akita.

***

It was nearing three in the morning and Albert, Corporal Van Dyke, and Sergeant Flint were still sneaking into the city. Albert hadn't yet fired his rifle, but Van Dyke and Flint were already a good way through their first magazines.

They were making their way toward an apartment building towering in the distance. The entire fifteen-story structure had been burned to a crisp, leaving behind charcoaled scree and debris at the bottom. It wasn't hard to see what started the fire weeks ago. Helicopter rotors stuck out from the top of the tower. Without a fire department to combat the blaze, it had torched much of the surrounding area. Albert's boots left tracks in the ashen carpet covering the street.

Flint led the small team through an alleyway to avoid

any contacts. The next street appeared empty. Most of the remaining residents were fast asleep, but it was the late-night prowlers that posed a threat.

They moved down another road clogged with stalled vehicles. At one point someone had attempted to push a few of them to the side, but had just ended up blocking the sidewalk instead. A charcoaled police cruiser was just ahead. Bullet holes riddled the side of the vehicle, and a skeleton was slumped next to the car, nothing but blackened bones.

That was the second police officer's corpse Albert had seen tonight. After a short prayer for his brother in blue, he moved his finger along the trigger guard. Whoever had killed that cop might still be in the neighborhood. They needed to find his sister—and fast.

Flint picked up the pace on the next street. He flashed hand signals, and the men fanned out in combat intervals, moving at a hunch and hugging the storefronts. Albert was growing more anxious with every step. What if Jacqueline wasn't there? What if something had happened to her already? It was a risk Albert had understood before setting out. He knew the journey could end with failure, even with his own death, but it was a risk he didn't regret taking.

A distant scream filled the night, stopping the men and sending them all crouching for cover. Albert searched the apartment building on the left side of the street. Hundreds of windows, some of them shattered, were directly overhead. In one of them, he saw a face looking down at him—a small one, perhaps just a child. By the time he brought his rifle up to zoom in with the scope, the person was gone.

The scream didn't come again. The city of Charlotte,

once the financial center of the Southeast, was shrouded in silence. The lack of noise chilled Albert to the bone. Gone were the sounds of human engineering: cars, sirens, televisions, cell phones. It was like a time machine had transported Albert into a bygone era.

Flashing another hand signal, Flint snapped Albert from his trance. They were coming up on a large, gated park. Another fire, still raging nearby, cast a glow over the area, illuminating hundreds of trees, a playground with slides and swings, and a cluster of gardens built around a central fountain. Albert did a quick scan for contacts and then joined Flint by a shrub that shielded their position. Van Dyke held security on the sidewalk, looking over his shoulder and whispering for them to hurry the hell up.

Flint held the map for Albert to see. "We're about two blocks away from your sister's apartment."

Albert nodded.

"When was the last time you were here?" Flint asked.

"Uh," Albert muttered, "I've never actually visited her here before."

Van Dyke flipped up his NVGs and wiped his forehead with a sleeve. "So you and your sister are real close, huh?"

The corporal snapped his goggles back into place. He didn't say another word, but judging by his tone, Albert could tell he was annoyed. Flint looked over his shoulder at them again, likely thinking the same thing. Captain Harris had sent them out into a warzone to find the sister Albert had never even bothered to visit.

The thought made Albert feel nauseous. His guts dropped farther when a shout rang out. Instinct took over, and he brought his rifle up at a man standing at the street corner on the east end of the park.

"What we got here?" the man yelled. "Nice hardware."

Five more shadowed figures strolled out onto the sidewalk and into the street, their bodies like green aliens in Albert's optics. He scrutinized them in the seconds it took the group to walk out into the open, his police training kicking in. All six were carrying weapons, from baseball bats to a shotgun. Most of them were Latino and sported multiple gang tattoos, including the five-point crown symbol of the Latin Kings.

"Back up, bro," Van Dyke said, directing his M4 at the man who had spoken.

Several of the gang members pointed flashlights at Albert, Flint, and Van Dyke. Albert continued scanning them, prioritizing who appeared to be the biggest threat. Five of the men were thin and muscular, but the guy carrying the baseball bat had tree trunk legs and a massive gut.

"Lower your fucking lights and get the hell out of here," Flint ordered. He moved his barrel from face to face. "Don't test me."

It took only a moment to see who the leader was. A Latino man with a Mohawk and neck tattoos strode forward with a machete in hand, his jeans hanging low and a gray sweatshirt tight across his muscular chest.

"Yo, you guys look like GI fucking Joe!" he said.

The other men laughed in sync.

"More like a bunch of terminators!" the fat man with the bat chuckled.

"Shut the fuck up and back up, or I'll shoot your little pecker off," Flint said.

Albert almost let out a sigh. Clearly Flint and Van Dyke weren't trained on winning the hearts and minds of the population. But it wasn't like these guys were the average civilian. Latin Kings were known for their brutality, just like MS-13, and the leader of this group was holding one of their weapons of choice, a sharp machete.

He took another step forward, twirling the weapon. His pants sagged farther down his butt, but he didn't bother pulling them up.

Flint pushed the barrel of his M4 in the man's direction, the red dot sight hitting him just below the belt.

"I said back the fuck off," Flint said.

The Latino man's eyes flitted down at the marker on his crotch. "All right, all right," he snarled. "But you and your GI Joes are in Latin King territory now, so you best watch your backs."

Flint and Van Dyke were slowly backpedaling. "Let's go, Randall," Flint said.

Albert didn't need to be persuaded. They all kept their guns shouldered, red dot sights flitting from chest to chest, ready to pull the trigger if the gang members so much as moved another inch. The leader watched them, nostrils flared like a raging bull, veins popping out on his muscular arms as he gripped the machete.

It was obvious the guy was waiting for the right moment to send his posse at the trio, but doing so would be suicide. They had automatic M4s, and these guys only had a shotgun and couple of pistols. As long as everyone stayed cool, they'd all make it out of the park.

A few steps later, a guttural crack sounded, and Van Dyke yelled out in pain.

Albert saw a flash of motion in his peripheral vision. Someone had flanked them. Another man with a baseball bat hit Van Dyke a second time in the back. The corporal crashed to his knees. Flint spun and pumped three holes into the attacker's chest, and then one in the head for good measure.

"Rear guard!" he yelled at Albert.

Albert was already moving. He fired a three-round burst into a man lunging forward with a knife, scoring shots to chest and gut. The gangbanger crumpled to the ground, blood gushing onto the road. Three more came at Albert, and Flint took two of them down with quick bursts.

The suppressed fire was answered by the boom of a shotgun. Flint cried out in pain and hit the ground not far from where Van Dyke was still gasping for air.

Albert roved his rifle toward the shooter and fired directly into the man's face, blowing out an eyeball and sending a round up his nostril. The corpse fell to the ground, leaving only two gangbangers standing, including the man with the Mohawk.

The second guy took off running, but the leader screamed in rage and ran at Albert with his machete raised and a flashlight directed at his optics. The bright light blinded Albert for a moment. He pushed his night vision goggles up and fired blindly, holding the trigger down and spraying in the direction of the light.

A scream followed and Albert backed away, blinking. When his vision finally returned, the gang leader was striding toward Albert, gripping a wound with one hand and swinging his machete with the other.

Albert brought his rifle up and parried the machete attack. The clang echoed over the groans of the dying men around them.

The leader had lost his flashlight, leaving them in almost complete darkness. Albert didn't dare reach up and pull his NVGs down, so instead he backed away and listened for footsteps. The move likely saved his life, as he felt the machete slash the air where he'd been standing. He swung the rifle again but missed.

Another slash came, this one scoring a line of fire down his right arm. This time when Albert swung his weapon, he caught the man in the face with the butt of the rifle. He flipped his NVGs back into position to see the leader sprawled on the ground, a mouthful of teeth on the concrete next to his shattered face.

Albert breathed heavily as he scanned the other fallen gang members. The violence had driven the air from his lungs. It was the first time Albert had ever killed anyone, and he felt like he was going to puke.

The fat man reached for his baseball bat and Albert raised his rifle.

"Don't!" Albert shouted.

The man gripped the bat and pushed himself up.

"Drop it!" Albert yelled, louder.

The man staggered forward, and then fell backward as gunshots riddled his gut and chest.

Albert lowered his rifle, seeing Flint had been the one to fire. The sergeant's hand was slick with blood. He reached back down and gripped his side where some of the shotgun pellets must have penetrated his vest.

"You hurt, Corporal?" Flint asked.

"I'm fine," Van Dyke said. "Just winded."

Flint nodded and pulled his hand away to have a look at his side. Albert tried to help, but the sergeant waved him away.

"Just a flesh wound," Flint grumbled. "Come on, let's go find your sister and get the hell out of this shithole."

— 10 —

General Dan Fenix was freezing his ass off. Morning was still hours away, and it was cold as hell. He'd had to leave his camp, his dying men, *and* the rest of the beer. To make things even worse, he was now lost in the goddamn woods with Doc Rollins.

Their escape didn't matter if he and Rollins didn't find shelter soon. Otherwise, they were going to end up as icicles.

The howl of a wolf sang through the forest. Fenix raised his M4, and Rollins brought his weapon up a moment later. The guns moved in opposite directions to search for the beast.

The sound faded into the night, leaving the two men in silence and shivering in their coats.

"You sure you don't got a cigarette, Doc?" Fenix asked.

"Carson had us hand in all of our reserves this morning."

Fenix thought of his right-hand man, the guy that had given his life to protect Fenix. He could clearly picture the dozen sharp spears of wood sticking out of Carson's back.

"Fucking A," Fenix said, his teeth chattering. "What a c-clusterfuck."

He hoped some of his men had survived the attack, but he had his doubts. For all he knew, Rollins and him were all that was left of their camp. There was only one way forward. He had to reach the closest Sons of Liberty outpost before he froze to death. Or got his balls eaten by a wolf.

"Come on, Doc," he grumbled.

They continued north through the forest, following the compass Fenix always carried with him. It was five miles to the shack where two of his sentries were posted. They were equipped with a working radio that would allow Fenix to contact his men in the other camps scattered across Colorado.

Now if he could just find his way back to the road...

Another howl sounded in the distance, but Fenix didn't stop this time. He pressed onward, his aging joints creaking like the canopy of pine trees overhead. The thought of a cigarette and warm coffee kept him moving as the temperature continued to drop. Rollins shivered behind him, his rifle shaking in his grip. For October, it was an unusually cold night in Colorado. A storm front had moved in, bringing with it freezing temperatures and the threat of snow. Fenix spotted heavy clouds rolling toward the moon. The last thing he wanted was to be caught out here in a snowstorm.

After another hour of heading north, he finally came up on a hill overlooking a country road. The sight of asphalt filled him with relief. He crouched next to a tree and aimed his rifle at a single car parked in the middle of the road. Rollins stopped on the ridgeline a few feet away from Fenix.

"Looks clear," the doctor said.

Fenix held up a hand. "Hold on, Doc."

He focused on the car. It wasn't as good as a cabin, but it was shelter from the wind and cold. Maybe they could hunker down for a few hours until dawn. Fenix moved to scope the rear of the vehicle. He cursed when he saw the shattered windows. It wasn't going to keep them warm or protected.

After another scan for contacts, Fenix waved Rollins onward. They carefully made their way down the side of the hill and moved onto the shoulder of the road.

Rollins took to the right side and Fenix moved to the left. They walked for another half hour, maybe longer. A snowflake fluttered onto his face, stinging his cheek. Looking up through his stolen NVGs, he saw a sky full of flakes, like green confetti coming down at a New Year's party. A long green streak of light flared across the horizon. At first he thought it was a shooting star, but then he heard the unmistakable bark of an M240 gun. Tracer rounds ripped through the darkness.

"Down, down!" Fenix yelled. He bolted across the road and hid with Rollins near the base of a tree at the edge of the woods.

"Who's shooting at us now?" Rollins asked.

Peeking around the tree, Fenix spotted the outline of a helicopter hovering over the forest to the west. The tracer rounds were centered on a hilltop position, which at least meant the bastards weren't firing on his sentry post. According to his map, the post was tucked in a ravine.

Was this the helicopter gunship that had attacked his camp earlier come back after refueling, or was this a new one?

He moved cautiously out onto the street, brought up the rifle to his NVGs, and zoomed in on the helicopter. It was a mile away, maybe more.

"Come on, Doc," Fenix said.

Rollins reluctantly moved back into the road. They

kept to the shoulder as they walked toward the battle, which lay between them and the sentry post. Ahead, the asphalt snaked around a corner that was blocked by more trees. Hills and snowy peaks protruded above the pines.

The snow picked up as the two men walked with their rifles aimed at the chopper. Flakes fluttered in front of his sights, and Fenix reached up to brush off the scope and his NVGs every few steps.

Over the din of automatic gunfire, he heard the faint rattle of an engine. He halted and then took a knee when he realized it was moving in their direction. The tracer rounds changed trajectory. One of them streaked down the road and hit a tree behind them.

"Shit!" Fenix yelled. He dove for cover just as a trio of pickup trucks rounded the corner ahead.

Fenix crawled behind a tree and was preparing his rifle when he saw men in black fatigues were firing from the beds of the pickup trucks at the chopper.

"Fuck yes! We got reinforcements, Doc!" he said.

"You sure those are our guys?"

Fenix wasn't sure. In fact, it didn't make much sense that they would run into the Sons of Liberty out here in the ass end of nowhere. But who else could they be? It had to be his men coming to rescue him, right?

"Give them some covering fire!" Fenix shouted. He pushed himself up and, using the tree for cover, roved his barrel at the helo. The suppressed crack of his rifle joined the chorus of war.

He held the trigger down with glee—sending rounds downrange was one hell of a feeling when you had your enemy in your sights, especially when the enemy wasn't firing back at you.

Smooth as shit, baby, Fenix mused.

He fired burst after burst, more rounds cutting through the darkness. The bird pulled up, but the door gunner continued firing, relentless. Flames burst from the pickup in the back of the column, the gas tank igniting and sending the men in the bed cartwheeling away in a brilliant flash.

Another bullet whizzed toward Fenix, pushing him back. He changed his magazine and waited for another opportunity to fire.

"Shoot your damn weapon!" Fenix yelled at Rollins.

The chopper continued its pursuit of the trucks, which were closing in on Fenix's position. Fenix palmed the fresh mag into the cold rifle and angled the carbine up toward the cockpit.

"Die, you fucking traitors," he growled.

The helicopter was heading right for him now, closing in on the trucks.

An explosion suddenly bloomed overhead, the bird blowing to pieces mid-air. Burning hunks of metal streaked through the sky, and a flaming corpse dropped to the ground like a flake of snow.

Fenix lowered his rifle and shielded his eyes with a gloved hand. The blast had been close enough that he could feel the heat on his face, and it felt damn good. He grinned and strode out into the road to link up with the Sons of Liberty soldiers that were apparently on their way to rescue his sorry ass.

"Doc," Fenix said. "Doc, come on."

He turned to see Rollins sitting in the snow near the tree, cross-legged, his hands on his stomach.

"Doc?" Fenix said. He hurried over and crouched down in front of Rollins, who looked up with sad eyes. His NVGs were pushed up on his forehead, and he seemed to be looking through Fenix instead of at him.

"I'm cold, General," Rollins choked, reaching up with one hand. "You got a cigarette?"

Fenix knew by the question that Rollins was a dead man. The doc might have been a drunk, but he wasn't forgetful. He put a hand on the doctor's shoulder and moved him back slightly to see the blood splatter on his stomach.

"I'll get you one," Fenix said. He stood and turned toward the approaching trucks. "Just hang on. I'm sure one of these boys can spare a smoke."

The rusty trucks and ancient Jeep eased to a stop, their engines coughing and whining. The front door of the lead vehicle opened, and a man with short-cropped gray hair stepped out. A hatchet and sheathed knife hung from a duty belt around his waist.

Fenix didn't recognize him, but new soldiers were joining the ranks of SOL every day.

"Hello, boys," he said. "You've got good timing."

The man looked over his shoulder at the others but didn't say anything. Several guns were still angled at Fenix.

"Lower your fucking weapons. It's me, General Fenix, and I really need a cigarette."

The man in camouflage laughed. "*You're* Dan Fenix?"

"Who the fuck are you?" Fenix snarled. He took a few steps forward to look at the face of the man that had disrespected him so blatantly. The move earned Fenix another four guns pointed in his direction.

The man wagged a gloved finger. "Now, now, General. If you'd be kind enough to stay put, I promise we won't shoot you dead."

Fenix narrowed his eyes. The guy had some sort of an

TRACKERS 3: THE STORM

accent he couldn't place.

"You don't look like much, if I'm being honest," the guy said. He shrugged and pointed a pistol at Fenix. "We've been looking for you for a while, but this is just too damn easy. It's almost like it was meant to be."

He reached down and pulled the hatchet from his belt. "I'm not sure how we're going to spend the ten million in gold bars, but I've got a few ideas…"

Fenix had just long enough to realize he was well and truly fucked before someone clocked him on the back of the head.

***

Colton punched the prisoner in the stomach for a third time. The man fell to his knees, hands cuffed behind his back, bald head dipped toward the concrete floor. He spat out a mouthful of blood and then looked up with a grin.

"You're a bigger pussy than that injun," he said.

Outside the jail cell, Raven unfolded his arms and strode forward, but Lindsey held out a hand to hold him back.

"Let me have a shot at this, Chief," Raven said.

Colton shook his head. The last thing he was going to do was let Raven in here with this piece of shit.

"I got this," Colton said. Without warning, he threw another punch at the man's jaw. The crack echoed through the small cell.

"I'm only going to ask you one more time who you're working for, asshole," Colton said. "And you're also going to tell me where your buddies are camped out."

The man cracked his jaw from side to side, chuckled,

and then spat at Colton's feet. Whoever he was, he was a professional, and he wasn't saying much so far. But they had plenty of time to interrogate him.

It was still dark in Estes Park, and Colton had just gotten their prisoner back to the station. The bullet Raven had fired had gone clean through, and the guy had patched himself up pretty well before they found him. Of course, he'd sustained a few more injuries since then.

Officer Hines was at the Estes Park Medical Center, where the doctors were removing the arrow Raven had accidentally fired into his shoulder. Tim Beedie, the volunteer that had accompanied Hines on the hunt, was dead, having bled out from a gunshot wound in Beaver Meadows.

One hell of a night, Colton thought as the man in front of him continued moving his jaw back and forth. He finally looked up and held Colton's gaze, narrowing a pair of blue eyes surrounded by bulging purple bruises. Raven had done a number on the bastard before Colton could cuff him. Creek had also done some major damage to his neck and right arm. Bite marks and lacerations still oozed blood.

"You want me to set the dog back on you?" Colton asked. "Talk!"

"Screw you," the man growled. "I'm not telling you jack shit without a lawyer."

Colton almost laughed at that. Lindsey couldn't resist, chuckling so hard she ended up bent over with her hands on her knees.

"We're under martial law in Estes Park," Colton said calmly. "The only person that you're going to talk to is me."

He leaned down, tired bones aching as he crouched.

"You killed seven residents of my town, and if you count Officer Sam Hines, you injured another seven. And for what?" Colton asked. He thought about hitting the man again, but he held back. Never in his career had he beaten information out of anyone before, but these were different times. The old rules of engagement didn't apply. That didn't mean he enjoyed it.

"You're not leaving me with many choices here," Colton continued. "You're either going to start talking or I'm going to start hurting you real bad."

Raven and Lindsey kept watch, their faces masks of worry, but Colton didn't let that distract him. He was determined to get this guy to talk with whatever means possible.

"Jason," the guy finally said. "My name is Jason. And what you don't understand is that nothing you can do to me will be worse than what my boss will do to me if I gave him up to a fucking pig."

Jason sucked in another long breath and then sighed, apparently done talking for now. His silver goatee was dripping blood from his broken nose, and his swollen eyes seemed to be getting worse.

Colton stood and let out his own sigh. He motioned for Lindsey to open the barred gate to let him out. Jason pushed at the floor with his cuffed hands and then sat on the single bench in the small cell while Colton left.

"Guess you won't mind me leaving you with Raven," Colton said. "I mean, he is a pussy and all, right?"

Jason's eyes flitted to Raven, who cracked his knuckles.

"He ain't a cop, either, so maybe you'll be able to have a more cordial conversation," Colton added.

"Doubt that, Chief," Raven replied.

Colton shrugged a second time and jerked his chin at Lindsey. "Come on, Detective, let's let Raven have a chat with our new friend."

"All of you are dead when they come!" Jason yelled. He staggered over to the bars, the veins in his neck bulging as he looked at them.

Colton turned halfway. "When who comes?"

Eyes wide like a wild animal, Jason retreated back to the bench. "There's a storm coming your way," he said. "And there's nothing you can do to stop it."

***

The situation room at Constellation was packed with military and civilian staffers with high-level security clearances. Doctor Peter Lundy, the leading scientist at the facility, sat at the far end of the conference table, stroking his red goatee and reading over reports. Colonel Raymond and General Thor were at the head of the table with several of their staffers standing behind them. Even President Diego had stayed up into the early morning hours to monitor this situation.

Covering his mouth to hide a yawn, Diego said, "We got a SITREP yet?"

"Sierra Team found Fenix's hideout about a mile from Apache Peak," Thor announced. "The Rangers took two of the SOLs captive, but Fenix escaped. We're still combing the area for him."

Charlize couldn't believe Fenix had gotten away a second time. It was taking every inch of self-control not to shout orders to find him at all costs.

Stay calm, stay in charge, she kept repeating to herself. She already felt guilty about pulling strings to rescue Ty and now Albert's sister. Good men had died to bring Ty home, and Charlize would have to bear the burden of her decision to send Lieutenant Dupree's fire team to Colorado. Sending more Americans into danger just to get revenge on the man who murdered her brother would be beyond selfish. Except that Fenix wasn't just a murderer—he was a terrorist.

The atmosphere now reminded Charlize of the moments before the nuclear explosion that had leveled Washington, D.C. and destroyed the PEOC beneath the White House. The room was tense, the air fraught with shouts and updates as they monitored the raid. But this time the enemy wasn't North Korea—it was domestic terrorists that called themselves the Sons of Liberty.

All across the country, groups like SOL were popping up and threatening the survival centers. Gangs, vigilantes, and other groups hell-bent on taking generators, food, water, and supplies were making it very difficult to keep any sort of order at the centers. They needed to cut the head off this particular snake to stamp out the Aryan Nation groups rising in Colorado and neighboring states.

Colonel Raymond walked over to a wall-mounted monitor. They didn't have a real-time feed of what was happening in Colorado, but they did have a map that showed the area. Charlize had practically memorized every mountain, road, and trail in the state of Colorado over the past month. They'd had plenty of false leads and tips that led nowhere. But this time the lead was real. Fenix and his men were out there, hiding like rats.

"This is where the SOL camp was located," Raymond said, pointing. "Sierra Team is searching this area for Fenix and any other men that may have escaped."

Thor leaned over for a report from a staff member

while Raymond continued briefing the president. Charlize took another drink of coffee. Not that she needed the caffeine. It was two a.m. and she was wide-awake. She just hoped Ty was sleeping peacefully. Maybe when he woke up in the morning, she'd be able to tell him that Fenix was dead and could never hurt him again.

Diego took a seat next to Charlize after Raymond finished his short briefing. The president offered her a tired smile.

"At least there's some good news," he said. "We've got more shipments of generators, oil, and other supplies coming in on the west and east coasts from our allies. The British and French have also sent us soldiers to help move these resources across to our SCs."

"That's great," Charlize said. She wanted to ask if it was too little too late, but every shipment meant more saved lives.

"More troops are coming home, too," Diego added. "More men and women to protect our assets and deliver them to the people that need them."

Charlize considered asking if there were enough troops to send to Houston to help with the cholera outbreak, but she knew there weren't. It wasn't just a matter of able-bodied soldiers, it was a matter of logistics and moving supplies.

"Shipments from Australia and New Zealand will be arriving in a few days as well," Diego said.

She took a deep breath, but before she could add her opinion, General Thor stood and said, "Mr. President, we just got word from Buckley AFB that Sierra team has gone dark."

"What do you mean *gone dark*?" Diego asked.

"The pilots aren't responding over the comms," Thor

said. "Buckley will continue trying to get through, but for now, we have no way to contact the pilots."

Charlize let out a huff of frustration. "Someone find out what the hell is going on," she snapped.

"We're doing our best, ma'am," Thor said. He sat calmly, eyes ahead.

Charlize was sick of sitting around calmly. The old military saying "Hurry up and wait" rang even more true now that communication happened at a snail's pace. The other staffers and officers went back to their duties while Charlize sat at the table, trying to keep her cool. Maybe she needed a break. She had been meaning to go check on Ty for over an hour now.

"We're going to catch him," Diego said quietly to her. "Fenix will not get away again. It's just a matter of time before he's in our custody."

Charlize thanked the president with a nod, but didn't reply. She stood and walked over to the wall-mounted monitor to look over the area herself. At least that would keep her busy. There wasn't much near Apache Peak, which made it one hell of a hiding place. The remote area gave them a ton of ground to cover, even for a helicopter, and especially at night.

"This is where we lost contact with the team," Raymond said. He pinched the touch screen together and zoomed in on a road. "The pilots said they were engaging a convoy of vehicles before going dark."

Charlize knew what the news meant. Sierra Team was gone, another victim to the Sons of Liberty.

"Goddammit," Diego said. He balled his bandaged hand into a fist and stopped just short of pounding the table. "How long until we can get another bird out there?"

155

Thor shook his head. "An hour, sir. Maybe more. By the time we send another team, the enemy will be long gone."

There was a long silence that seemed to linger. They were all aware that sending another bird wouldn't find Fenix; all it would do was recover the bodies of the previous team. How many more men would die at the hands of these terrorists?

Diego shook his head, his bewildered expression like a poker player that had just lost a hand he'd been certain of winning.

"Send another helo to recover our boys and look for any survivors," he said.

General Thor reached up to make a call when a knock came on the door. A female officer peeked inside.

"Sorry to interrupt, but there's someone here that needs to see Secretary Montgomery," she said.

Charlize craned her neck to look for the visitor, expecting an officer or scientist to be standing outside with more bad news. Instead she saw Ty, sitting in his wheelchair wearing his NASA t-shirt instead of pajamas.

He raised a timid hand.

"If you'll excuse me, Mr. President," Charlize said. She shot up from her chair and hurried out of the room, heart beating even harder now. The door closed behind her with a click, and she bent down in front of Ty.

"What's wrong?" she asked.

"I... I can't sleep. I keep thinking about *him*...have you caught him yet?"

— 11 —

Raven walked out of the Estes Park police station at sunrise. He sheathed his bloody knife and held a battered hand up to his face like an addict after a bad night, shielding his eyes from the rising glow of the sun. He *felt* like an addict after a bad night.

It was a new day in Estes Park. In a way, he felt like a new man—but not in a good way. He'd spent the past two and a half hours beating the living shit out of Jason Cole, a former Special Operations soldier and world-class asshole. It had taken some work, but Jason had finally come clean about his actions over the past few weeks.

What Jason had told Raven made him want to puke. The guy had taken the same oath as Raven to uphold the honor and safety of his country above all else. Instead, Sergeant Jason Cole had spent the past month raping, pillaging, and killing his way through Colorado with a group of bandits and raiders from Fort Collins. Who they were, exactly, he wouldn't say, but Raven knew enough now to take the information to Colton.

Creek trotted out of the station and followed Raven around the side of the building, looking up every few steps to check on his handler. Dogs could sense when someone was in pain. They picked up on the subtle signs humans could never see. Creek would do everything in his power to protect and comfort Raven. Now that was loyalty. That was honor.

And Creek wouldn't judge Raven for what he'd had to do to Jason.

Damn, I need a drink.

Raven shook his head. "No you don't, Sam."

Drinking was actually the last thing Raven wanted to do now. He was a changed man in more than one way, and he wasn't going back to his old habits. Sam Spears had made promises, and to keep them, he needed to be of sound body and mind. Right now, he had to find Colton to explain what Jason's "storm" really meant.

He found the chief of police talking to the refugees in Bond Park. Even from a distance, Raven could tell Colton hadn't slept for more than an hour. Maybe not at all. That made two of them. Sleep, like New Zealand chocolate or a nice medium-rare steak, was a luxury Raven wasn't going to be experiencing for a very long time.

"Chief," he said.

Colton pivoted away from a tall, slender woman and a girl that looked to be about eight or nine. The girl straightened a multi-colored wool cap over her braided hair and looked at Raven, her eyes widening at the dried blood on his clothes.

"You got news?" Colton asked.

Lindsey made her way over, her smile slipping off her face at the sight of Raven.

I must really look like shit, he thought.

"Best we talk in private, Chief," Raven said.

"All right." Colton gestured for the street, and Raven followed him away from the park.

"Sir," the girl said as Colton walked away. "Can we stay or not?"

The tall woman put her hand on the girl's back and

looked at Colton. "Sorry. Sarah's just anxious."

"I'll make my decision soon. In the meantime, please make sure your people stay in Bond Park, Jennie."

Jennie smiled politely and ushered Sarah back toward the tents. Smoke rose from the fire barrels, filling the area with the scent of cedar and metal.

"How'd it go with Jason?" Colton asked. His eyes flitted to Raven's bloodied knuckles.

"He's still alive, if that's what you mean," Raven said. He swallowed and forced the memories out of his mind. There was a mess to clean up, but that was the least of their worries right now.

Lindsey finally walked over and folded her arms across her chest. "What's going on?"

"Like I thought, Jason is a former Special Ops soldier. He's well trained, and I'm guessing the other raiders are too. He wouldn't give up his friends, but there are definitely more of them out there."

"You think he's part of the Sons of Liberty?" Colton asked.

Raven shook his head. "Nope, and he's not aligned with Redford's posse either. He's one of the raiders that have been terrorizing the cities east of the mountains. Sounds like he's from Fort Collins, but I couldn't get much more out of him. He's more afraid of his 'boss' than my blade."

"Great, more psychopaths to worry about," Colton said, heaving a sigh.

"I told you, Chief," Raven said. "We've got enemies barreling down on us from all directions. We need to send out scouts, beef up our security, and make some friends."

"We can start with them," Lindsey said, jerking her

chin toward the refugees. "They want to help."

Raven wasn't sure that welcoming so many refugees into town was the right move, but it wasn't his call.

"All right, I've made up my mind," Colton said. "Lindsey, change of plans. I want you to stay here while I go to the FEMA camp outside Loveland. Start arming the refugees and assigning them to roadblocks and other facilities. Then, I want you and Raven to head to Storm Mountain and convince John Kirkus to fight with us. Tell him about Jason and what's headed our way."

Raven raised a brow when Colton looked at him, knowing exactly what was coming next. He almost protested, but he shut his mouth and put his battered hands in his pockets. He had expected different orders, but he wasn't complaining. He needed to get home to check on Sandra and Allie.

"But, sir, you can't go by yourself," Lindsey protested. "It's far too dangerous."

"I've got to do this on my own. We can't afford to take another person off our barriers in town," Colton said.

"At least get a few hours of sleep first," Lindsey said. "You can't go out there exhausted. You need to be sharp. Besides, the FEMA camp hasn't sounded the all-clear yet."

Colton hesitated and finally nodded. She was right; he couldn't go out there until they had signaled the attack was over.

"I'll head home and grab a few hours of shut eye and say goodbye to my wife and daughter. Radio me if you hear the all-clear. As soon as you do, I'm heading out there to see if I can track down Sheriff Gerrard. We're going to need help if we have any hope of standing against men like Jason."

***

Sergeant Flint grimaced as he joined Corporal Van Dyke and Albert at the window. The sun was up and the city had come alive outside the apartment building where they were hiding out.

Albert kept to the shadows as he watched the street below fill with people. Some of them seemed to be normal citizens: men and women that looked like average office workers and neighbors, but a closer look revealed filthy faces, thin frames, torn clothes, and desperate eyes.

Everyone was looking for something, and most everyone was starving or on the verge of starving.

Albert took a drink of his water bottle. This was supposed to be a quick in and out, all under the cover of darkness, so they hadn't weighed themselves down with rations. But now they were going to need to wait until night to sneak back into the SC—assuming he was able to find Jacqueline first.

He shook his head. They were just a few blocks away from his sister's apartment, but after the attack in the park, the team had been forced to find cover and lick their wounds. Van Dyke had suffered two nasty strikes from a baseball bat, and Flint had been hit by the shotgun blast. Their armor helped save their lives, but they were still hurting.

Albert wondered if they were in any shape to move. Maybe he should tell the men to return to base without him while he continued the search for Jacqueline. This wasn't their fight, and he didn't feel right about putting them at risk for his sake.

"This is messed up," Van Dyke said, moving away from the window. "Soon as we show our mugs, we're going to get annihilated down there. Last Humvee that went outside the SC hardly made it back at all. Looked like it had passed through a gauntlet of machine gun fire."

"Captain Harris warned us," Flint said. "MS-13 and the Latin Kings are terrorizing this area. We're on their turf. You know what happened to…you know."

"What?" Albert said, turning from the window.

Van Dyke and Flint exchanged a glance.

"Is there something I don't know and need to know?" Albert asked.

"I'm sure you heard there is major gang activity in these areas," Flint said, pausing. "However, I doubt Harris told you details. A few weeks ago a group of National Guard soldiers were taken hostage. We found their bodies hanging from a bridge. All of them were skinned alive."

"My God," Albert said.

"We're lucky, man," Van Dyke said. "Back at that park, if those guys had captured us, we'd be the ones hanging from a bridge."

Flint pointed to the closet. "See if you can find any clothes and some backpacks. We'll change clothes and take what we can. I'm sure as hell not leaving these NVGs behind, though. Harris would shit a brick."

Albert went back to look out the window. A dark-skinned man wearing a track jacket was standing on the hood of a vehicle halfway down the street. He cupped his hands over his mouth and shouted something Albert couldn't make out.

"What's he saying?" Flint asked. He moved over for a better look, one hand on his injured hip.

"Not sure, but looks like it's got the attention of everyone down there." Albert pulled the drape back for a better view as a crowd formed around the man. Several were carrying shotguns and rifles. Most everyone had a pistol holstered or wedged under a belt. There was enough firepower on the street to start a bloodbath.

"It's all girl shit," Van Dyke announced as he finished going through the closets. A pile of discarded shirts and pants were on the floor.

Flint looked over his shoulder. "Then go find another empty apartment and bring some stuff back."

"You got it, Sarge," Van Dyke said.

"Go with him," Flint said quietly. "Last thing I need is Van Dyke getting spooked and blowing away some civvies."

Albert nodded and followed Van Dyke toward the door. They removed some of their gear, including their packs, and proceeded out into the hallway with their weapons raised. It was quiet. The carpet reeked of stale piss.

"Clear," Van Dyke said.

Albert followed him down the hallway. It felt odd walking through an apartment building wearing combat gear and carrying a machine gun, but he was slowly getting used to treating everyone like an enemy. People were shooting each other for cigarettes, and the gangs were committing unthinkable crimes.

Van Dyke stopped at an apartment halfway down the corridor. The corporal stopped and knocked on the door. When no one answered, Van Dyke nodded at Albert, who in turn kicked the door off the frame. A moment later they strode into the apartment with their M4s sweeping over the space.

"Clear," Van Dyke announced in the living room. He flashed a hand signal, and Albert proceeded toward a hallway, barrel roving to the left and then the right. Van Dyke followed him into the open passage and moved to the left bedroom while Albert took the right bedroom.

A stench hit his nostrils before he even opened the door. Raising his rifle in his left hand, he slowly pushed the wood door open with his right.

"Get out!" someone screamed.

Albert lowered his gun and reached out toward the boy that bolted from a hiding spot in the corner of the room. The kid dove for the twin bed before Albert could catch him.

"Shit," Albert muttered.

The boy wedged his body under the bed and growled like a dog. Albert got down on his knees and looked under the side at an angle.

"I'm not going to hurt you, kid," Albert said.

The boy appeared to be maybe seven years old with shaggy black hair. He was shirtless, and wore a pair of filthy jeans. The stink wasn't just body odor—this kid had clearly soiled his pants.

"Where are your folks?" Albert asked.

The boy bared his teeth and growled again.

"Stop doing that," Albert said. "You're not a caveman."

"Get out!" he screeched.

Albert held up his hands and slowly rose to his feet. "Okay, kid, just chill out." He walked a few steps away, bringing a finger to his lips when Van Dyke moved into the doorway. Then Albert pointed at the bed, drawing the corporal's gaze.

The boy peeked out a moment later and screamed again.

"GET OUT!"

Van Dyke laughed, but Albert shook his head.

The corporal backed into the hallway. Albert went to follow, but something made him pause. The kid looked like he hadn't eaten in days, and he smelled like a dumpster. Albert couldn't just leave him here like this. He pulled out his water bottle and put it down near the edge of the bed. Then he gestured for the energy bar he knew Van Dyke had in his vest.

"Hell no," Van Dyke said.

"Don't be an asshole," Albert replied.

Van Dyke snorted and pulled out the bar. He tossed it to Albert, who set it on the floor beside the water. A hand shot out from under the bed. The water bottle and bar both vanished.

Albert listened to the kid eating, and waited a few minutes before speaking again.

"Can you come out now and talk to us?"

Van Dyke whispered, "What the shit for? We can't help him."

"Go find some clothes like Sergeant Flint ordered," Albert said, shooting him a glance.

"Fine. Whatever, man."

Albert bent down and sat on the floor casually, just like he would have done with his own kids. "Where are your parents?" he asked.

"They left me here. All by myself."

"When?"

The boy's dirty face peered out from under the bed.

"I don't know," the boy said. He wiped his lips and slowly crawled out. His ribs were showing. Red sores

165

covered his stomach from scratching.

"My parents were on a trip to the White House."

"The one in Washington, D.C.?"

A nod.

"They just left you here?" Albert asked.

"I had a babysitter, but she took off a long time ago." He looked at the ceiling as if in deep thought. "She's dumb anyway."

Albert narrowed his eyes. He wasn't sure what to make of this kid. "What's your name?"

"Dave, but my friends call me D-Money."

"I'm Albert, but my friends call me Big Al."

Dave bit off another hunk of the energy bar and chewed noisily.

"How old are you?" Albert asked.

"Almost eight. You a football player or something?"

Albert smiled. "I was."

"I'm going to be a pro someday. My dad said that I got some growing to do, but…" Dave flexed his right bicep.

"Impressive," Albert lied.

Van Dyke returned a few minutes later with clothes draped over his left arm and two backpacks over his shoulders. "Found us some stuff. We better get moving. Sarge is waiting."

Dave, still chewing, looked up at Van Dyke with a scowl. "Those are my dad's clothes."

"Yeah, well your dad ain't here now, is he?"

"He's coming back. You can't have those," Dave replied.

Van Dyke chuckled. "Whatever, kid."

"Knock it off, Corporal," Albert said. He stood and motioned for Van Dyke to get out of sight. The man looked like he was going to protest, but then just shrugged.

"I'll meet you back in the other room in a few," Albert said. "Me and Dave need to have a chat."

Van Dyke left without a further word, and although Dave watched him go with the same scowl, he too remained silent.

"I don't like that guy," Dave said a moment later.

"He's okay," Albert replied. He let out a short sigh and said, "I got to be honest with you. Your parents probably aren't coming home."

Dave lowered the bar and stopped chewing. "Why would you say that?"

"Because Washington is gone. My family was there too, and they died. There was a bomb. I came here to find my sister, and I think you could help me."

For a moment Dave just stared at Albert. Then the tears came racing down his dirty face, burning away the grime.

"I'm sorry," Albert said. "Losing loved ones is hard, but you got to keep fighting. Even when your team's down, you can't give up."

Dave's sniffles gradually subsided, and he nodded firmly. "Okay, Big Al. I'll come with you on your quest. It'll be like the Fellowship of the Ring."

Albert laughed. "Something like that… I guess." He gestured toward the closet. "Change out of those clothes, okay? Grab something warm to wear."

While Dave dressed, footsteps sounded outside the door. Albert raised his rifle but then lowered the barrel when Van Dyke and Flint moved into the room, frantic looks on their faces.

"Get out of your gear right now," Flint said, shutting

the door behind them.

"Why? What's wrong?" Albert asked.

"That guy in the street earlier," Flint said. "I heard what he was saying. Apparently those guys we killed last night weren't just some low level gangbangers. One of them was pretty far up with the Latin Kings. They're looking for three soldiers in black body armor."

"We got to ditch the kid," Van Dyke said. "He'll slow us down."

Albert looked at the boy, who was halfway into a sweatshirt. Dave pointed at Flint. "You're Legolas, 'cause you got big ears," Dave said.

Flint raised a brow. "No, I'm Sergeant Flint."

"Leave the goddamn kid," Van Dyke insisted.

"We need him," Albert said. "Those people are looking for three soldiers, right? Three guys and a kid won't be as suspicious, then."

Flint snorted. "Okay, fine, whatever, but we need to get moving, stat."

Dave threw on a Ninja Turtles sweatshirt, and grinned to reveal two missing teeth. "Let the Fellowship of the Ring begin!"

— 12 —

The radio crackled, stirring Colton awake.

"Chief, this is Don, you copy, over?"

Colton groaned in his bed and picked up the radio. He paused for a moment to sit up and then said, "Copy, Don. Go ahead. Over."

"The FEMA camp is all clear. Detective Plymouth said you wanted to know."

"Roger that. I'll be at the station shortly, over."

Colton rubbed the sleep from his eyes and looked out the window. He had no idea how long he'd slept, but it was still light outside. The bedroom door creaked open and Colton's wife, Kelly walked in holding a cup of coffee.

"I thought I heard voices," she said.

Colton swung his legs over the bed and she brought him a warm mug.

"It's pretty watered down, but I'm rationing."

"This is great, thank you," Colton said.

For several minutes he sat on the edge of the bed drinking the watery coffee. Kelly watched in silence, waiting for him to speak. He was so exhausted he couldn't find the right words. Instead, he stood and walked downstairs to the kitchen table. Kelly joined him, and a few more moments of silence passed.

"I don't like you going by yourself," Kelly finally said. "In fact, I hate it. I can't believe I'm saying this, but maybe you should take Raven with you."

Colton shook his head. "No, he's needed here. I can't risk pulling a single man away from our barriers right now, either. We need all the firepower in Estes Park that we can manage."

He took another slug of coffee. The caffeine was starting to kick in, but what he really needed was another five hours of sleep. After a second gulp of the weak brew, he set the cup back on the kitchen table and went over the checklist he and Kelly had created to help their family get through the winter. Colton noted with pride that forty of the fifty items had already been completed.

"This is good, Kelly. While I'm gone, I'd sure appreciate it if you could get—"

"Marcus, I really don't want you going by yourself," she interrupted.

He looked up to meet her gaze. "I have to go."

She folded her arms across her chest. "So I don't get any say in the matter? That's what you're saying?"

Colton waited a moment before replying. He was on edge from the lack of sleep and the violence of the previous day. The last thing he wanted to do was get into an argument with his wife right now, especially before heading out on a dangerous mission.

"I have to do this for our town, and our family," he said. "We're not going to make it without help."

To his surprise, Kelly nodded and said, "I know, Marcus. I've never been able to talk you out of anything you were determined to do. It's just…we need you to come home, okay?"

He covered her hand with his. "I promise, love."

After a moment, she grabbed the checklist and looked it over. "I'm behind on a few things you asked me to do, but I'll get caught up today. I'm heading into town with the Travises from next door."

A spike of fear went through him. "No, dammit! I told you a dozen times already that you have to stay inside," Colton snapped. His words were sharper than he meant them to be. "I'm sorry. I'm exhausted. But it's not safe out there. We lost seven people yesterday. I don't want you going anywhere until I'm back. We have plenty of food, water, and supplies until then."

Kelly reared back to study him. "Keep your voice down, Marcus. Risa is already worried enough. Frankly, I'm worried too if you're keeping things from me. What's going on out there?"

Colton stood from the table and gestured for his wife to follow him to his office, where they could talk in private. Risa looked up from the book she was reading on the couch as they passed.

"We'll be right back, sweetie," Kelly said.

Colton quietly shut the door to his lightly furnished office, taking a moment to look at the snow-brushed boulders in their backyard right outside the window.

"I'm sorry about cursing," he said.

Kelly held his gaze for a moment and then nodded. "I understand you're tired, and that you have a major burden trying to keep everyone safe, but don't snap at me. I'm your ally, not your enemy."

"You're my rock." Colton reached out, and Kelly hesitantly accepted a kiss to her forehead.

"I'm scared, Marcus," she said when he pulled away. "What if something happens to you out there? Isn't there anyone else you can send on your behalf or take with you?"

Colton thought for a moment, but who could he send?

He didn't trust Don, and it was too dangerous to send Lindsey. The detective was tough and savvy, but a pretty young woman like her would be a target for every raider from here to Loveland. Raven didn't know the first thing about negotiation. There wasn't anyone that could do this job but him.

"I'm sorry, but there's no one else that can do it."

Kelly wiped at her eyes, smearing a tear into her hair. "I wish Jake could go with you. He always had your back."

Colton glanced at the picture of him and Jake Englewood on his desk. They were younger men then, and stronger. God, how Colton wished he was still here to help fight the coming battles. Kelly stepped over to his bugout bag and rucksack on the floor in front of his desk. His gear was all spread out, including his weapons and ammunition.

"Looks like you're preparing for a war," Kelly said.

"I'm preparing for the future," he said. For the past month he'd shared most everything with his wife, trusting her to handle the harsh realities of their world with the same strength and grace she'd always shown during their marriage. But now, as he was about to leave Estes Park for the first time since the bombs dropped, he feared telling her what Jason Cole had said. It would only make her worry.

"What else aren't you telling me, Marcus? I know there's something…"

He almost laughed; she was sharp as ever. "Raven and I both think a fight is coming. Not like the skirmish with the raiders or the sporadic violence we've seen in the past few weeks. Something much, much worse. That's why I'm going out there to find help."

Kelly was silent for a moment, fear radiating from her eyes. He wrapped his arms around her and held her for several moments. "How bad is it out there?" she asked.

"It's getting worse every day," Colton said. "The FEMA camp outside Loveland was attacked, Fort Collins is in shambles, and Denver is hell."

Kelly placed a hand on her heart, silent.

"We've been lucky compared to the cities east of the mountains, but the violence that's torn those communities apart is headed our way," Colton continued. "I have to find allies to help us keep order until the government can make it out this way and get the grid back up. I just hope we can survive until then."

Kelly locked eyes with Colton. "Can't Secretary Montgomery help?" she asked quietly, like she knew it wasn't possible.

"She's got her hands full with a thousand other communities that need help. Estes Park already got more than most."

The door creaked open and Risa walked into the office. She clutched her stuffed donkey to her chest, the one Colton had wanted her to give up. He was glad she'd kept it.

Risa looked at the rucksack and bugout bag, tilting her head curiously. "Papa, are you going somewhere?"

"Yes, sweetie, I'm going to meet some friends."

"Can I come?"

"I'm sorry," Colton said. "I need you to stay here, okay?"

Kelly gestured for Risa. She walked over, and Kelly wrapped her arms around their daughter. Having his wife and daughter staring at him with fear in their eyes broke Colton's heart—but it was the exact reason he had to leave them tonight. This was the best way to protect them.

"I'll be back in two days," he said. "I've already told Raven and Detective Plymouth to check on you guys."

Kelly nodded. "Okay."

He hesitated, and then said, "You still have that thing I gave you?"

"Yeah." Kelly lifted up her shirt slightly so Colton could see the grip of the pistol without Risa seeing the gun.

"Good," he said. "Remember to keep rationing the food and water. If something happens, go to the safe room in the cellar."

"I hate that place," Risa said. "It's dark, and cold, and…"

"It's a safe place, kiddo," Kelly said, running a hand through Risa's hair.

"Actually, let's go take a look at it before I go," Colton said. "I'm going to grab some more gear from there."

They made their way through the house to the basement, where Colton had installed a safe room after the 2013 floods. Usually they used a bookshelf filled with paint cans to hide the steel door, but he'd gone inside for gear earlier and had pushed it aside.

Colton clicked on his flashlight and walked into the large room that was built directly under their deck. Bunk beds were positioned against the north wall, and barrels of fresh water and crates of MREs lined the west and east walls.

"If something happens, this is where you're going to come with your mom," Colton said to Risa. "Do you understand?"

Still clutching her donkey, she just stared into the

dimly lit space.

"When I'm gone, you listen to your mom, okay?" Colton said.

This time Risa nodded, once.

Colton continued into the room and grabbed a box of the MREs. He wasn't planning on being gone long, but he would take them just in case. He set the box outside the door, closed it, and then pushed the bookshelf back into place.

A few minutes later, they were loading his gear into the Jeep outside. Colton threw the rucksack on the passenger seat. Next came his rifles: an M14 and an AR-15. He kept one Colt .45 holstered and set the other on the seat.

"I love you both," Colton said after shutting the passenger door. "I'll see you in two days."

Risa hugged him around his waist and buried her head against his chest. Kelly kissed him, hugging both Colton and Risa tight. Something about the moment seemed final, like...

No, don't even start thinking like that, Marcus.

"I'll see you soon," Colton said. He jumped into the Jeep and waved as he backed out of the driveway. As soon as he pulled onto East Elkhorn Avenue, the questions and doubts in his mind vanished. He remembered the oaths he'd sworn to his country, his family, and his town. Sometimes an oath required a man to pick the safety of others over his own. Colton would protect Kelly, Risa, and all the other people of Estes Park, no matter the cost to himself.

He drove with a renewed sense of purpose and made good time to downtown. Colton spotted Lindsey and Don talking outside Bond Park. The patrol sergeant's presence at the refugee camp was a bad sign. Colton sped down the final stretch of street and then parked outside town hall. He motioned for Lindsey and Don to come over to the Jeep.

Lindsey leaned down to the truck and said, "Thank God you're here, Chief. We heard some crazy news. I'll let Don tell it."

Don pulled off his cowboy hat and scratched at his thinning hair. "I was finally able to reach someone at the Larimer County's Sheriff's Office with the radio," he said. "Sheriff Gerrard was shot dead by raiders. Apparently one of his deputies, Mike Thompson, has taken over."

"The UFC fighter?" Colton asked.

"Yeah, that's the one. Real gunslinger with a killer instinct," Don said, stepping up to the Jeep.

Colton tilted his head. "Sounds like he's the guy I need to talk to, then. Do you know where he's holed up at?"

"Fort Collins," Don said.

"I guess that will be my second stop after the FEMA camp." Colton paused to look Don in the eye. "The FEMA camp is all clear? The attack is over?"

A quick and firm nod from Don. "That's right. You're good to go, Chief."

"Okay," Colton said. "I'll head inside now to listen to the broadcast and see if I can arrange a time to meet up with the new sheriff."

Colton went to shut off his Jeep, but Don stopped him with his hand. "I heard from the station at Fort Collins that Thompson just left with several deputies. I'll radio him and let him know you're coming. It will save you some time."

"Sounds good," Colton said, anxious to get moving. "I better get going."

"Good luck," Don said. He spat chewing tobacco juice on the pavement and put his cowboy hat back on. Lindsey looked over her shoulder as he strode by Bond Park. She scowled as Don eyed the refugees with distaste.

"He said anything about my decision to let them stay yet?" Colton asked.

"Said you weren't thinking with your head. I told Donnie he needs to try thinking more with his heart."

Colton smiled. "Not sure he has one."

"That prick should be the one going out there to meet with the sheriff," Lindsey said with a snort. "Personally, I don't trust Thompson. I heard he's got a temper and has multiple pending cases against him for using excessive force."

"Another reason I should be the one to meet him," Colton said. "I wouldn't trust Don to make us any friends."

"Agreed."

"Just keep things in line here and make sure Raven stays out of trouble," Colton said. "Where is he, by the way?"

"He's spending some time with Sandra and Allie at his place. We're going to leave for Storm Mountain later today to see if we can get a meeting with John Kirkus and his men. Anything specific you'd like me to say or offer Kirkus?"

Colton paused to think, then said, "I'd like you to talk to John about establishing an outpost there to warn us of attack along Highway 34. If they say no, you're authorized to offer them a few horses and some diesel for their generators. If they say no to that, tell them they can have all the access they want to the park to hunt in return for their help."

"Roger that. What are you going to offer Sheriff Thompson for his help?"

"I'm honestly not sure yet, but I've got a good drive ahead of me to think about it."

She patted the Jeep door, her gaze moving toward the front of the police station where Mayor Andrews and Tom Feagen were standing. Colton waved and then put the Jeep in gear. The last thing he wanted to do was talk to either of them.

"Good luck, Chief," Lindsey said.

"You too, Detective." Colton paused and glanced back at Lindsey. "One more thing. Tell Raven to keep his mouth shut on Storm Mountain. He's there to protect you, and that's it."

She patted her gun and grinned. "More like I'll be the one looking out for him."

Colton smiled and waved goodbye. He glanced in the rearview mirror as he drove away, studying the crowd in Bond Park. Something told him he was going to have more problems on his hands when he came back...assuming he came back at all.

***

Fenix stood by the window of his cell looking out over the snowy forest, trying to figure out where the hell he was being held prisoner.

The good news was these guys weren't military, but the bad news was they were going to hand him over to the military as soon as they could secure their ten million dollars in gold.

Fenix pounded the concrete wall with his palm.

In a single night, he'd lost most of his inner circle and

TRACKERS 3: THE STORM

was completely cut off from the rest of his network. They were probably out there looking for him right now, but if he didn't make it back in a few days, his power would transfer to Zach Horton, a former Army Sergeant that Fenix had known for over a decade. He liked Zach, but the man wasn't ready to lead the Sons of Liberty.

I have to get back to my men. I have to finish what I started.

"Let me out of here!" Fenix yelled at the top of his lungs.

The noise attracted the attention of one of the guards. The steel door creaked open, and a man with silver hair stepped in. Fenix recognized him as the bastard who'd shoved a gun in his face last night on the road. Two more men stood sentry in the hallway, all of them wearing fatigues. These men, whoever they were, didn't have any symbols or logos on their outfits. So who the hell were they?

"Shut your trap before I shut it for you," the guard said.

Fenix snarled. If it weren't for the cuffs on his wrists, he would have dropped this guy with a punch to the throat.

"Where the fuck am I?"

"You're in a prison cell."

Fenix clamped his jaw shut and managed his anger for a moment before replying. "You do realize my army is going to be coming after me, right?"

The man stared at him, sizing him up, and Fenix did the exact same thing in return. The guard stood at least six feet tall and had sharp features. His fatigues were tight enough that Fenix could see sculpted muscles beneath the fabric.

"You going to tell me your name?" Fenix asked.

179

"Hacker." He pulled the duty belt up around his waist, rattling two sheathed knives, a pair of pliers, and the hatchet he'd pulled out on the road the night before.

Fenix laughed when he made the connection. "Hacker, like you hack people up? That's fucking funny."

The guard smiled back. "I'm not worried about your racist, ignorant friends, to be honest. They didn't do very well against the United States military last night, now did they? Us on the other hand...well, you saw that helo go down in a hail of gunfire."

Fenix felt his face warm. Footfalls in the hallway distracted him momentarily. They weren't the heavy echo of military boots, but rather the click of dress shoes. A man Fenix hadn't seen before rounded the corner, dressed in a pinstriped suit with a red pocket square in the breast pocket. Black leather shoes, polished to a shine, clacked on the floor. His long dark hair was combed back into a neat ponytail. Like Spears, he seemed to be some kind of Indian. Fenix couldn't be bothered to guess what type. They were all the same, anyway.

"That will be all, Hacker. I'll take over now," the man said.

With a nod, Hacker moved out of his boss's way.

"I've met Hacker, so what the fuck is your nickname? Crazy Horse?" Fenix asked.

Hacker stepped forward, drawing a buck knife, but the well-dressed man held up a hand. "Hacker's been instrumental in collecting many debts over the years for me. I really don't think you want to see how good he is with his tools."

"Yeah, I get the point, but that's a pretty stupid name if you ask me," Fenix said.

Hacker twirled the knife and said, "Please give me a

few minutes with this asshole, sir."

The man in the suit raised a hand to silence his subordinate. Hacker backed off immediately, and Fenix felt the first trickle of fear. Whoever this guy was, even the knife-toting psycho respected him.

"So who the hell are you?" Fenix asked with furrowed brows.

Tightening his tie, the man directed his cold, bottomless gaze at Fenix. "You can call me Mr. Redford."

***

Sandra sat on the swing on Raven's porch. His land was on the edge of Rocky Mountain National Park. Aspen and ponderosa trees formed a natural fence around the yard. A creek meandered along the foothills. She listened to the trickle of water and the whispering wind as it worked its way through the canopy of trees.

Allie giggled as she chased Creek across the yard. The dog left tracks behind in the thin carpet of snow. It was getting colder by the day, and soon Sandra would be getting out her winter jacket and gloves. The thought of winter made her shiver, and she folded her arms across her fleece jacket.

A creaking sounded behind her as the front door swung open. Raven stepped out holding a jar of tea and a plate of crackers and elk jerky. He placed them both on the table within reach of the porch swing and then took a seat next to Sandra, letting out a relaxed sigh. She tried not to look at his battered hands. Sandra suspected that he'd busted his knuckles open interrogating the man who'd shot him. Still, the nurse in her reached out to check them.

"What am I going to do with you, Sam?" she asked.

Raven pulled his hand back and brought his fingers up to his sheared-off ear.

"Don't touch it," Sandra said. "If you get an infection, you're going to lose the entire thing. Listen to my advice for once in your life."

He lowered his hand. "I never ignore your advice. I just choose to go my own path."

Sandra wagged her head and reached across Raven and plucked a couple of crackers off the plate. She popped one into her mouth. They were stale, but she didn't care. They couldn't afford to be picky about food these days.

"You're going to get yourself killed, and then what are Allie and I going to do?"

"I've proven I can take care of myself," he said.

"You've proven you're tough as hell, but a man can only sustain so many broken bones and bruises before he ends up in a grave. How are your ribs, by the way?"

He patted his chest gently and shrugged. Then he hollered at Allie and Creek.

"You guys want something to eat?"

Sandra tried not to let her frustration bleed through, but every time her brother went on a scouting mission, she wondered if it was the last time she would see him. Now, more than ever, they needed to stick together. That's what families did when times got tough.

Allie and Creek joined them on the porch, and for the first time in days, they sat sharing a meal and listening to the sounds of nature. Sandra decided to give up on talking to Raven about his Rambo antics and just enjoy the moment.

The sense of peace didn't last.

A memory of the conversation with Teddy and Allie

back in the hospital surfaced in her mind. She felt helpless to protect Allie from the death surrounding them. The wave of violence heading their way wasn't going to stop, and Raven couldn't protect them forever.

"Can we go play more?" Allie asked after a few minutes.

Sandra nodded. Grabbing a few more pieces of jerky, Allie then ran back out into the yard with Creek. Sandra and Raven sat in silence, watching the little girl and the dog, impossibly gentle no matter what Allie did.

"What do you plan to do next?" she asked after a while.

Raven rubbed at his eyes and stifled a yawn.

"I'm going to head up to Storm Mountain with Lindsey to see if we can get John Kirkus and his boys to form some sort of alliance or something."

"And then what?" Sandra asked.

Raven glanced over at her. "We identify our weak points, secure our borders, make some friends, and prepare for what comes next."

"Which is what?"

"War," he said. "We have enemies on all sides. Estes Park is doing well, relatively speaking, and there's a lot of people faring way worse than our town. I'm surprised we haven't seen more refugees, to be honest."

Sandra zipped her fleece jacket up to her chin, suddenly freezing. Her final question was the one she had been dreading to ask, but she had to know.

"Do you still plan on going after Nile Redford and that Nazi asshole?"

Raven leaned back on the swing, the wood creaking.

"My priority is to keep you and Allie safe."

Sandra smiled at his response. Maybe she could even

convince Raven to give up his quest to kill Redford and Fenix. She hated Fenix for killing Nathan, but she couldn't bear the thought of losing her brother too.

Her heart broke all over again when she thought of the pilot. They'd never had a chance to find out whether they had a future together. He'd been a good man—one of the best she'd ever met. And Fenix had taken him from her, just like Brown Feather had tried to take her daughter and Redford had taken the town's supplies. There were too many men out there who took what they wanted without regard to the damage they did. If Raven kept going after them, he would end up dead, just like Nathan.

"What's wrong?" Raven asked, sensing her sadness.

"Nothing, I was just thinking."

Raven studied her for a moment, and then stood to stretch his back and arms. He stepped over to the porch stairs and looked back at her. "Now I have a question for you, sis."

"What's that?"

Raven pulled the Glock out of his waistband and held it up. "Which one of us is going to teach Allie to protect herself?"

— 13 —

Albert slowed to look at their reflection in a Radio Shack window as he passed by with Sergeant Flint, Corporal Van Dyke, and their new sidekick, Dave. Aside from the weapons the men carried, Albert and Flint looked like they were about to go on a Caribbean cruise. They were dressed in tight button-down shirts sporting palm trees and umbrellas. The only things missing were flip-flops and sunglasses. They were the only clothes Albert had found that actually fit him and the sergeant, and "fit" was not exactly the proper way to describe these jeans.

Albert loosened the belt another notch, but that didn't help the fact the jeans were still several inches too short and far too tight in the legs, more like women's Capri pants than anything. At least the shirt covered his body armor.

Thankfully Van Dyke had found something that didn't look ridiculous. He wore an Under Armor shirt and cargo pants, and his backpack was stuffed full of their night vision goggles and extra magazines.

They were an odd-looking bunch, and Albert was starting to wonder if they wouldn't have been better off wearing their fatigues or simply staying put until nightfall. Sergeant Flint however, had been adamant about getting back to the SC as soon as possible.

The group cut through alleyways, avoiding the roads

on their way to the apartment building where Albert hoped to find his sister. He looked up at the gray sky, wondering what time it was. The team had already wasted time looking for more clothes and then another two hours avoiding the groups of civilians prowling through the streets. They'd had to stop several times to change Flint's dressings. His wound was still bleeding, and the threat of infection had Albert worried.

A gunshot cracked in the distance, but none of the group, not even Dave, stopped to take cover. They were all used to the noise now.

"When do I get a gun?" Dave asked.

"Frodo had a sword, not a gun," Albert replied. Dave had already decided he was the Hobbit hero of the group, since he was the shortest.

"Okay, then I want a sword."

Flint and Van Dyke both chuckled, but Albert stopped and turned to Dave. He reached into his backpack and pulled out his tactical knife. Dave's eyes widened and his lips curled into a grin that showed off his missing teeth.

"Can I have it? Does it glow when bad guys are around?" Dave asked.

"No, it doesn't glow," Albert said when he realized Dave was serious. "Don't take it out of the sheath unless I tell you."

Dave picked up the knife, holding it aloft in both hands reverently, like it was a holy relic. "Thank you, Mr. Big Al."

"Come on," Flint said.

They continued onward, walking casually but cautiously. Flint and Van Dyke avoided flashing hand signals or talking in military lingo. Instead, the sergeant and corporal played the part of lost tourists trying to

186

make their way out of the city, something they had discussed before leaving the apartment earlier.

So far it was working.

The people on the street paid them little attention. The only thing that could possibly give them away was their rifles, but pretty much everyone was armed out here. Only a few civilians looked in their direction. From the conversations they overheard, it seemed like the majority of people were heading toward the SC or out of the city.

"They were giving out food last night," Albert heard a woman say as they passed her. The dark-skinned woman had two small children with her, a boy and a girl, their hands gripped tightly in hers. "They might do it again today, so we've got to go see."

"But we have to wait for daddy," the girl said.

The woman didn't respond as she hurried down the sidewalk away from Albert and his team. He considered warning her against going to the SC, but they were so close to his sister's apartment and he had his hands full with Dave. The kid had stopped to look at a pile of trash on the side of the street, bending down to examine something while the soldiers continued down the sidewalk.

"Let's go," Albert said.

Dave looked up with his fingers clamped on his nose. "It smells out here."

"So stop sniffing everything like a dog," Flint said. He waved them toward the street corner that Van Dyke was already approaching.

Two Caucasian men and a woman were hanging out on the patio at the abandoned Starbucks. Albert, in police mode, scanned them for weapons, but he didn't see any on them or in the bags they had stowed under the metal tables. The trio looked in his direction briefly, but then went back to talking.

A skirt of glass surrounded the front entrance where someone had thrown a chair through the window. From a quick glance, Albert could see the coffee shop had been raided weeks earlier. Another group of civilians caught his attention across the street. The man leading the group held a shotgun, and one of the women had a pistol tucked in her waistband. The man dipped his head at Albert, and Albert returned the respectful but wary gesture.

In some ways, trekking through Charlotte was like being in the Wild West, where everyone was packing heat and no one knew who they could trust.

Albert looked back at the people sitting outside Starbucks. He gripped his own carbine tighter and looked for weapons again, even more suspicious now that he didn't see any. One of them was smoking a joint, filling the air with the scent of marijuana.

Dave skipped alongside them, clutching the sheathed blade in both hands, oblivious to all the possible threats around them. He no longer seemed to care that Albert and the soldiers had taken his dad's clothing. He'd retreated into his own little fantasy world and seemed to be enjoying his role as an adventurer for now. But the kid was going to crash eventually, especially when it sank in that his parents weren't coming home.

"We're hobbits, Mr. Big Al," Dave was saying. "Hobbits need a second breakfast, and I'm hungry. Can we stop for some taters?"

Flint glared over his shoulder. "Shut up, kid. You're driving me crazy."

"Yes, sir," Dave said, halting to throw up a salute.

Flint pointed to the set of old apartment buildings at

the end of the next block. They were at least five decades older than the more modern construction around the area. Albert's twin sister had always enjoyed older things—books, architecture, hot rods…men.

"That's our target," Flint said.

"Just a little bit farther until we're home," said the corporal loudly, playing the part of civilians in case anyone was listening.

Dave stopped next to Albert and looked up at him. "We're adding your sister to the fellowship now?" he asked curiously.

"I sure hope so, buddy."

"Well, what are we waiting for?" Dave said, his brown eyes lighting up with excitement. "Lady Big Al needs rescuing!"

Albert smiled. He was really starting to like Dave.

They continued down the sidewalk, approaching the intersection.

"Those are some nice machine guns," said one of the men sitting on the Starbucks patio.

Flint and Van Dyke stopped in the intersection while Albert hung back with Dave on the sidewalk. The two men and the woman stood and blocked the path in front of them, but their attention was on Van Dyke and Flint.

"What's in the bags?" asked the woman. He guessed she was in her twenties, but too much tanning and substance abuse had added an extra ten years to her appearance.

"None of your business," Flint said.

The two men grinned. Albert scanned them again, but they wore long sleeves and pants that hid any potential gang tattoos. The guy on the left had a black stocking cap on, and the one on the right wore a Panthers hat.

"Those automatic rifles?" asked the guy with the stocking cap.

"Sure looks like 'em, Johnny," said Panthers hat.

"Military-issue M4s with suppressors," Johnny said. "Where'd y'all get those, if you don't mind me asking?"

"I said it's none of your business," Flint said. He waved at Albert. "Come on, man."

The two men and their female friend turned to look at Albert and Dave.

"Oh, you got one of them fancy guns, too," the woman said.

Van Dyke and Flint both raised their rifles, and Flint jerked his chin at Albert, a sign that said, *Get your ass moving.*

"Stay behind me," Albert whispered to Dave.

Instead of keeping back and silent, Dave waved and held up his knife in the other hand. "Do you like my sword? I'm gonna use it to slay Orcs!"

The trio blocking the sidewalk all burst out laughing. Flint shook his head and shot Albert a glare, but Albert's focus flitted to the woman, who was reaching for something in her backpack. Van Dyke saw it at the same moment.

"Don't fucking move!" yelled the corporal.

She slowly withdrew her hand and said, "You're them soldiers the Latin Kings are looking for, aren't ya?"

Flint and Van Dyke trained their guns on her.

"Step away from your bag, ma'am," Flint said.

"You sound like a soldier or a cop," she replied. "We don't like either."

Her two companions both took a step forward, and Albert moved his finger to the trigger guard of his rifle. He quickly searched the area. The African-American man with a shotgun that they had passed earlier was looking in their direction.

Potential combatants on all sides, Albert thought.

There were more civilians down the street, and several of them were armed. Only a block separated him from the building where he hoped to find his sister, and he had a feeling all hell was about to break loose.

"Those guys you killed have powerful friends, and they put a nice price tag on your heads," said the guy with the Panthers hat.

The woman snickered. "They're going to skin you alive when they find you. Then they're going to hang you."

Johnny wagged his finger twice. "Or burn you alive."

Van Dyke backpedaled, trying to put distance between himself and the trio. Flint motioned for Albert with one hand, but kept his other on his carbine.

"We didn't kill anyone," Van Dyke said. "We're just trying to get home."

"Right," replied the woman. "Well, you better be on your way then."

Johnny clicked his tongue like a handler would to a horse. "Go on and get outta here."

Van Dyke and Flint continued to move away slowly, but as soon as Flint turned, Panthers hat suddenly reached behind his back, earning himself a three-round burst to the chest from Van Dyke's rifle that sent the guy crashing into the metal tables.

"No!" the woman screamed. She pulled a knife from her bag and lunged at Flint, who dropped her with a single shot to the skull. Johnny managed to pull out a Glock before Albert took him down with a burst to the chest.

He fell to his knees, gasping for air, his eyes locked on Albert.

"You..." he wheezed.

Albert didn't let him finish the sentence. He squeezed the trigger again, firing a round into the center of his stocking cap that sent him crashing backward. The shock of seeing his brains on the ground made Albert freeze.

Dave stood paralyzed too, mouth agape. A stream of piss trickled down his jeans. Somehow, he'd kept hold of the knife, but it hung loosely by his side.

"Move it, Randall!" Flint shouted.

Albert snapped out of the trance, grabbed the boy, and pulled him past the carnage. The other soldiers ran from the intersection with their rifles shouldered. Shouts and screams rang out from all directions as they bolted around stalled cars.

Looking over his shoulder, Albert searched for other hostiles. His gaze found the man with the shotgun. For a second, Albert thought the guy was going to raise the gun and fire at them, but instead the man simply dipped his head again and then corralled his family in the opposite direction.

There were still good people out here, people that just wanted to protect their kin. The end of the world drove some folks crazy, and Albert hoped he would never stop being sickened and disturbed by the evil that some people did in the absence of law and order. But the killing was starting to get easier and easier each time he pulled the trigger, and part of Albert wasn't sure if his soul would survive this new world.

"Contacts!" Flint shouted.

Albert looked to the left side of the street and saw several men with rifles flooding out of a building. Bullets whizzed in his direction.

"Run!" Van Dyke shouted. "RUN!"

***

Charlize sat in the cafeteria watching her son eat lunch. She was still exhausted even after sleeping for five hours straight, but being able to sit and have a meal with Ty reminded her how lucky they were to have a roof over their heads, plenty of food, and electricity. Over ninety-nine percent of Americans were fighting for basic survival.

But if she was so damned lucky, then why did she feel so terrible?

Ty scooped a spoonful of vegetables into his mouth and looked across the room at Melinda Collins, the resident teacher at Constellation. Ten kids his age sat around a white table with her.

"You sure you don't want to eat with your friends?" Charlize asked.

"Maybe tomorrow." Ty picked at his food, eyes downcast.

Charlize knew how important it was for Ty to be around other kids his age, but selfishly she was glad he wanted to eat with her. She had tried to give him space and not press him on what had happened at the Castle. Seeing him like this made her wonder what horrors he'd witnessed. Ty had been too young to clearly remember the car wreck that had killed his father and left him paralyzed, but he'd been right there when Fenix executed Nathan. It was too much for anyone to bear, and she wished he would talk to her.

Glancing up from his food, Ty asked, "Do you have to work tonight?"

"Some, but I promise I'll read to you tonight, okay?"

Ty picked up a carrot, dropped it, and then took a bite of his peanut butter and jelly sandwich instead.

Charlize finished her chicken salad and washed it down with a Red Bull. She knew it wasn't good for her, but she needed the caffeine. Boots clicking on the tiled floor commanded her attention, and she turned to see Colonel Raymond crossing the room. He stopped at their table.

"Sorry to interrupt your lunch, Secretary Montgomery, but General Thor would like to speak with you in the situation room. President Diego will join later to brief you on another situation."

Ty finished chewing and politely said, "May I come?"

"Not this time, sweetie," Charlize said. "You have to go back to class with Miss Collins."

The teacher was already corralling the other kids out of the dining hall.

"But Mom..." Ty began.

"I'll be right there, Colonel," Charlize said.

"Sounds good, ma'am, I'll be waiting in the hallway."

"Do you think General Thor found him?" Ty asked.

Charlize stood and grabbed the handles on his wheelchair. "I sure hope so."

He was quiet for a moment, and then twisted around to look at her, his face solemn. "Mom?"

"Yeah?"

"I'm sorry."

She brushed her hand over his hair. "Sorry for what, sweetie?"

"I'm scared. I know I shouldn't be, but I'm scared all

the time," he said.

"Don't apologize. You should never be afraid to be afraid. Real men get scared, and anyone that says otherwise is not being honest."

"I know, but I'm scared to be alone. I keep having these dreams where *he* comes for me. Sometimes, when I wake up and you're not there, I think I'm still at the Castle."

Charlize's heart shattered into pieces. "Oh, Ty. I'm the one who should be sorry. The president needs my help for a little while, but I will come back. In the meantime, why don't you spend some time with the other kids? Miss Collins will keep an eye on you. Maybe you'll even make a new friend."

Ty nodded his head several times. "Okay," he said. "Okay, I'll try."

She kissed him on the cheek and watched him wheel across the room to Miss Collins and the children.

Exhausted but anxious for news about Fenix, Charlize followed Colonel Raymond back to Command. The room was bustling as usual. General Thor was waiting for her in the situation room. Colonel Raymond shut the door behind them.

"The remains of Sierra Team have been recovered," he said as soon as she took a seat. "Their helicopter was shot down over a country road on the west side of Apache Peak."

"Do we have any new leads on Fenix?" Charlize asked. A nice lunch with Ty and several hours of sleep had helped refill her depleted energy reserves, but her patience was already slipping away. Why couldn't these men ever get to the point?

"Negative, ma'am," Thor said. "We recalled our

second Black Hawk to Buckley and are waiting for new intel."

Charlize took a breath before answering. "I understand, General. Do not send out anyone else until we can confirm his whereabouts. We can't afford to lose more good men and women."

"Understood," Thor replied.

"Anything else to report?"

"No, ma'am."

Charlize wondered if this five-minute briefing was worth cutting her lunch short for, but she said nothing. Thor gathered his folder and walked out of the room with Raymond on his heels.

"The president will be in shortly," Raymond said before closing the door.

Charlize sat alone in the room, mind racing. It wasn't often that President Diego requested a one-on-one meeting, and her gut told her this wasn't going to be about anything good. A few minutes later, the president walked into the room, offering a quick nod but no smile. Dressed in a suit with his dark hair slicked back, he looked more like a mobster than a politician. General Thor returned to the room with him. Next came Doctor Peter Lundy, the head scientist at Constellation.

So much for this being a one-on-one.

"Good afternoon, Mr. President," she said, standing.

He nodded and dropped a folder on the table. Thor and Lundy took a seat across from Charlize, and Diego sat at the head of the table. He passed over a confidential folder to Charlize, and she quickly broke the seal.

"Read the first page. Then I'll go into more details," Diego said.

Charlize thumbed to the opening of the memo,

anxious to see what had the president on edge. It only took her a few moments to read the front page, and she quickly realized his bad mood wasn't from some disaster at a SC or the further spread of cholera like she feared—it was due to a major development in foreign aid.

"The People's Republic of China is offering us quite the deal," Diego said. "Five hundred ships full of heavy duty machinery and enough supplies to help us rebuild our power grid. They're even including some new locomotives and equipment to help us get our rail system back up and running."

Impressive, Charlize thought to herself. If anyone had asked her before the attack whether China would end up being one of their biggest allies and benefactors, she would have been skeptical at best.

"I'm sure you're thinking the same thing I've been thinking since I saw this come in over the wires," Diego said.

"That there's a catch? That maybe China did have something to do with the North Korean attack?" she said.

The president ran his uninjured hand through his hair. "I'm not sure about the latter, although I've wondered. Thing is, why would China want our country to collapse? It hurts their economy. It would make no sense to aid North Korea in an attack that would devastate the world market."

"True, but an attack would also open the door for the Chinese to become the most powerful nation in the world," Charlize said.

Lundy nodded. "She's right. They stand to make trillions off helping us rebuild. But what choice do we have?" He looked to President Diego. "Sir, as you know, I've been tasked with helping get the power back on, but

I simply don't have the resources or logistics to do that on a wide scale right now. I was optimistic two weeks ago, but we're running into so many unforeseen issues, especially the extreme violence on the highways and in the cities. Simply put, we need help."

"That's why we need to get our railways working again," Charlize said.

"It's not enough, Charlize, and we don't have the time or resources or the soldiers to guard the rails," Diego quickly said, cutting her off.

Lundy nodded. "It's a great idea, but the President is correct."

Diego looked down at his folder before talking. He might look like a low-level gangster gone to seed, but behind that façade was one of the smartest men Charlize had ever worked with. "The Chinese have promised to help us with our logistics safety issue," Diego said at last. "Turn to page three."

Charlize thumbed through the document and then bit her lip when she saw what was written on page three. Now the truth was starting to surface. In addition to sending material goods, the Chinese were also proposing to send fifty thousand workers to help repair the grid— and twenty-five thousand troops to support their crews.

"I want your honest thoughts," Diego said. "Do you think they had something to do with the attack? Because if they did, and we open the floodgates to twenty-five thousand Chinese troops, then you can kiss our recovery efforts goodbye. We'll be at war."

Charlize looked at the ceiling, trying to digest the information. After a few seconds she shook her head, unsure. "I want to believe the Chinese are simply trying to help us, but I'm with you, sir, and I'm not ready to agree to a military occupation. It's one thing to have British and French soldiers working alongside our own troops, but what are people going to do when they see Chinese soldiers on our soil?"

Diego folded his hands and leaned back in his leather chair, heaving a sigh. "I agree, but we can't get the grid back up on our own. I'm afraid we might not have a choice. If we let the Chinese construction crews into the country, we could save millions of lives. At this point, I'm not sure we can say no."

— 14 —

Boulders sheeted with moss and snow covered the side of Highway 34. Raven rode Willow, while Lindsey rode Colton's horse, Obsidian. The beasts didn't seem to mind the cold, but Raven did. And he really didn't like the idea of sneaking up on John Kirkus at night, either. The preppers living up on Storm Mountain were a mixture of millionaires and backwoods rednecks, but they were all paranoid and armed to the teeth. Raven had a feeling they weren't going to like a cop and a Native American popping into their neck of the woods at this hour.

Raven zipped his coat up to his chin and tightened the Shemagh scarf around his neck. Lindsey wore a fleece-lined hunter's cap, scarf, and her Estes Park police all-weather coat. At least they were both prepared for the cold.

The only good thing about this mission was spending time with Lindsey. He had jumped at the chance to tag along, thinking that he might finally be able to charm her into agreeing to that drink. But tonight they weren't joking around like usual.

Willow rounded a bend and the final roadblock along Highway 34 came into view. Several men and a woman Raven didn't know were manning the post, rifles angled east toward the canyon walls. The roar of Big Thompson River rose over the click-clack of horse hooves on the asphalt shoulder of the road.

"I still think we should have waited until morning," Raven said.

Lindsey didn't bother turning in her saddle, but Creek looked up at the sound of Raven's voice. He had stopped to mark yet another bush, painting it with piss before trotting onward.

"We don't have time to waste," Lindsey said. "Tomorrow we're going to be needed in Estes Park, so tonight we need to secure a deal with Kirkus and his men to help protect this side of the valley from raiders. We can't wait any longer."

"Well, we could have at least had Colton drop us off. Save us the long trip."

This time she did twist in the saddle to glare at him. "It's only another three miles from here, Raven. I could run that far. We'll be there by nine, and I'll have you home before bedtime, I promise."

Raven chuckled, possible innuendoes swirling through his brain. "Has anyone even been up to Storm Mountain lately?" he asked instead.

"Colton sent a volunteer to warn them of potential fallout right after the bombs. I think Don's been up there a few times to scope things out, but Kirkus and his boys don't really like visitors."

"So I've heard."

A bitter wind bit into Raven, and he hunched down as their horses slowed to a stop at the roadblock. Creek sat on his haunches, tongue lolling.

"Where are you two headed?" asked a thin, bearded man wearing a heavy coat. He looked familiar, but Raven couldn't think of his name.

"We're on our way up Storm Mountain, on orders from Chief Colton," Lindsey said.

The other three people at the roadblock were wearing scarves or bandanas to cover their faces, something that made Raven uneasy. Hiding your face was never a good thing; it meant you were doing stuff you didn't want to be seen doing—in this case, turning away refugees or shooting at people that might come back hell-bent on revenge.

The thin man scratched his beard and then looked back down the road. "It's dangerous out there, ma'am, especially for a woman."

"I'm well aware," Lindsey replied.

The woman at the roadblock pulled her scarf down. "Mitch is right. We've heard some pretty atrocious things are happening in Loveland and Fort Collins."

"She's capable of taking care of herself," Raven chimed in. He shrugged a shoulder. "Besides, she's got me to watch after her."

Lindsey rolled her eyes. "I'd rather rely on the dog. Let us through, Mitch."

Raven remembered the guy with the beard now. He was a high school teacher with a drinking problem. They had spent the night in jail together a year ago. Raven hardly recognized him with the beard, though. He'd also lost about twenty pounds in the past month.

Creek was the first one around the concrete barriers. Raven used the reins to direct Willow through the gap after his dog. Every gaze focused on him and Lindsey as the horses trotted out into no man's land. The golden glow of a gorgeous sunset divided the bluffs of the valley ahead, bathing part of the land in light and shrouding everything below the rocky cliffs with shadows. Raven wanted to be off the road before it got dark.

"Where's the trail?" Lindsey asked.

"It's a Jeep path about a mile before we get to Drake. Should be there in about fifteen minutes at this pace."

"So let's pick it up," Lindsey said with a grin. "Come on, I'll race you."

Before Raven could reply, she grabbed the reins and gave Obsidian a good kick. The horse broke into a lope that quickly turned into a run. Lindsey bobbed up and down with her AR-15 slung over her shoulders.

Raven shook his head and whistled at Creek. The wind rustled Raven's hair, which was hanging out below his cap, and stung his injured ear as Willow increased her pace.

"Let's go, lady," he said.

The horse fell into a trot. By the time she was running, Obsidian was a good two hundred feet ahead of them. Lindsey shot him a glance over her shoulder and grinned.

Raven hollered after her. "Slow down!"

It was too dangerous to be playing games on the open road. Willow snorted into the cold wind while Raven scanned the road for any sign of hostiles or refugees. The way was clear, and Lindsey continued to ride Obsidian into the waning light at a breakneck pace. The river bubbled on the right side of the highway, clear water churning through the canyon. Raven loved that sound, along with the clean scent of cedar, but he was too on edge to enjoy it tonight.

The road turned ahead, providing a view of the minivan that he remembered seeing the night of the bombs when he had driven Sandra to Loveland to pick up Allie. The mountains swallowed the retreating sun, casting shadows over the entire valley. Raven made a clicking sound and pressed his heels to Willow.

You want to race, fine.

He sat up straight in the saddle, kept his heels down, pelvis tilted forward, and his butt relaxed as she picked up speed. In moments, the horse was moving at an all-out gallop on the side of the road along the river's edge. Creek wouldn't be able to keep up for long, but they weren't going much farther. The road continued to twist, and the trees along the shoulder blocked his view around the bend. Lindsey moved out onto the asphalt and rounded the corner, vanishing from sight.

What the hell? Is she trying to impress me, or has she lost her mind?

He gave Willow her head, riding low over her neck. The mare was fast, but Obsidian was faster. The freezing wind bit Raven's exposed skin and worked its way into his ear. Now he was just mad.

"Goddammit, Lindsey," he cursed.

Willow tore around the trees and onto the road, hooves clicking on the concrete. By the time Raven saw Lindsey, she had brought Obsidian to a halt on the side of the road under an umbrella of pine trees, a wide grin on her freckled face.

"I thought you'd put up more of a fight," she said as Willow slowed to a trot. Then she pointed at a gated trail to the left of the road. "That's the way up, right?"

Raven settled back in his saddle. "Yeah, that's it."

He took a moment to scan his surroundings. The dog caught up a few minutes later, tongue hanging out and panting in the cold air.

"Sorry, boy. Lindsey thought it would be fun to race."

"It was. I had my eyes on the road the entire time, Sam. You worry too much."

"I thought I didn't worry enough. But in this case, you got me a bit riled up."

Lindsey's smile vanished, her cheeks flaring as red as a tomato. "I'm sorry." She paused for a moment to stroke Obsidian's mane. "You know, I've been giving that drink some thought. Since you saved my life twice now, I'm considering it."

Raven perked at that. "Well, uh, I guess I do deserve…"

Creek looked up at Raven, then to Lindsey. The dog sneezed, shook himself, and trotted away, uninterested. The Akita wasn't used to sharing Raven's attention with anyone, but Creek quickly found something else to occupy his time. He chased a rabbit through the snow and under a bush.

Lindsey took a sip from her water bottle and then screwed the cap back on.

"You going to let him wander off?" she asked. "We need to get moving again."

"Creek?" Raven asked. "He'll catch up with us in a bit. Likes his independence. Sometimes I think he's more cat than dog. Besides, dog food is hard to come by and everyone's got to eat."

"True," Lindsey wiped her lips. "I'm not a fan of cats, by the way."

"Me neither. Guess that's something else we got in common."

"I was kidding. I like cats."

Raven narrowed his eyes.

"I'm just joking around, Sam!" Lindsey grinned again. "Come on, let's—"

The sound of a vehicle cut her off. Raven unslung his crossbow and Lindsey grabbed her AR-15. They dismounted from the horses and shooed the beasts away from the road.

"Creek!" Raven yelled.

The dog was nowhere in sight.

"Come on," Lindsey said.

Raven followed her to cover behind a pair of pine trees. The rattle of the engine filled the air again, but this time it seemed to be coming from all directions, an effect of the canyon.

Lindsey checked her rifle while Raven loaded an arrow into his bow. A moment later, headlights flooded the road, hitting the two from behind. The vehicle was coming from Estes Park, not Loveland.

"Who the hell could that be?" Lindsey said.

She strode out into the road, her rifle lowered. Raven slowly followed her out with his crossbow cradled over his chest. The Estes Park Police Department's Volkswagen Beetle putted around the corner, and Raven raised a hand to shield his face from the beams.

"Shut off the lights," Lindsey said in a voice just shy of a shout. She walked a few steps toward the vehicle. The driver kept the engine running while the passenger stepped onto the pavement.

To Raven's surprise, it was Don and Officer Sam Hines. The sergeant gestured for Raven and Lindsey. Hines, his right arm in a sling, eyed the crossbow suspiciously as if he thought Raven might shoot him again.

"What the hell is going on?" Lindsey asked.

"Raiders, more of them from the south," Don said. "We need Raven's help tracking them."

Raven looked at the horses. "It'll take time to ride back."

"Tie them to a tree and jump in with us," Don said. "Got no time. I'll send someone for them later."

Lindsey slung her rifle over her back, and Raven did the same thing with his bow. They hurried to Willow and Obsidian. Heart pounding, Raven grabbed the reins and looped them around a thick ponderosa.

"You'll be okay here," he whispered to the horse. Willow let out a snort.

"What are you doing?" Lindsey said.

Raven thought she was talking to him, but when he turned, he saw two guns pointed in his direction. Don spat tobacco juice on the ground and pumped his shotgun.

"What the hell is this?" Raven said.

Hines raised a Colt .45 at Raven's forehead, the hammer already pulled back.

"It's time to clear the shit out of Estes Park," Don said. "No more refugees, and no more Raven Spears." He glanced at Lindsey. "Sorry, Plymouth, but you've got to disappear to make this work."

"You son of a bitch," Lindsey growled. "You can't do this!"

Don moved the shotgun toward her as she took a step forward.

"Listen," he said calmly. "I tried to do things the easy way. Redford's boys were supposed to kill Raven and burn the refugees out of the Stanley. But then Raven had to complicate things by getting the government involved. Now that Colton's chief again, I had to take matters into my own hands—and this time it requires blood."

Raven took another step forward, his fists clenched.

"Go ahead and try it," Don said, moving the barrel of his shotgun toward Raven's belly. "I'll blow your guts all over the road, and then I'll make sure Sandra and Allie suffer." After a pause, he added, "Or if you don't resist, they can continue living their lives."

"You're going to kill us in cold blood?" Lindsey snapped. "You're supposed to be a police officer!"

"These are different times," Don said without moving his eyes off Raven. "Turn around and start walking."

Raven considered his options. He could charge the cops, but doing so would earn him a bullet or blast from the shotgun. He had to be smart. If they were going to execute him in the woods, he would make his move then. Plus, Creek was likely watching and waiting for an opportunity to strike.

"Colton won't let you get away with this," Lindsey said.

Don laughed. "Colton isn't coming back."

"What do you mean?" Lindsey said.

"I said start walking," Don replied, jerking the barrel of his shotgun at the Jeep path across the road.

***

"We can't go back out there. It's not safe," Van Dyke said. "We're lucky we didn't get shot up on the road."

Albert stared out the second story window of the office building. His sister's apartment was still two blocks away, but this section of the city had turned into a warzone. The violence outside the Starbucks had set off a chain of events that had led to several groups engaging in a firefight.

He stepped away from the window to scan the offices that were furnished with about a dozen desks, and a conference table. A single locked door led to an outside hallway, restrooms, and a staircase to the first floor. Van Dyke waited at the door, listening for anyone that might be sneaking into the building.

"We're screwed," Van Dyke muttered every few minutes. The others ignored him.

Flint paced, gripping his injured side. Dave remained hiding under a desk. Albert wasn't sure he would be able to get the boy to move anytime soon.

"I'll go out there alone and sneak into my sister's building," Albert said. "You guys stay here with Dave. If I'm not back in three hours, take him to the SC."

Flint and Van Dyke exchanged a glance.

"I know our mission was to find your sister, man, but it's way too fucking dangerous right now," Flint said.

The pop of gunfire echoed from the street, and a round punched into the side of the building, punctuating his statement. Dave let out a cry, and Albert bent down to calm him. The boy sat under the table, knees to his chest, rocking back and forth.

"It's okay, buddy," Albert said soothingly. Dave didn't seem to hear him.

He stood and moved back to the windows, keeping to the side to look for contacts. Across the street, three men with rifles strode down the sidewalk. The leader, an Asian man with a ponytail, stopped and squeezed off several shots. Return fire hit the sidewalk, and the trio took off running for cover.

"Man, this is crazy," Albert whispered more to himself than anyone.

He retreated back to the desks. "I need to get my sister to the SC before this entire area falls into anarchy. She's not good at looking after herself."

"Too late for that," Van Dyke said. He moved away from the door. "Charlotte is toast. There's no coming back from this. I doubt the SC will hold much longer, either."

"Don't say that," Flint snapped.

Van Dyke shrugged. "Sorry, Sarge, it's just... I want to get home. I'm worried about my wife and daughter."

It was the first Albert had heard Van Dyke speak of a family. He wasn't the most likeable man in the world, but Albert did appreciate Van Dyke coming out here, especially when he had his own family to worry about. It was yet another reason Albert needed to go on his own. He checked his gear and prepared his weapon while the two soldiers argued.

"We all have families, but we also have a job to do," Flint said. "Don't forget that, Corporal. I need you to stay focused. It's the only way we're getting home."

Van Dyke sank to the carpet near the door, resting his back against the wall. He took in several deep breaths. "I know, man, I'm sorry. I just miss Margo and Penny."

"You'll see them again," Albert said. He grabbed his gear and walked toward the door.

Flint held up a hand. "I'll come with you. Van Dyke, you stay here and look after Dave."

Van Dyke pushed himself up. "You serious, Sarge?"

Dave slowly crawled out from under the table. "You're leaving, Mr. Big Al?"

"Just for a little while," Albert said. "Remember when the Fellowship split up?"

A slow nod. "Yeah."

"It's just like that," Albert assured Dave.

"Okay." The boy retreated back into the darkness. "Don't let the Orcs catch you," he said from under the table.

Albert grabbed his M4 and met Flint's gaze.

"I think I should go on my own," Albert said. "You're injured, and I don't like leaving Dave here with Van Dyke."

The corporal shot Albert a glare, but he shrugged. "You're not very good with kids, Corporal."

Flint scratched at his face, thinking. "I could stay here and send Van Dyke with you instead."

"Hell no! That's worse than babysitting," Van Dyke protested.

"I'm better off on my own," Albert said.

"Fine," Flint finally replied. He unzipped his backpack, pulled out a radio, and handed it to Albert.

"Where did you get that?" Albert asked.

"Harris gave us two of them just in case we ran into any problems. We're not supposed to use it unless absolutely necessary," Flint said. "Go on, take it. This way you can stay in contact with me if anything happens."

Albert grabbed the radio and tucked it into his own backpack.

"Good luck," Flint said.

"Stay safe, and don't take your eyes off Dave."

A few minutes later Albert was working his way through the offices on the first floor. The street outside appeared empty, but it was draped in shadow. Then he saw the body.

The small figure lying on the sidewalk across the street was just a kid, not much older than Dave. Albert took a deep breath, looked to the left and right side of the street for contacts, then moved out. He darted across the street and crouched by the boy lying face down on the concrete. Using the utmost care, Albert slowly rolled him over, revealing three small bloodstains on the front of the kid's shirt, and a pistol gripped in his hand.

The boy was maybe ten years old, and he had been forced to fight for his life.

Albert reached down and closed the kid's eyes. Then he glanced over his shoulder to look up at the office building. Flint was standing at the window, but the sergeant couldn't see Albert from this angle.

He dragged the boy off the street and positioned his body under a tree. There wasn't time to bury him right now, but perhaps someone else would take the time after the sun came up. At least he wasn't sprawled on the street like roadkill anymore. Albert closed his eyes and muttered a prayer for the child.

During his training and his career with the Capitol police, Albert had seen some terrible things, but nothing compared to this nightmare—and it was only going to get worse.

The next street was free of contacts at first glance, but Albert remained behind a brick building for several minutes to listen for sounds: footsteps, gunshots, voices, or anything else that meant potential hostiles. Hearing nothing, he moved around the corner and hugged the side of the shops to the right of the street. Several cars blocked the road, providing perfect ambush points.

Gunfire erupted just outside the Starbucks where Albert had taken a life several hours earlier. He ducked behind a car and peered around the bumper. The Asian man and his two friends were back, firing at contacts in the courtyard of his sister's apartment building.

Albert took off running, moving toward the courtyard in the shadows of the building. The three men firing from the Starbucks had their backs turned to his position. If he could just get around them, he would be able to take a back route into the apartment complex.

A scream rang out just as he was about to slip into an alleyway. Shots tore into the hedge in front of him, and a bullet streaked by his head. Another round splintered the bark of a large tree ahead. He took cover behind the wide trunk, counted to three, then bolted for the alley between a fence and a long two-story office building.

Trash swirled in the narrow space from the gusting wind. He ran as hard as he could down the passage, his muscles moving almost as fast as they used to when he'd been running down a football field. But this wasn't a game. All around him the sound of gunfire echoed through the city.

He could see his sister's building in the waning sunlight at the end of the alley. A gate was the only thing separating him from the courtyard outside the apartments. He barreled into the three-foot gate, slamming it open. Shouts came from the street he'd left behind, and another bullet whizzed past him, closer this time. He continued through the weeds and overgrown grass filling the courtyard.

Two large oak trees provided a canopy of red and brown leaves overhead. Several fluttered in his path. He looked over his shoulder at the Starbucks, but the three men were gone, probably headed down the alley to flank him. Albert ran for the side entrance to the apartment building, sucking in air. He stopped and raised his rifle at the alley when he was halfway across, squeezing off a three-round burst that hit the gate.

The men remained out of sight, and he used the opportunity to run to the side entrance of the building. A white door hung half open. Albert slipped inside and quickly cleared the hallway. Then he shut the door and bolted for the staircase at the other end of the passage.

He knew his sister lived on the second floor, but he wasn't sure at what end of the building.

Once he reached the second floor, he stopped to listen for anyone that might be following him, but all he heard was his own labored breathing. He moved slower now, carefully clearing each stretch of hallway, and followed the signs pointing to apartments 250-300. He jogged down another corridor, cleared it, and finally stopped when he reached a door marked *291*. Instead of knocking, he reached for the doorknob and twisted. It clicked, locked.

"Jacqueline," Albert said in a voice not much louder than a whisper. His heart was beating so loudly that he was afraid he wouldn't be able to hear a reply.

When no one answered, Albert kicked the door open and strode into the apartment. The living room was sparsely furnished with a single table and a raggedy couch. He checked the kitchen to the right, but it too was empty.

Turning, he shut the door and used the chain lock to secure it now that the bolt lock was destroyed. Then he made his way deeper into the apartment.

"Jacqueline, it's your brother, Albert."

He passed the bathroom, stopped, and took a step back.

A foot was hanging over the side of the bathtub, but a curtain blocked his view of whoever was inside the tub. Heart firing like an automatic weapon, Albert crept into the bathroom and pulled back the curtain.

His sister lay there, eyes closed, chin slumped to her chest.

"Oh God, Jackie," Albert said. "Oh Jesus, no."

He didn't need lights to see the track marks on her arms or the needle in her left hand. She had been using again, and it looked like the addiction had finally gotten the best of her.

He gently set his rifle down and knelt next to the bathtub. The stench of body odor and human waste was almost unbearable, burning his nostrils and filling his lungs. He reached out to feel for a pulse. Her bony wrist was so light in his massive grip.

There was something there…or had he imagined it?

"Jackie," he repeated, tapping his fingers against her cheek. "Jackie, wake up."

"Who da fuck?" mumbled a voice behind him.

Albert whirled toward a man standing outside the doorway. The barrel of his rifle was directed at the face of a sinewy African-American man with gray hair wearing nothing but a pair of white briefs.

Instead of being afraid, the guy swatted at the barrel clumsily. He stumbled to the side and then righted himself, eyes wide as he ran a hand over his matted hair.

"Get back," Albert said. He directed the man into the living room, leaving his sister for a moment to deal with this new threat, and made him take a seat on the couch.

"Who are you?" Albert asked.

"I'm motherfucking Santa Claus. Who da fuck are you?" the guy growled, spit dripping off his lips.

Albert slowly lowered the rifle, seeing the only threat this guy posed was to himself.

"I'm Albert," he said. "Jacqueline's brother."

That seemed to get the man's attention. He looked up, narrowed his unfocused eyes, and tilted his head.

"Jackie has a brother?" he slurred. "She never nothin' 'bout you before."

Colton didn't like driving at night, but it was far less dangerous than driving during the day. He kept both of his Colt .45s on the seat next to him and his M14 rifle and AR-15 propped up against the passenger seat. In the place of his uniform, he wore a black Estes Park sweatshirt over a ballistic vest, gray cargo pants, and hybrid trail running shoes. It was his attempt to not look like a cop.

For the past hour he'd been parked behind an old shed, scoping out the area for contacts, but everything west of Loveland was pretty well abandoned. The action seemed to be in the east, where he could make out the glow of fires from the FEMA camp. More plumes rose to the north, but these were too thick to be coming from campfires or chimneys. A fire was raging somewhere in Fort Collins, and it looked massive.

So far the trip had gone flawlessly. He'd met only a few contacts on the road, and none of them had tried to attack him. But the sun had receded over the mountains, and he feared the darkness would bring out the real threats. The gangs, especially the Russians that had moved into the area around Fort Collins to benefit from the legalization of marijuana, were well-organized, well-armed, and extremely violent. His gut told him some of the raiders were affiliated with the Russian Mafia.

A year back Colton had worked jointly with Sheriff

Gerrard on a homicide that left three Russian mobsters dead, mutilated, and buried in shallow graves just outside Rocky Mountain National Park. Those murders were some of the worst Colton had ever seen. But he had a feeling he was going to be seeing more atrocities—and, like in Afghanistan, he wasn't sure if he would be able to tell the enemy apart from the general population.

Colton's experience in scanning for potential threats was nearly worthless in this new, lawless landscape. Since he'd left the final roadblock outside Estes Park, he'd driven by two men walking along Highway 34 and several teenagers riding bicycles. Any of them might have fired at his Jeep. Since there was no way of knowing what he'd find at the FEMA camp, he decided to head out to meet with Sheriff Thompson first. The lawman and cage fighter would know better than anyone what the conditions were around here—and if Colton could hope to get any help from the Feds at the camp.

He took a drink of water, carefully placed the bottle back in the cup holder, and pulled away from the shed. To his left was Glade Road, a less-traveled route to Fort Collins. He kept the speed of the Jeep around twenty miles an hour. The light snow hadn't accumulated on the road, which meant no tracks. He hoped he'd be able to make it to Loveland without leaving a trail to follow.

You're getting paranoid, he chided himself. Except it wasn't really paranoia when anyone he met might be a hostile.

As soon as he was sure there wasn't anyone on the street, he pressed down on the pedal and continued into the darkness, using the full moon to guide him around the abandoned vehicles. Drab fields framed the road on both sides, and rolling hills rose above them. The arid terrain was far removed from the lush landscape in the Estes Valley.

Most people used Highway 287 to get to Fort Collins. This route would allow him to take the back way in, which was the reason he'd selected it in the first place. Still, the threat of snipers, raiders, and gangs had Colton on edge, and driving without headlights made it even worse. It wasn't much different than driving with his eyes closed, something he used to do as a teenager with his friends, daring each other to keep them shut for as long as they could.

Although he kept both hands on the wheel, his weapons were just a heartbeat away. He scanned the concrete and fields on both sides for any sign of a flashlight or movement, but Glade Road appeared to be empty.

This was worse than driving in Afghanistan on night missions. At least then he'd had Jake and his other brothers with him. It was every soldier's worst nightmare to be heading into potential battle alone.

An abandoned pickup truck blocked the road around the next turn, and Colton eased off the gas. With one hand on the wheel, he reached for his Colt .45. For several minutes he sat in the vehicle, eyes darting over the landscape for any sign of hostiles. Shadows seemed to move back and forth on the road. He looked toward what appeared to be a person crouched in the field to the right, but saw it was just a bush.

Take it easy, Marcus. You're freaking yourself out.

He steered around the pickup truck. Once clear, he pushed down on the pedal, giving the engine plenty of gas to speed away. He passed the mailboxes of ranch homes with boarded up windows. *No trespassing* signs were raised in front yards, but nobody seemed to be home.

Glade Road turned into County Road 38 E, and Colton got his first glimpse of Horsetooth Reservoir, the water sparkling in the moonlight. Several abandoned cars dotted the road along the water's edge. He passed them on the right side, giving himself plenty of clearance.

A rocky overpass blocked the view of the city, making it a great place to scope out things to the east. He drove onto the shoulder, checked the road for contacts, and then shut off the engine. He grabbed both of his rifles and locked the Jeep.

The climb up the rocky hill only took him a few minutes. At the top, he set his rifles against a boulder and looked out over the flat terrain bordering the Rocky Mountains. A fire raged in the heart of the city. Aside from the wind, it was quiet—almost unnerving.

To the east, a wall of black clouds made it almost impossible to see anything. He brought up his rifle and zoomed in. They weren't clouds at all. The black wall was more smoke. Colton crouched there for several moments, breathing heavily at the sight. Had something else happened to the FEMA Camp? Don had said it was all clear. So why did it look like the entire area was on fire?

He pivoted back to the city of Fort Collins. Several headlights were moving down a street to the east. Deciding to risk using his flashlight, he pulled out his map and marked the roads that appeared blocked by barriers or vehicles. It didn't look like there were any good routes to the sheriff station.

After a few more moments studying the city, he picked up his weapons and headed back to the Jeep. When he got to the vehicle, he crouched once more and searched for any hostiles, but the road still looked empty. He loaded the rifles and fired up the Jeep.

This time he drove with both hands on the wheel and the Colt .45 on the dashboard. A fence of trees lined the road to his right. He kept to the left and prepared to gun the engine down what appeared to be an open stretch. Just as his foot pushed down, a silhouette burst from the wall of pine trees.

More massive shapes powered through bushes and around trees a moment later to move into the street. Flashlights flickered on all around, painting the Jeep with bright beams. In the glow, he saw a dozen horses, all mounted by armed men directing rifles at the windshield of his Jeep.

He slammed on his brakes and then put the vehicle in reverse. Looking over his shoulder, he saw more men on horses flanking the Jeep.

Colton pulled to the left side of the road, but that earned several warning shots that came dangerously close to the hood. He pushed down on the brakes again, coming to a stop with the front of the truck angled downward into a ditch. With nowhere to run, he put both hands on the steering wheel, knowing it was his only chance to get out of this alive.

A man wearing a bandana dismounted and walked over with a shotgun. Three other men followed, all of them carrying rifles. Colton kept his breathing steady and his hands in sight. The guy with the shotgun used the barrel to tap the window lightly.

"Roll down your window and then shut off the vehicle," the man said.

Colton obeyed the order and cool air rushed into the vehicle. He caught a scent of something else too—

something burning.

"Evenin'," the man said, leaning down. Colton got a good look at him then—forty or so, dark eyes and hair, and a handlebar mustache. "What brings you to Fort Collins?"

"Got a meeting with Sheriff Thompson," Colton said. He decided to give his name after a brief pause. "I'm Estes Park Police Chief Marcus Colton."

The man turned and looked up to the road. "You hear that, boys? This here is a police chief all the way from Estes Park, and he's here to see Sheriff Thompson."

Someone laughed. Colton felt as though he were missing something. The men weren't threatening him—they were *mocking* him. But why?

"So that's what you guys are calling Thompson, eh?" the man said.

"I was told Sheriff Gerrard was killed by raiders and Thompson replaced him," Colton said.

"Second part is true," the man said.

Colton narrowed his eyes. "My patrol sergeant said…"

His words trailed off when he realized that no one had confirmed Don's story. Colton cursed himself again for driving out here without doing more research. He had made a rash decision, and this time he feared it would get him killed.

"On second thought, I think I should be getting back to Estes Park," Colton said. "Would you men be kind enough to let me through?"

The guy propped his shotgun up on his shoulder and grinned, revealing a gap between his front teeth. "You just got here, Chief, and now you already want to go home?"

"Yes, sir," Colton said.

"Well, that ain't very polite of you. How about you get out of the Jeep? We'll take your guns, and then we'll take you to meet 'Sheriff' Thompson."

***

Fenix had yet to see Nile Redford smile. Talking to him was like talking to a carved block of cedar—albeit one with a very large vocabulary. But this was only their second conversation, and Fenix was going to do everything in his power to get his ass out of here, even it meant joking with a damn redskin.

"What if I told you I could make you a better offer than ten million in gold?" Fenix said.

"I'm a businessman first and foremost," Redford said. "Usually I wouldn't listen to anything a racist prick like you had to say, but these are challenging times. I'm willing to give your misguided views a pass if you can do something for me."

Redford sat in a red leather chair behind a fancy wood desk. Weapons, including several spears and bows, hung on the wall. Pictures featuring Redford and celebrities like Benjamin Bratt, Mike Tyson, and Angie Harmon were displayed between the weapons.

"Impressive place," Fenix said.

Redford opened his desk drawer and pulled out a tobacco pipe. He lit it and took a puff, blowing out the smoke in Fenix's face. It took everything in his power not to reach out, grab the pipe, and jam it down Redford's throat.

Instead, Fenix glanced out the second-floor window, which overlooked a town he didn't recognize. It was Colorado, had to be. But where, he wasn't sure.

"I'm also a man that doesn't like to waste time," Redford said after taking another drag off his pipe.

"Nor do I," Fenix replied. He coughed, and raised his handcuffs. He tried his best to hide his anger and disgust, reminding himself that at one point the United States military fought alongside some redskin tribes in the battle for the American West. Fenix was willing to do the same thing now if it meant achieving his end goal.

"I have over five hundred soldiers spread throughout Colorado," Fenix said. "Men that have been preparing for this for years. We have weapons, supplies, vehicles, and communication equipment that is far more valuable than gold."

Redford leaned back slightly in his chair. He took another hit of the pipe, blew the smoke into Fenix's face, and gestured for him to continue.

Fenix coughed a second time and then gave Redford his best smile.

"The Feds 'might' give you ten million in gold bars for catching me," he continued, tracing quotation marks in the air with his cuffed hands. "But what if they don't? Judging by the looks of this place, and the fact you got a dude named Hacker working for you, I'm willing to guess you're some sort of high-level loan shark at best and organized crime boss at worst."

That got Redford's attention. He straightened in his chair and narrowed his dark eyes.

"So my question, again, is, what makes you think that Montgomery bitch is going to give you shit for handing me over?" Fenix paused for a moment. "I, on the other hand, can ensure you make out real good if you get me back to my men."

Redford finally smiled, just a quick flash of the whitest

teeth Fenix had ever seen.

"And what makes *you* think I would trust a Nazi asshole like yourself?" Redford asked, leaning forward. He set the pipe down on his desk. "Hacker thinks we should cut your balls off, scalp you, and then tell the Feds which tree we hung you from. I'm inclined to agree."

Fenix chuckled. "I like how he thinks, but I promise that would be a very bad idea."

"Oh?" Redford relaxed back in his chair and folded his hands together. "And why is that?"

"Because those five hundred soldiers I told you about? Well, they're out there looking for me," Fenix said. He swallowed, hoping Redford couldn't see his bluff. In reality, he had only half that many men, and he doubted they were mounting some sort of SEAL Team Six-style rescue mission.

Fenix placed his cuffed hands back in his lap. "Join up with me and my men, and let's take over Colorado. You'll have hundreds of millions of dollars' worth of loot. Maybe more."

"I do that, and I'll have the government coming after me," Redford said. "I'm a very rich man, partly because I like to keep a low profile."

He stood behind his desk and sighed. "I thought you had something real to offer me. Instead you've wasted my precious time."

Fenix wasn't the type of man to beg—and it pained him to even be negotiating with an Indian—but the alternative was ending up in a dark prison cell for a few months before the Feds gave him the gas chamber. That was, if Hacker didn't cut his nuts off first.

"Hold on, now. Don't be hasty. There's something else I haven't told you yet." He waited for Redford to take a seat. When the man had settled back into his plush leather chair, Fenix brought out the big guns. "I've got more than ten million in gold, silver, and weapons stowed away. You let me go and I'll have it delivered to a place of your choosing. The government doesn't have to know you ever met me."

Redford stared at Fenix like a poker player trying to get a read on his opponent. Fenix tried not to let the fact that he was lying show on his face.

"That does sound tempting, but before I agree to anything, I think we need to have a little test. There's something else I want. I heard you want it as well, which should make this mutually beneficial," Redford said. "I want Raven Spears."

Fenix cursed. The goddamn injun again.

"I understand Mr. Spears ambushed and slaughtered at least a dozen of your men," Redford said. "Word travels fast over the radio channels that still work, and my men intercepted a transmission."

"Yeah," Fenix replied. He wasn't sure if Redford was a friend of Raven's or not, so he kept his answer simple.

Redford walked over to the pictures hanging on the wall of his office. He stopped to look at one.

"Raven killed one of my best enforcers and sent my cousin to jail. I retrieved Theo, and I've made Estes Park pay for their error in judgment. But frankly, I've taken a liking to the town. I want Raven captured and the way cleared for me to take over Estes Park. Do you think your men can handle that?"

Fenix nearly licked his lips at what sounded a lot like a proposition. "We'd be happy to help. Hell, I had similar plans, to be honest."

Redford clasped his hands behind his back. It wasn't

the handshake Fenix was hoping for, but a quick nod from the well-dressed man told him that maybe this partnership wasn't going to be such a bad thing after all.

***

Charlize was half asleep when she heard a knock on her apartment door. Ty heard it too. He sat up in bed and looked over at her with rumpled hair and squinty eyes.

"Mom, someone's here," he mumbled.

"I know. Go back to bed, sweetie."

Ty remained sitting up as Charlize left the room. She threw on a large t-shirt and opened the door. Colonel Raymond stood in the hallway.

"Ma'am, I'm very sorry to bother you, but we just got word from Charlotte. I thought you would like to know immediately."

"What is it? Is Al okay?"

"Albert Randall has located his sister, but his team is trapped. They encountered more resistance than expected."

"I'll come to the Command Center and monitor the situation myself," she said. "Just give me a few minutes."

Raymond held up a hand. "Ma'am, there's something else."

She hesitated, the door half closed.

"The SC in Charlotte is under a major attack," he added. "It's not random, either."

"What do you mean?"

Raymond took a moment to think, or perhaps to choose the right words. "It appears to be a coordinated attack by several gangs. Captain Harris is requesting reinforcements."

Charlize hesitated, recalling what had happened on her flyover. If she authorized aircraft to transport more troops, they could be shot down. A single crash would kill hundreds, if not more, in the teeming crowds surrounding the SC.

Charlize stood in the doorway. So much was happening, and it was all happening so fast. "We can't let that SC fall," she said.

"Yes, ma'am," Raymond replied, apparently just now noticing her baggy t-shirt and shorts. Charlize had never been vain, but the look of mingled pity and horror on his face when he noticed her burn scars made her want to cover up. She made her way back into the bedroom and kissed Ty on his forehead. He was wide awake now.

"What's going on, Mom? Did something happen to Big Al?"

Charlize shook her head and ran her hand through Ty's thick hair. "Big Al is just fine. I'm going to go see if I can help him to get home, okay?"

Ty nodded. "Okay. Tell him I said hi."

A few minutes later and Charlize was back in the situation room. It was quiet compared to the usual bustle, but several officers and General Thor sat with laptops and satellite phones. The clock read 0100 hours, but Charlize didn't feel tired.

"Who's got a SITREP on the situation in Charlotte?" she said as soon as she entered the room.

Thor stood. "Good eveni—morning," he corrected himself. "I'm afraid I've got some bad news."

Charlize remained standing. "Yes?"

"The east wall of the SC just came down, and people are pouring in. Captain Harris has ordered everyone to fall back. I doubt they will be able to hold the line through the night."

"Recommendations?" Charlize asked.

"It's a charnel house there, but there's nothing we can do to stop it at this point," Thor said. "I would highly recommend not sending any troops until the sun comes up. It will only escalate the violence."

Raymond nodded. "I'm afraid Captain Harris and the others are on their own for now."

"No," Charlize said. "We can't abandon them. Where's the closest base?"

Thor looked to Raymond. The colonel stepped over to a map and pointed.

"We have several birds on a carrier off the coast, here."

"Fire them up and send them to support Harris," Charlize said.

Charlize looked around the half-empty Command Center. She could almost picture the figures of all those she had failed to save. Her colleagues from the Senate, Lieutenant Dupree's fire team, the children at the Easterseals camp. Every room she walked into was full of ghosts these days. Nathan was always there, front and center, his face solemn. If she failed to hold the SCs, hundreds of thousands of deaths would be on her. She couldn't live with herself if that happened—and more importantly, her country wouldn't survive it.

She squared her shoulders and turned to Raymond. "Have one of the staffers put on a fresh pot of coffee. It's going to be a long night. We have to save as many lives as we can."

— 16 —

This wasn't the first time Raven had a gun at his back, but he was starting to think this was going to be the last.

Don kept a shotgun leveled at him and Lindsey from behind, and Hines carried a Colt .45. The gun made him think of Colton, and Raven wondered how the chief was faring. It sounded like Don had sent him into a trap.

The march continued onto a narrow path off the Jeep trail. Raven searched the forest ahead of them, hoping to see a glimpse of Creek's tail. Don believed the dog was back in town with Sandra and Allie, but Raven kept hoping his furry friend would pop out and save them. The Akita was pretty much their only hope at this point.

"Keep moving. We're almost there," Don said.

Lindsey shot a glance over her shoulder. "It's not too late to change your mind. I promise—"

"Shut up for once in your life," Don said. He jammed the barrel of the shotgun hard into the small of Lindsey's back, and she cried out in pain.

Raven gritted his teeth. He was going to tear Don's throat out as soon as he had the chance. But first he had to figure a way to get out of his restraints. He searched the forest in his peripheral vision again for Creek. Had something happened to him, or was the dog just waiting for a chance to strike?

You better hurry up, pal.

They continued up a narrow trail fenced on each side

by aspen trees. Ponderosas towered overhead, their branches weighed down by snow. To the left, a ridgeline looked over a valley. A stream churned a hundred feet below. Raven had a feeling he knew where Don was taking them.

"Look, I'm sorry about your shoulder, Hines," Raven said, doing his best to sound sincere. In truth, he was wishing he'd aimed better last night.

"Just keep walking," Hines said.

Lindsey almost tripped over a root. Raven wanted to reach out to steady her, but he couldn't with his hands bound. They were nearing the crest of the hill, and he could see the rocky platform where Don no doubt planned to push them both to their deaths. It was easier than digging graves, and it might look like an accident if anyone found their corpses. Raven used to take tourists up here sometimes; it was a breathtaking overlook. Now it seemed like it might be the last thing he ever saw.

Oddly, all he could think about in this moment was how much he loved it out here. The scent of cedar, sound of the river, whistle of the wind. Nature set Raven free, and if he was going to die, at least he would die in the heart of one of the most beautiful places on earth.

He stopped at the edge of the path where the dirt met the surface of the rocky ledge. Below, the clear water rushed over the rocks. It was a three-hundred foot drop.

"Move it, Spears," Don said. He followed Lindsey onto the rock platform, her red hair whipping in the wind like a wildfire.

"Please, don't do this," she pleaded.

It was the first time Raven had ever heard Lindsey beg. The tone of her voice broke his heart, and then it pissed him off.

"Cut their restraints," Don said.

Hines walked forward and sliced through the rope binding Lindsey's hands, and then the rope binding Raven's. He considered making a move, but Don had the shotgun barrel aimed at his back.

"Keep walking," Don said, flicking the barrel. Hines sheathed his knife, and pulled his pistol out. He pointed the gun at the back of Lindsey's head.

"Sorry, but it has to be this way," Hines said.

Side by side, Raven and Lindsey walked out onto the ledge. She was shaking, and a tear streaked down her cheek.

"I'm sorry," Raven whispered. "I'm sorry I got you into this mess."

A click sounded as Hines pulled the hammer back on his pistol.

"Any last words?" Don asked.

The forest seemed to freeze in that moment. Raven's eyes flitted to the churning water below. The stones, which had been smoothed by thousands of years of water rushing over them, seemed to sparkle in the moonlight. In a few seconds his bones would crack on those polished rocks as he bled out into the gushing water.

His mind jumped to his family. Sandra, Allie, and Creek were out there, waiting for him to come home. Raven had made them promises. If he didn't return, they would suffer. A storm was coming. That's what Jason Cole had said. Bad people were headed toward Estes Park, and Raven couldn't leave his family alone. He had to do something, and he had to do it soon.

"Nothing? Then go ahead and jump," Don said.

Hines remained silent. So did Lindsey. She held her head up high and glanced over at Raven. There was nothing either of them could do now. He should have made his move earlier, but he had been waiting for Creek.

Where the hell are you, boy?

Raven leaned over the edge and looked down. There were several dirt ledges fifty feet down. Maybe, if he jumped, he could land on one of those…

No, that's crazy.

The mind did crazy things when faced with death. This wasn't the first time Raven had been in a situation where he thought he was going to die, but this time he didn't see any way out of it.

"Jump," Don said. "If you jump, it'll look like an accident. Raven Spears will die a hero. Otherwise…well, I'm sure everyone would believe that you murdered dear Detective Plymouth after she turned down your advances, and that I was forced to shoot you in self-defense when you resisted arrest. Which story do you think your family will like better?"

An eerie, deep-throated howl answered him. Raven turned just as Don and Hines did. There was a flash of snow-colored fur amidst the dark trees. Then Creek was there, his powerful jaws latched onto Don's arm. The patrol sergeant shook him off and aimed a kick at the dog's side.

"Run!" Raven yelled at Lindsey.

Neither of them wasted any time. She vaulted onto the dirt path and took off running. The boom of the shotgun broke the silence of the night, and the crack of the .45 followed. A yelp sounded.

Creek was hurt.

Raven roared, ducking as Hines turned to fire at him. Two bullets streaked by Raven's head. Hines then turned the gun on Lindsey, who barreled into him. She didn't weigh much, but she was moving fast and low. She threw Hines off-balance, and they both went down.

Creek limped away from Don, who was holding his arm. The shotgun had fallen several feet away. Raven ran toward the gun, but just as he was about to kick it away, Don threw a right hook that hit Raven square in the nose. Pain lanced up his sinuses. He staggered backward several steps. Warm blood flowed from his nose. He held up his hands to fend off the continuing barrage of punches from Don. One of them hit Raven's wounded ear.

He glimpsed Hines and Lindsey wrestling on the ground about ten feet away. Hines screamed out in pain as she hit his injured shoulder. Lindsey dug her thumb into the wound.

Don landed another hit to Raven's head. His brain rattled inside his skull. He'd always thought of himself as a tough bastard, but his body had taken major punishment over the past month. The officer ran at him again, plowing his shoulder into Raven's chest. He fell onto a boulder, cracking the back of his head on the moss-covered stone.

Creek yelped again in the distance.

The sound of his dog's pain snapped Raven into focus. He had to save Creek and Lindsey. He fought his way upright and head-butted Don in the face. The blow shattered the officer's nose with a satisfying crunch.

Don rolled off him and Raven pushed himself up, placing one hand on his pounding head. He looked over at Lindsey and Hines. She was on the bottom of the pile now, and Hines had his hands around her throat. Creek was slumped in front of a tree, but Raven saw his head move, which told him his dog was still alive, at least. It hurt his heart, but there wasn't anything he could do for his best friend until he took down Don and Hines.

Raven kicked Don in the gut while the patrol sergeant was still down and then reached down to grab the blade on his duty belt. Don grabbed Raven's wrist before he could pull the knife, and then kicked Raven's leg out from under him. He fell to the dirt and Don scrambled away.

A guttural choking sounded, and Raven looked to his right as he pushed himself up. Lindsey had stripped Hines of his knife and plunged it into the bottom of his chin. She held the grip steady, a look of fury on her face, until Hines stopped kicking.

The sound of a shotgun shell being pumped sent a chill through Raven. Don had found his gun.

"I've been waiting for this, Spears," Don said, his voice thick. Blood sluiced down his face. He aimed the barrel at Raven's heart and used his shoulder to wipe the blood away from his lips.

A flash of motion came from the side as Don pulled the trigger, knocking the gun to the side. Lindsey shouted a wordless cry like a bird of prey as she smashed into Don, sending them both stumbling toward the ledge. They grappled for a moment before teetering over the edge. Raven flailed for Lindsey's leg, but it was too late. She vanished over the side with Don.

"No!" Raven yelled.

He scrambled over and looked down. At first he didn't see anything besides the rocks below. But as he leaned farther out, he saw a face looking up at him.

"Help!" Don yelled. He was holding onto the roots of a tree growing out of the side of the slope. "I'm sorry, Sam. I'll let you go, just help me up!"

Lindsey was hanging onto a limb a few feet away. She kicked Don in the side, once, twice, then a third time.

"You little bitch," Don growled.

Raven reached down for her hand. "Grab it!" he shouted.

Lindsey reached up, but Don latched onto her. "If I go, she goes with me!"

Raven drew back. Just to his left, the shotgun lay in the dirt where Don had dropped it. He made sure Don couldn't see what he was doing, and when he had the gun in his hands, Raven brought it up to his shoulder and aimed it at the patrol sergeant's face.

"No, please, don't!" Don shouted.

Raven pulled the trigger without hesitation. The blast caught Don in his already broken nose, erasing his features in a spray of blood, bone, and gore.

His body fell away from the cliff, plummeting into the valley below. Raven checked the shotgun chamber for another shell, and when he found it was empty, lowered the gun down to Lindsey. She grabbed the stock, and he pulled her to safety.

For a moment, he held her against his chest. They were both breathing hard, and the scent of her hair filled his nostrils as he inhaled.

"Are you okay?" he asked.

"I think so. Thank you, Sam. Thanks for saving my ass."

Lindsey's shoulders twitched and he let her go and turned to look for Creek. The dog looked up as Raven called out, one of his eyes a bloody mess and his coat spotted with blood. The sight took Raven's breath away. He hardly managed to choke out, "Creek."

Raven crouched down to check his best friend's wounds. The shotgun blast had sprayed the dog with multiple tiny projectiles. One had hit his eye, and several others were embedded in his shoulder. If Raven could get him back to town, they might be able to save him.

"You're going to be okay, buddy," Raven said. The dog whined as Raven picked him up gently.

Lindsey joined him, her eyes wide when she saw how badly Creek was hurt. Raven looked over at Officer Hines's still body and decided to leave him for the wild animals.

"I'll gather their guns and ammo," she said.

"No, we'll come back for it later, we have to get Creek help."

She nodded and followed Raven back to the path.

"I never saw this coming," she said, still panting. "Hines wasn't a bad man; he was just a dumb one."

Raven didn't reply. He moved down the trail as quickly as he could without jostling Creek too much. The dog whimpered in his arms and tried to lick Raven's hand.

"Just hang on," Raven whispered.

After they'd been walking for a few minutes, a dozen flashlights emerged from the woods, carving up the darkness with high-powered beams. Raven and Lindsey froze. They waited to see who these newcomers were in silence. As they approached, Raven saw they were all armed, and most of them were on horseback.

A large man with a white mustache and an expensive white cowboy hat to match moved into view. He sat astride a massive black horse that rivaled Obsidian in size.

"That's John Kirkus," Lindsey said.

She stepped out from behind a tree and said, "Hold your fire."

Several guns pointed in her direction, and then Raven's, as he stepped out, still holding Creek.

"Detective Plymouth, is that you?" Kirkus asked.

"Hi, John," she said.

"We heard gunfire," he said. "You want to explain what the hell is going on out here?"

Lindsey nodded. "Yeah, but we need to get Raven's dog to a doctor first."

Kirkus's eyes flitted to Raven and then to Creek. Something in his stern expression softened when he saw the dog.

"Follow me," he said.

***

Colton sat in a cramped holding cell in the Larimer County Jail, cursing his luck. He never should have come here. That's what desperation did to a man; it pushed him to make poor decisions.

At least he was still alive. For now.

"Hey. Hey you, over there," whispered a voice.

Colton made his way over to the bars of his cell. Across the hallway was a man in a larger cell, what some cops referred to as the "drunk tank." A single candle burned from a wall mount, providing enough light for Colton to make out the swollen face of a guy looking through the bars at him.

"I heard you're a cop," the guy said. "That right? Did you come to help us?"

When Colton didn't reply, the man raised his voice and continued, "Hey man, don't ignore me. You gotta…" His voice trailed off and fell silent at the sound of footfalls at the opposite end of the hallway.

"Shut your trap or I'll stomp it shut," said a guard Colton couldn't see.

Colton sat down on the cot in his cell. He'd always

wondered what it was like to be on the other side of bars. It was worse than he'd imagined. With no idea what the hell was going on, there was nothing to do but wait until someone came to talk to him. Had Don set him up, or was this some sort of mistake? Colton's gut said it had been treachery.

The door at the other end of the hallway opened and then clicked shut as the guard left. The man with the bruised face wasted no time in resuming his one-sided conversation.

"Hey man, talk to me. I'm a friend."

Colton stood again and walked over to the bars. The man across the hall wore a flannel shirt, jeans, and a tattered Colorado Rockies baseball hat. Someone had given him a good beating. Several of his teeth were missing.

"Who are you?" Colton asked.

"I'm Clint Bailey. Own a small chicken farm a few miles outside town. They took it from me when I wouldn't give them all my birds. They killed one of my workers, too, and they...they..." Clint reached up and put his hand over his eyes, a sob wracking in his chest. "They raped my wife and..."

Colton put a finger to his lips. "Quiet. I'm sorry about your wife, but—"

The door at the other end of the hallway opened again. Footfalls clicked on the floor and Clint scooted away from the bars. Colton took a step backward and waited.

Three men walked into view, their faces illuminated by the candlelight. Two of them stopped and held sentry, but the third man dressed in a sheriff's uniform made his way over to Colton's cell. He was young, maybe thirty-five, with a five o'clock shadow hugging a square jawline.

Colton noticed that his ears were deformed, bulging from the fluid that caused cauliflower ear, which told Colton this was the cage-fighting sheriff himself, Mike Thompson.

"Chief Colton, sorry to keep you waiting," the man said with surprising politeness. He pulled out a ring of keys and opened the jail cell. "I've been out and just got back."

Colton stepped away from the barred door, watching Thompson warily.

"My men operate on the policy of better safe than sorry," he said. "If I had been here, I would never have thrown you in a cell."

Thompson offered his hand. "I'm Mike Thompson. I haven't been the sheriff long, so you might know me better as Spartan. That's the name I used in the cage."

Colton shook the man's hand. Thompson certainly had the grip of a Spartan warrior.

"So what brings you to Fort Collins?" Thompson asked.

"Sergeant Aragon with the Estes Park police said he spoke with you over the radio. I'm here to talk about forming an alliance. We've been hit by raiders, and I don't have enough men to defend our borders. I was hoping we could help each other."

Thompson scratched at the back of his ear, turning slightly. "Sergeant Don Aragon? Doesn't ring a bell. You sure he said he talked to me?"

Colton nodded. "That's right."

A shrug from Thompson. "I can't say I remember any such conversation."

"Must have been a misunderstanding, then."

Clint looked up at Colton across the hallway and

slowly shook his head, tears still flowing down his face. He seemed to be trying to warn Colton. Thompson seemed nice, but something didn't add up. Actually, nothing added up. Still, Colton had only one hand to play, and it was the same hand he came here with.

"But either way, I'm here to talk to you. I've heard you're having problems with raiders on this side of the Rockies. A single attack killed seven of my people. We captured one of the men, a guy named Cole, and from what he told us, things are getting even worse out here. I'm here to discuss an alliance between Fort Collins and Estes Park."

Thompson watched Colton in the flickering candlelight, sizing him up like he would an opponent before getting into the octagon. Colton used to do the same thing before a boxing match, and what he saw in Thompson's eyes scared him.

"I'm also planning to visit the FEMA camp and try to work something out with the National Guard stationed there," Colton continued when Thompson didn't respond. "Estes Park has resources Fort Collins might need, and I'm willing to offer supplies, food, water, and weapons."

"Chief, I think you misunderstand the situation," Thompson said at last.

"Oh?" Colton said, lifting a brow. Although he kept his tone light, he was tensing up as if his body expected a fight at any moment.

"We have things well under control here, but I'm afraid you'll be a bit disappointed by the FEMA camp," Thompson said. "Follow me—I'll let you see for yourself."

***

Albert slipped the radio into his backpack after reporting in to Flint, and leaned down next to his sister. She lay on the couch, eyelids cracked open halfway. He tipped her head up and helped her take another sip of water from his bottle.

"Jackie, can you hear me?" he asked.

Wayne, his sister's boyfriend—or the man that claimed to be her boyfriend—paced near the doorway behind them.

"You gonna get us the hell out of here or what?" he kept asking.

Albert was about ready to answer the question with a right hook, but he was honestly scared doing so would snap Wayne's neck. Both he and Jacqueline had wasted away during their bender, no doubt more interested in drugs than food. He focused back on his sister, trying to ignore her crazy lover.

"Jackie, please wake up. It's Albert."

She finally opened her eyes fully, and for the first time since he arrived at her apartment she looked at him— really looked at him.

"Al?" she whispered. Her lips cracked into a smile, revealing several broken, yellowed teeth.

Albert gripped her hand in his own. "Yeah, it's me. I'm here to rescue you."

She pulled out of his grip and her lips straightened into a line. Her features went back to the stone-cold look he remembered from their childhood.

"Rescue me from what? Why are you really here, Al?"

Albert had a hundred things he wanted to say to her, but they didn't have time to rehash the past.

"Because I love you, and because I'm sorry," he said.

"Yeah, yeah, we all love Jackie. Now give me some of that water," Wayne said.

Albert glanced over his shoulder, firing an icy glare that made the man stop pacing.

"Yo, my brother, I just want a drink," Wayne said.

"How long you been holed up here with my sister? You the one who's been giving her those needles to stick in her arm?" Albert rose to his feet. He towered over Wayne.

Wayne took a step back. "Jackie, tell him that shit ain't true. I didn't make you take any of that candy."

Jacqueline sat up on the couch. She rubbed at her eyes and then scratched her right arm. The track marks were in plain view.

"What do you call those?" Albert asked, pointing.

When he turned back to Wayne, the man had drawn a knife. He held it in a shaky hand. Albert didn't have time to regret the fact he hadn't patted Wayne down earlier. The man jabbed the blade at Albert's face, slicing his cheek wide open. He cried out in pain and backed away.

"I'll kill you!" Wayne shouted. He thrust the knife at Albert's chest, but Albert jumped back.

"Stop it!" Jacqueline yelled, her voice raspy. She tried to stand up, but her legs gave out. She landed on the filthy carpet with a yelp.

Albert planted his feet and waited, warm blood rushing down his cheek. He could tell the cut was bad and would probably require stitches. Definitely antibiotics; who knew where that knife had been? Wayne's wild eyes locked onto Albert's. His frail body trembled, and his face twitched.

"Get out of here!" he yelled. "Jackie's mine. I take care

of her. She don't want you here!"

"Stop it, Wayne," Jacqueline said from the floor. She struggled to push herself up.

"Put the knife down," Albert said calmly. "I don't want to hurt you, but I will."

"Stop!" Jacqueline shouted. "Both of you, stop it."

Wayne looked over at her. "Shut up, whore!"

The insult sent Albert over the edge. He lunged like his days on the football field after a snap. Wayne didn't have time to react before Albert barreled into him and picked him off the ground. He crushed the smaller man against the wall, and the knife clanked onto the floor. Albert backed away, and Wayne's sinewy frame crashed limply to the ground with a thud.

"No one talks to my sister like that," Albert said.

Jacqueline managed to stand and walk over with tears welling in her eyes. She stared at Wayne's prone form for a long moment before looking up at Albert.

"You never did know how to pick 'em," Albert said.

17

The settlement on Storm Mountain was even more impressive than Raven remembered. He carried Creek in his arms toward a twelve-foot cedar fence. Judging by the fresh scent, the fence was new.

Lindsey walked next to Raven, her eyes fixed on the walls built around the mansions beyond. Several guard towers stood along the perimeter, and each was manned with more men and women.

Through the opening gate, a bonfire burned in the middle of the street. Apparently Kirkus and his friends had been very busy since the bombs dropped. They had turned the neighborhood into a fortress.

"Almost there, buddy," Raven whispered to Creek.

The Akita whimpered, and his flesh quivered beneath his fur. If Raven could have taken the dog's pain, he would, but there wasn't anything he could do for Creek besides rush him to someone who could help.

The massive gates continued to open, revealing several modern houses on a street ahead. John Kirkus dismounted from his horse and walked over to Raven and Lindsey.

"I'll take you to the doc's house first," he said. "Then we can talk."

Raven and Lindsey followed quickly after Kirkus and several other men to a white two-story house. A man in a leather coat stood on the front steps. He removed a pair of glasses and wiped them off on his shirt, then put them back on.

"Doc Meyers, this is Sam Spears and Detective Lindsey Plymouth from Estes Park. They were on their way to meet with us but were ambushed by two officers that were apparently working with outside forces to take over Estes Park."

Despite his worries, Raven was impressed with how concisely Kirkus had summed up their situation.

"I'd say I don't believe it, but after this past month, I'll believe about anything," Meyers said with a huff.

"Creek here is hurt real bad," Kirkus said.

Meyers nodded at Raven and Lindsey and then opened the door to his house. "Come on in."

Raven hurried inside, talking as he did. "He was hit in the right eye and his right shoulder. I've stopped some of the bleeding, but I can't tell how bad the wounds are."

"Let's take him into the kitchen," Meyers said. He led them through a beautifully-decorated living room with vaulted ceilings. On the second floor, two kids and a woman looked over a balcony as Raven passed below. He entered a hallway and then a kitchen lit by oil lanterns and candles. Meyers pointed at a granite tabletop where Raven carefully set Creek down.

"Easy, boy," Raven said soothingly. "You're going to be feeling better really soon, I promise."

The dog slowly moved his head toward the doctor, then to Lindsey, and then back at Raven. His tail thumped once against the table.

Meyers grabbed a box of supplies from a cupboard and walked back over to Creek's side.

"Hold him down," Meyers said.

Raven and Lindsey both carefully restrained Creek

while Meyers checked his eye. A low growl came from Creek's throat, but Raven calmed his dog by whispering in his ear.

"You're with friends, buddy. Be good and I'll give you a treat. Nice, tasty elk jerky. Maybe a rabbit, too."

Creek's muscles relaxed, responding to the tone of Raven's voice more than the words, allowing Meyers to pull back the bloody fur covering his right eye. Raven glimpsed the wound for the first time in the light and felt his gut sink. It was destroyed.

"I'm going to need to perform surgery, but I can already tell you that I won't be able to save his eye."

Raven choked out a response. "Whatever it takes, Doc. I'll pay you whatever you want."

Lindsey put a hand on Raven's shoulder. Creek's left eye flitted from face to face, and he let out a low whine that broke Raven's already shattered heart.

"I'll sedate him first," Meyers said. "Don't worry, he won't feel a thing. He's going to be okay."

"Thank you," Raven said. He bent down and kissed Creek on the forehead. "I love you, boy. Be brave."

Raven and Lindsey stepped back outside, where John Kirkus had gathered with several of his men.

"How's the dog?" Kirkus asked.

"Doctor Meyers says he'll pull through, but he's going to lose his eye," Lindsey replied when Raven didn't answer.

Kirkus dipped his cowboy hat. "Doc's good. He'll fix your hound up in no time."

"Thank you," Raven said.

"So tell me again what happened on that bluff," he said. "Then we can talk about our other business."

Raven let Lindsey tell the story, everything from Don

working out a deal with Nile Redford that ended with the burning of the Stanley to sending Colton to Fort Collins to meet with Sheriff Thompson.

"He ain't no sheriff," Kirkus replied with a shake of his head. He looked at Lindsey. "With Colton gone and Captain Englewood and Sergeant Aragon dead, you may have just gotten a promotion, Detective."

"What do you mean he isn't a sheriff?" Raven asked.

"Thompson?" Kirkus said. He gestured toward the fence surrounding the mountain community. "That son of a bitch is the reason we built these walls."

***

It was still dark in Fort Collins, and the moon rode high in the night sky. Colton sat in the passenger seat of Raven's Jeep with the same guy that had captured him back on the road. His name was Jango, and he was irritatingly cheerful about having Colton along for the ride. The engine hummed as they idled outside the sheriff's station.

"Where are we going?" Colton asked.

Jango massaged his handlebar mustache, running his fingers along the top and all the way down the sides. Two passes later, he said, "Wait till you see it."

Colton raised a brow. "See what?"

"What the government has done," Jango replied.

The side doors to the building opened, disgorging Thompson and a dozen other men, all armed to the teeth.

Jesus, they look like they are going to war, Colton mused.

"Here we go," Jango said. He patted the steering wheel. "Nice Jeep, by the way. We can always use—"

The three trucks ahead pulled away, and the sound of

engines drowned out Jango's voice. Colton had a feeling he knew what he was going to say, but he didn't respond. If they wanted to commandeer his ride, there was nothing he could do about it at the moment. For now, he was playing it cool until he knew exactly what the hell was happening in Fort Collins and the FEMA camp. Not that he had a choice. The men had taken every single one of his weapons, even his damn pocket knife.

The lead truck, an old Toyota, turned right. Jango followed the other two trucks down a road to the left. For several minutes they drove silently through the empty streets. No one was out, which struck Colton as odd. Back in Estes people would walk around at all hours, but Fort Collins looked like a ghost town. There must be a curfew here.

The headlights swept over several houses that were burned to charcoal. Half the city seemed to have burned over the past month, and the fire to the east continued raging.

"What is that?" Colton asked, pointing to the blaze.

"That? Oh, that's a very unfortunate situation."

Colton strained to get a better look as the convoy moved closer to the fire. Soon he glimpsed the stone façade of an old church. The burning steeple reached toward the moon like a flaming spear. Smoldering lumps littered the front lawn beneath a shattered stained-glass window. Colton tried to process the information his eyes were feeding his brain, but it couldn't be real...

The Jeep turned slightly, and the headlights hit the double doors of the church. A chain and padlock had been looped around the handles, securing the entrance. That's when Colton understood. The trapped people had clawed their way out the shattered windows, but had perished from the flames anyway.

"What the hell happened here?" Colton asked.

"Like I said, it's an unfortunate situation."

The convoy passed the front lawn, and Colton saw one of the smoldering bodies was still moving, crawling across the ground and reaching up with a burned hand.

Is this what Thompson wanted Colton to see?

The lead truck continued driving right past, the driver not even slowing at the sight of the dying person that was so badly burned Colton couldn't even tell the gender. He managed his breathing the best he could, but the horrendous sight made his heart kick. For the next thirty minutes he sat in silence. He considered opening the door and jumping out, but where the hell would he run?

The distant glow on the horizon continued to brighten, and Colton finally realized where the convoy was heading. Normally this would be the point where Colton would palm a magazine into his rifle. Weaponless, he felt almost naked. His thoughts shifted from Kelly and Risa to Raven and Lindsey and the rest of Estes Park. What the hell was Don up to, sending him out here to meet with Thompson on false pretenses? Was something happening back in the town?

Not only did he feel naked, he felt helpless, unable to defend his people. He'd come out here to build an alliance, but it seemed he'd left his friends and family in more danger.

The scent of charred wood and burning rubber filled the Jeep as they drove farther away from Fort Collins. The lead truck slowed on the next hill and shut off the headlights. Jango followed suit. The vehicles parked side by side on the crest of the hill. Doors opened and men jumped out of the beds onto the concrete, fanning out across the pavement.

Jango jerked his chin. "Let's go, *Chief*."

The first thing Colton did when he stepped out was scan the area just in case he was going to have to make a run for it, but there wasn't anywhere to go. Surrounded by rocky fields and rolling hills, the drab landscape provided little cover. The air was thick and heavy from the distant smoke, and the other men pulled up scarves and bandanas over their faces.

Thompson strode through the group and gestured for Colton. Jango followed them to the top of the hill, where Thompson put a muscular arm around Colton's shoulders. Colton was too busy staring at the view to pay much attention to the odd gesture.

Dozens of poles had been constructed on the shoulder of the highway, and a body was hanging from each of them. Several of the silhouetted figures seemed to be writhing, but Colton couldn't be sure they were still alive until a voice pleaded for help.

"You wanted to see the FEMA camp," Thompson said, pointing at a field of charred tents, trailers, and small buildings about a mile past the poles. Fires continued to eat the structures, filling the sky with smoke.

Colton tried to speak, but nothing came out. The refugees were right; the FEMA camp was hell on earth.

"We had a good deal with Captain Moraine. The camp was supposed to give us a shipment of supplies every few days, but Sherriff Gerrard screwed things up. He found out what we were doing and tried to stop me."

He raised his right hand and waved it back and forth. "Bullets started flying, and one thing led to another. Next thing you know, the entire place is burning."

Jango chuckled behind them. "Serves 'em right."

"Come on," Thompson said after lowering his hand. "I want to show you something else."

Colton followed Thompson and Jango down the hill toward the first of the poles. A darkened body hung from the wood about six feet down. The clothes were completely burned away, leaving behind raw flesh and bone.

The man had been dead for a while, judging by the scent. Colton brought his sleeve up to cover his nose.

"You came here to see if the Feds would help you, right?" Jango said, stopping right next to the body. He pulled out a knife and prodded the dead man on the pole. He'd been burned so badly that his skin looked like jerky.

"Sorry to break it to you, but Captain Moraine here won't be providing you much help at all, nor will Sheriff Gerrard." Thompson pointed the knife at the next pole, where a second body had been burned to a crisp.

After shrugging his muscular shoulders, Thompson sheathed his knife and jerked his chin back toward the trucks. He patted Colton on the back as they walked.

"I thought I'd give you the opportunity to see what happens to those that don't follow the laws, Colton, since you seem to have broken one already," Thompson said. He halted and moved in front of Colton so they were facing one another. "You do know what I mean, right?"

Colton waited for Thompson to explain, stony faced and sick to his stomach.

"That's disappointing, Chief. You don't remember capturing one of my men? You told me about it earlier."

"Shit," Colton muttered.

"There you go. You remember," Thompson said, slapping Colton harder on the shoulder. "Anyways, I'd like Jason Cole back. Once that happens, I'll see if you and I can work out some sort of 'alliance' between Estes Park and Fort Collins. I've heard a rumor that you've got a nice cache of supplies to trade. Otherwise, I'll ship you back home in several small boxes."

***

Fenix awoke sometime in the middle of the night inside the cold jail cell. The bastards had only given him a shitty blanket and no pillow. He shivered on the hard floor, mind racing. Would Redford really give him a chance to take Estes Park? In a few hours, he would find out. In the morning Redford and his men would either lop off his nuts and hand his mutilated body over to the Feds or they would set out together to destroy a mutual enemy.

At some point Fenix finally drifted off to sleep, only to be awakened by a loud banging. The door to his cell creaked open, and Hacker stood there holding a lantern, illuminating the tools hanging from his duty belt.

"Get up, you pig fucker," Hacker said.

Fenix slowly rose to his feet. Half asleep and furious, he considered throwing a double fisted punch, but Hacker didn't give him the chance. He reached out and grabbed Fenix by his shirt to drag him from the cell.

"Let's go," he said. "Redford wants to see you."

Hands still cuffed, there wasn't much Fenix could do but follow. The lantern rocked back and forth as Hacker walked down the hall, shedding light on several other empty rooms. Fenix wasn't sure where the man was leading him, but he followed like a good sheep, biding his time and hoping he wasn't being led to slaughter.

A sour sensation worked its way through his gut, partly from the shit dinner they had fed him and partly from anxiety. He calmed his nerves by imagining all the ways he could kill Hacker. His favorite involved gouging out the man's eyeballs and filling up the sockets with burning lamp oil.

Hacker led them down a concrete staircase several floors beneath the ground. A radiation sign hung over a steel door at the bottom.

"Where you taking me?" Fenix asked.

Hacker grabbed the door and pulled it open to reveal a wide room lit by more lanterns and candles. Several hard looking men sat around a poker table in the middle of the room. They looked up from their cards, their smiles all folding into frowns when they saw Fenix.

"What the fuck is this racist sewer rat doing here?" said a guy with a red bandana tied around his head.

Fenix almost laughed at the stereotypical Rambo wannabe, but he kept his mouth shut and scrutinized the other men. Two of them appeared to be American Indians. They wore necklaces with feathers and bracelets made of bone. There were dozens of poker tables, roulette tables, and blackjack tables set up in the small underground casino.

Redford sat at the bar along one wall, still dressed in a colorful blue suit with a red pocket square. He turned and looked at Fenix, then said, "Finish your game later, boys."

The men got up and started walking, their eyes all on Fenix.

"He doesn't belong here," said the guy with the bandana.

Fenix ignored them and crossed the room with Hacker at his back.

"In there," Redford said when they got to the bar. He gestured at a red door on the adjacent wall. Hacker opened it and ushered them inside toward a desk stacked with radio equipment that looked older than dirt. The man sitting in front of the equipment pulled off headphones.

"I want you to radio your second in command and tell him about the attack on Estes Park. We will need fifty men and several vehicles. They will meet us at these coordinates in three days," Redford said. He handed Fenix a piece of paper.

"Sounds like a plan to me, boss." He walked over to the equipment and waited for the other man to get up.

"I don't like this, Nile," the man said to Redford.

"It's my decision, Theo."

"This isn't the right move," Theo said as he stood. "Teaming with a bunch of neo-Nazi fuckers isn't going to go over well with the other men."

"Hey, I really object to the harsh language," Fenix said.

Redford directed his gaze at Theo. "This man can help us get Spears without putting our own men in jeopardy. I'd rather a few Nazis were lost in taking Estes Park than our men." He glanced back at Fenix. "No offense."

Fenix snorted and shrugged. It was good to know where the redskin stood, at least. They would work together for now to achieve their goals, but one of them would eventually stab the other in the back—it was just a question of who got there first.

"Don't you want justice for Alex?" Redford asked Theo.

"This ain't justice, and Alex wouldn't have wanted us to join this piece of shit to avenge him." Theo walked away, using his shoulder to hit Fenix on the way out of the room.

"You're lucky you're blood," Redford said.

Theo slammed the door behind him, and Hacker looked uncertainly at Redford. It seemed everyone but Redford wanted Fenix dead. But that was fine, as long as the boss made the decisions.

Fenix sat down at the radio before Redford could change his mind. He picked up the receiver and scrolled to the channel the Sons of Liberty used. Then he relayed his message to Sergeant Zach Horton, his second in command. Fortunately for Fenix, his soldiers were more loyal and respectful than Redford's men. It only took a few minutes for Horton to reply. The plan was set. In three days, Raven Spears would be dead, and Estes Park would belong to the Sons of Liberty.

18

Albert snuck a look around the corner to check the road for contacts. After finally getting his sister back to the office building where Sergeant Flint, Corporal Van Dyke, and Dave were hiding, they were preparing to move again.

The night vision optics allowed him to see in the darkness. In the green hue, he didn't spot any contacts—just empty sidewalks and a street devoid of any foot traffic. But there were plenty of places for people to hide among the abandoned vehicles or in one of the many apartment windows towering above the street.

Most of the fighting seemed to be coming from the SC though, and despite the early morning hours, the violence had hardly calmed. Sporadic gunfire and even small explosions rocked the airport where the masses were attacking the walls and barriers.

He returned to the alley where Sergeant Flint waited with Jacqueline and Dave. The two people they'd rescued were shivering—although her shakes were from withdrawal, while Dave was almost paralyzed by fear.

Flint flashed a hand signal to Albert, indicating that Corporal Van Dyke hadn't returned from scoping out the other end of the street. They waited in the alley for several minutes, listening to what sounded like a full-fledged battle in the distance. Albert kept his breathing steady, but the rotting scent of death and trash made it difficult and he found himself holding his breath.

"We're going to have to find a way around the fighting to get back to the SC," Flint said.

"Have you been able to get ahold of Captain Harris?"

"Negative. I'll try again." Flint moved to pull out his radio, but gripped his side instead, wincing in pain.

Flipping up his NVGs, Albert glimpsed fresh blood on Flint's uniform.

"I'm fine," Flint said before Albert could say a word.

A shadow darted into the alleyway, and Albert raised his M4. Flipping his NVGs back into place, he saw it was Corporal Van Dyke.

"The other way isn't safe," he said. "Need a detour."

"Jesus, don't sneak up on us like that," Flint said.

Van Dyke sulked. "Sorry, Sarge."

Albert reached down to help his sister up. She was too weak to move on her own, and with Van Dyke's help, Albert hoisted her over his shoulder in a fireman's carry. Once she was secure, he took Dave's hand.

"Stay close," Albert said.

Dave nodded back. He was still gripping the sheathed knife.

Flint took point and moved out of the alley, striding onto the sidewalk and sweeping his carbine high and low. Albert followed close behind. With one hand still clasped around Dave's and the other ensuring his sister didn't fall, he wasn't able to raise a weapon. He shifted Jacqueline higher onto his shoulders. She was so frail, and he hardly noticed the additional weight with the adrenaline pumping through his veins.

They moved down the side of the street at a good pace. Flint stopped at the next intersection and flashed a hand signal to proceed after a quick scan. The sound of gunfire continued in the distance, the pop of small arms answered by the crack of automatic rifles. Harris's men were fighting back now, which told Albert things were spiraling out of control at the SC. How could they hold back tens of thousands of desperate, starving people? Smoke fingered into the skyline over the airport, and as they approached, Albert saw the flames for the first time. Multiple locations at the SC were burning.

"Contacts," Van Dyke whispered from the rear guard.

Albert quickly took cover in an enclosed brick entryway to an office building on the corner of a four-way intersection. Dave tucked his small body behind Albert while Van Dyke and Flint found cover behind a Jeep Wrangler in the middle of the road.

"You sure you saw them?" a man said.

"Pretty damn sure. They had automatic weapons and moved like soldiers."

Dave pulled on his hand. "Mr. Big Al, are those Orcs looking for us?"

"Shhhh," Albert whispered. He carefully placed his sister on the ground. She winced in pain, her eyelids flickering. She was slowly slipping away. He had to get her to a doctor before she lost consciousness.

Across the street, Flint and Van Dyke were hiding behind the Jeep with their rifles angled upward. Both men had their NVGs flipped into position and glanced over at Albert. He nodded, weapon readied.

The voices were coming from the street they had just left, and Albert could make out the footfalls now. There were at least four men. He stole a glance, seeing five Latino men about three hundred feet away, all of them carrying rifles except for one that held what looked like an Uzi. Quickly pulling back, he motioned to Van Dyke and Flint, signaling five hostile contacts.

Taking them down shouldn't be a problem, especially with the advantage of night vision optics, but Albert feared a stray round might hit his sister or Dave. Albert prayed that they would pass by. Still, he slowly readied his rifle, fully prepared to step around the corner and empty the magazine into the men hunting them.

Very carefully, he peeked around the corner again. The men were close enough that Albert could see the five-point sacred crown tattoo on the neck of the closest guy. Definitely Latin Kings. They were now less than one hundred feet away.

"I can't see shit, Jose," one of the gang members said. "Can I use my flashlight now?"

"No, and keep your mouth shut, you dumb shithead," replied another man.

"This is fucking stupid. Why are we looking for a few soldiers out here? The airport is where the action is," said another guy. "I'm ready to carve some mofos up!"

"'Cause these are the pricks that killed Del and Fernandez. The airport will be ripe for the taking tomorrow. Let the civvies do the hard work for us. We'll move in when they're done."

Twenty feet away, Flint and Van Dyke were moving into firing positions. Albert balled his hand to tell them to hold their fire. It was too dangerous to engage with Jacqueline and Dave so close. Plus, if these guys weren't using lights, then maybe they would just continue walking.

The first of the armed men took a left and moved into sight, heading right for the Jeep. Albert nudged Dave back until he was up against the door. The boy had pulled out his knife. He stood next to Jacqueline and said, "I'll protect her."

Albert heard the strength in Dave's voice and saw it in the boy's stance.

"Thank you," Albert whispered. "For now, keep back and stay quiet, okay?"

He took a knee and aimed his rifle at a short man with a bandana covering his features and a wide chain necklace hanging down his chest. Just as he prepared to squeeze off a shot, the crackle of a radio sounded behind the Jeep. Albert cringed at the noise.

"Sierra 1, this is Echo 1. Do you copy? Over."

It was Captain Harris trying to raise Sergeant Flint, and the message came at worst possible moment.

"There!" yelled one of the Latin Kings. All five gang members raised their guns at the Jeep and fired. The shots lanced into the side of the vehicle, shattering windows, deflating tires, and punching through metal.

Dave yelled, "Shoot 'em, Mr. Big Al!"

Albert pulled the trigger and hit the guy with the chain necklace in the temple. His skull shattered and gore exploded into the air.

The next guy turned to fire his Uzi, but Albert dropped him with a shot through the neck that obliterated his crown tattoo. As the man fell, he managed to fire a burst. Bullets zipped into the brick wall to Albert's left, and one of them hit the ground in front of his feet.

Dave let out a cry and grabbed onto Albert's belt, but Albert kept firing. By the time the other three Latino men knew what was happening, two of them were on the ground, bleeding out from mortal wounds. The fifth and final guy took off running.

Albert moved out, Dave still clinging to his back. He fired several shots at the fleeing gangster who vanished around a corner. In a quick motion, Albert pulled out his spent magazine and jammed a fresh one home. Then he raised the carbine in the direction of the guy that had fled, just in case he returned.

"Watch over Jacqueline," Albert ordered Dave. The kid let go of his belt and hurried away. Albert kept his rifle trained on the corner.

"Sergeant, Corporal, you okay?" Albert called out when he deemed the area clear. He backpedaled toward the Jeep to check on Flint and Van Dyke, who were still crouched behind the cover. Flint made a thumbs up sign and then pulled out his radio to send a message to Harris.

Albert moved over to the downed men. Three of the four were clearly dead, but the fourth was on his back, kicking at the ground. He clutched his neck, blood streaming between his tattooed fingers. Albert kicked his gun away and then bent down for a look. The guy couldn't have been more than eighteen years old, if that. They locked eyes and the young man's lips moved, trying to speak.

Another kid, Albert thought. He considered putting him out of his misery, but Van Dyke beat him to the punch by firing a shot in the center of the young man's forehead, ending his suffering with a crack that echoed through the night.

"Piece of shit," Van Dyke said, spitting. "These are probably the guys that hung those guardsmen from the bridge after skinning 'em."

Flint strode over and looked down. "Nice shooting," he said.

It took Albert a moment to realize Flint was talking to

him and not Van Dyke. In less than a minute, Albert had killed three men. Technically four, if you counted the one Van Dyke had finished off. A shiver rolled down his back. In his entire career, first as a police officer and then as head of Charlize's security detail, he'd never been involved in a fatal shooting.

"We need to move before they come back. I've got the evac coordinates," Flint said.

"What evac?" Albert asked.

"You got friends in high places, brother," Flint said. "Apparently there's a Black Hawk heading to a park three blocks from here. They'll be here in thirty. The other birds are on their way to the SC to evacuate personnel."

"Fuck yes!" Van Dyke said, too loud. "We're finally getting out of this shithole."

"Let's move," Flint said.

Albert hurried back to get his sister. "You okay?"

She worked her dry, cracked lips for a moment before responding. "Cold...so cold..."

"Just hang on," Albert said. He bent down and picked her up. Flint was waiting in the street with Dave. They continued onward at a quick clip, anxious to get away from the carnage and reach the evac point.

The first block was clear, and Albert started to relax. They were almost there, but by the time they reached the second block, Albert realized they were heading to the same park where they had killed those men, setting off the chain of events that had put a price on their heads.

The team cleared the trees surrounding the park and then moved through a gated entrance where they stopped at the sight of a man hanging by a noose from a tree limb. It was another National Guard soldier.

He pulled Dave close and told him to shut his eyes.

For once, he was grateful that Jacqueline was too out of it to notice anything.

"What kind of animals could do this?" Flint said, even though he already knew. Whatever sense of law and order that had kept the most vicious gangs somewhat in check was gone now. They were living in a world without rules, without morals, and Albert was starting to think that the few remaining good people were no match for the bad.

He forced himself to look at the body as they approached. The clothing and skin had been stripped away, leaving ribbons of bright muscle exposed. Pinned to the man's chest under the dog tags was a sign that read, *This land belongs to the King.* A five-point crown was drawn below the words.

"Cut him down," Flint said.

Van Dyke nodded and ran over to the tree. He climbed up and, using his knife, sliced through the rope. The body crashed to the dirt and Flint bent down to retrieve the dog tags. Dave pulled his hands from his eyes to watch.

"Was that a person?" he asked.

Albert turned to look back the way they had come, anxious to get out of there.

"He deserves a proper burial," Flint said. "He's one of us."

"All due respect, Sarge, but we got to get to that chopper," Van Dyke said.

Flint hesitated for a moment before he continued through the open gates, reaching up to wipe something from his eyes. He didn't strike Albert as a sentimental man, but the sight of a fellow soldier skinned to the bone would break any man.

They took a trail through the woods that ended at an

open area of playground equipment and fountains.

"There," Flint whispered, pointing to the basketball courts at the edge of a lake. "That's our evac."

When they reached the courts, Albert lowered his sister to the ground at the foot of a wide tree. Van Dyke and Flint took up position with their rifles angled toward the playground. It was a good location; the lake made it virtually impossible for anyone to sneak up on them in that direction.

Albert scanned the area. A hellish orange light raged in the direction of the airport. The forest bordering the tarmac of the SC must be burning.

"Is that Mordor?" Dave asked, stepping up next to Albert's side.

"Contacts," Flint said before Albert could answer.

Albert turned to see flashlight beams crisscrossing through the trees. Albert moved Dave to sit by his sister. Then he took a knee behind a boulder and aimed his rifle at the approaching figures. To his right, Van Dyke and Flint were both lying in the grass.

"How long till evac?" Albert asked.

"Ten minutes," Flint whispered.

Armed men moved into view. Albert spotted the guy that got away earlier leading the group, but this time the gangbangers were more cautious. They fanned out like soldiers, weapons shouldered and flashlights raking across the park. He counted at least a dozen beams.

As they moved out around the playground equipment and fountains, Albert heard the thump of the incoming Black Hawk.

"We have to take these guys out or that bird isn't going to land," Flint whispered.

Albert nodded. He prepared to take his first shot,

lining the sights up on the face of another young man wearing a bandana over his head.

Forgive me, Lord, he prayed as his finger tightened on the trigger.

Van Dyke fired first, sending a burst downrange. Flint and Albert followed a split-second later, and Albert's target dropped from one shot to the skull and two shots to the chest.

Return fire exploded across the park, muzzle flashes lighting up the area like massive fireflies. A round whizzed past Albert's head, and another hit the tree behind him, shattering the bark.

"Stay down!" he yelled to his sister and Dave.

Albert squeezed off a burst in the direction of the closest muzzle flash, dropping another gangbanger. Two more men ran for the playground equipment. The squeeze of the trigger brought one of them down in the sand. A second hit the other guy as he attempted to scramble up a plastic slide. The man slid back down, leaving behind a smear of red on the surface.

Flint and Van Dyke fired calculated shots, cutting down three more contacts. Albert focused on a group of four men behind a fountain. They popped up one at a time to fire, forcing Albert back behind the boulder. These guys were smart enough to take cover, but fortunately they couldn't shoot for shit.

Albert fired a burst, scoring a hit that dropped one of the men into the pool of water with a splash and a choking scream.

Van Dyke suddenly cried out, "I'm hit."

Albert kept his sights on the fountain and shot another man who was making a run for their position. Then he looked over to Van Dyke. He was trying to raise his rifle, but dropped the weapon and hit the ground.

"Keep firing!" Flint yelled at Albert.

Pushing his rifle back up, Albert counted three more contacts in the green view of his NVGs. The men had all shut off their flashlights, but he could see them with his optics. One man snuck around the fountain at a crouch, and Albert nailed him with a burst to the upper body. He jerked several times before collapsing.

Return fire rang out, and Albert crouched back behind the rock. Bullets kicked up dirt to his right. He pushed his body against the boulder, doing his best to keep his large frame hidden.

"How bad is he hurt?" Albert asked.

"We need to get him out of here fast," Flint said.

More muzzle flashes came from the playground as the chopper approached, descending over the basketball courts. The sight of the bird brought out courage in the remaining Latin Kings. Bringing down a Black Hawk would be a badge of honor for these assholes.

Flint looked over at Albert. "Get Dave and your sister out of here! We'll hold these fuckers back. I'm not leaving until every one of them is dead."

Van Dyke choked out, "Just don't leave without us, bro."

"Never," Albert said. "We're all getting out of here. Just hang on."

Albert took off running for the chopper, shielding his sister and Dave with his body. A flash of motion came from his right. Before he could raise his rifle, a bullet slammed into his side, knocking him to the ground and seizing the air from his lungs. His night vision goggles rolled onto the dirt, and he looked up with naked eyes.

To his right, a man with lip piercings and a thin

mustache walked into view. He was holding a Glock. He grinned as he aimed the barrel downward.

Albert focused on the cold, dark eyes of the Latin King. Tattoos covered his face and neck. Was this really the last face Albert would ever see?

"Fuck you, nig—" the man began to say when his words were cut off by a scream of pain.

Albert's eyes flitted to a short figure standing behind the gangbanger. It was Dave, and the boy had plunged his knife into the man's back. He pulled it out and then jammed it in a second time.

"For Gondor!" Dave shouted.

Albert quickly pushed himself up, gritting his teeth at the pain. The gangster howled and reached with one hand to grip the knife sticking out of his back. He aimed his Glock at Dave with his other hand but never got the chance to pull the trigger.

A three-round burst hit the guy in the chest, sending him sprawling backward. Albert turned to see Flint, his rifle raised.

"Go!" Flint yelled.

More flashlights were approaching from the opposite end of the park. Reinforcements had arrived. Albert picked Dave up under one arm like an over-sized football. They returned to the tree where Jacqueline lay, feebly groaning.

"Y'all stop all that noise," she groaned.

He reached down to help his sister up, but the gunshot wound was too painful. "You've got to get up," he said.

"Just lemme sleep," she said, turning her head away.

"Come on, Jackie!" he shouted, watching as the chopper landed on the courts. A team of soldiers jumped out and Albert waved at them and yelled, "Over here!"

More gunfire cracked behind them, Van Dyke and Flint exchanging rounds with the advancing gangbangers. The next few seconds dragged by with agonizing slowness.

The pain was intense, and Albert could feel the lifeblood gushing from the wound in his side, warming his belly and chest while turning his limbs cold. He tried to run, but his legs wouldn't respond. They gave out on him and he collapsed in the dirt.

The soldiers reached them a moment later. Two of them hauled his sister and Dave away.

"Mr. Big Al!" Dave yelled.

A third man with the bulky build of a linebacker bent down and helped Albert up. Using the big soldier as a crutch, Albert hurried toward the bird.

Flint and Van Dyke abandoned their position, but they were still firing as they retreated. A dozen muzzle flashes came from the trees. Van Dyke stumbled, and as Flint leaned over to offer him a hand, bullets tore into his back and side. He fell with Van Dyke, both men tangling on the ground.

"Sergeant!" Albert yelled. He pulled away from the soldier helping him and stopped. "We can't leave them."

The soldiers that had helped Dave and Jacqueline into the chopper returned with their rifles shouldered. They fired at the final gangbangers while two of them ran to help Van Dyke and Flint.

Albert wanted to help, but the pain was too intense. He couldn't even walk on his own. Red encroached across his vision. By the time he reached the chopper, his body was numb. He collapsed to the floor of the troop hold and forced his eyelids open. A small face stared down at him.

"Please don't die," Dave sobbed.

"I won't leave you, buddy," Albert said. He looked over to his sister. A medic was crouched next to her, applying an oxygen mask to her gaunt face. A second medic bent down by Albert to check his gunshot wound.

The soldiers that had run to help Van Dyke and Flint were returning now with both men over their shoulders. As soon as they made it to the chopper someone yelled, "Go, go, go!"

As the pilots pulled the bird into the air, he heard a voice say, "He's gone."

Van Dyke lowered his head next to the limp form of the sergeant. Flint had taken a round just below the temple. There was nothing anyone could do for him now. Albert closed his eyes and prayed for the man's soul.

The chopper pulled away from the city, providing a view of the airport. The eastern fence had come down, and thousands of people had streamed inside. Fires raged throughout the camp, and the scene sparked with gunfire.

"It's a damn warzone down there," one of the soldiers said as the Black Hawk pulled away into the night sky. "SC Charlotte has fallen."

— 19 —

Charlize stood on the bottom floor of Central Command with her arms folded across her chest. Dr. Lundy and General Thor flanked her, and President Diego stood in front of them. Everyone was focused on the large, wall-mounted monitor at the front of the room. Her mind was consumed with worry about Albert, but right now she needed to focus on the situation at hand.

On screen, hundreds of ships with Chinese markings were cutting through the water, leaving the shores of China for the United States.

The Chinese government must have been preparing the ships for days if not weeks, knowing that President Diego would likely agree to their offer, and now the fleet had embarked with billions of dollars' worth of industrial equipment and containers packed full of supplies.

But their help came at a cost. Twenty-five thousand Chinese soldiers were also aboard those ships. Their presence in the United States would bring with it the first occupation force in the history of the country.

Agreeing to China's terms felt like betraying her country, but the loss of multiple SCs to violence and disease had forced her hand. Word had come in over the night that another SC had fallen just outside Loveland, Colorado, not far from the town of Estes Park. It had been burned to the ground by raiders. The devastating news continued to flood in over the scrambled comm systems.

The war with North Korea might be over, but the United States was losing the fight against its own people. Now they were at the mercy of a foreign government that had long been an uneasy ally at best.

She wasn't the only one with mixed feelings. The images on screen weren't received with applause or celebration, but skeptical looks from nearly everyone. Each officer or staff member around her seemed uneasy about the idea of armed Chinese soldiers walking freely around the United States.

As the ships sailed on the screen, President Diego turned and used the opportunity to address the gathered members of his cabinet, his generals, and everyone else that had arrived over the past few weeks. The conversations died down, silence shrouding the Command Center as he began to speak.

"I'm sure I don't have to tell you that we're entering a new phase of American history," Diego said. "A phase that will either lead our country toward a brighter future, or one that will be the end of our republic. Like the Romans and so many other great empires, we're faced with war, famine, disease, and uncertainty about the future. Every decision we make moving forward will determine if we crumble like the Romans or whether we rebuild and restore the United States of America."

Diego paused for a moment, tightened his tie with his still-bandaged hand, and took a moment to scan the faces around him, stopping on Charlize. She offered her support with a brisk nod. Although it pained her, this was the only way to save what was left of their country. She just hoped it didn't backfire. They couldn't afford a war against the Chinese.

"I'm confident that the Chinese government and our other allies will help us get back on our feet. This will save countless American lives and put us back on a path to prosperity. I reached this decision with the help of my cabinet, and while I know the decision won't be popular, I feel it is the correct one. I ask you all to work with me with optimism as we move forward. Together we can be strong, but divided we will not succeed."

Charlize continued nodding, and soon most everyone in the room was dipping their heads in support. Still, there was no applause.

"Thank you," Diego said simply.

The moment felt as though the United States had reached a crossroads. One day, perhaps, historians would look on President Diego as a great leader who brought America out of darkness. On the other hand, he might be reviled as the man who sold his country out to China.

Charlize had no way of knowing which way things would turn out. She could only pray that there would be a future where someone was left alive to write those history books.

As everyone went back to work, Colonel Raymond walked over to Charlize and whispered in her ear, "Ma'am, I've got news about Albert Randall."

The words flooded her with the anxiety that had momentarily gone away during Diego's short speech. She followed Raymond to a conference room and waited for him to shut the door.

"He found his sister. He's on his way back here via Black Hawk, but Albert was shot, and the sergeant leading the mission was killed," Raymond said.

Charlize slumped into a chair." How bad is Albert?"

"He's going to make it, but his sister is in pretty bad shape. Apparently she was using heroin," Raymond said.

Charlize closed her eyes as her heart rate began to slow down to normal speed. It wouldn't be a popular move bringing Jacqueline to Constellation, but she'd made Albert a promise, and she was going to keep it. She hoped the facility's clinic was prepared to treat a heroin addiction.

"They also rescued a young boy about Ty's age. A kid named Dave," Raymond said. "His parents were in D.C. the night of the North Korean attack."

"Two civilians out of how many?" she mumbled, more to herself than to Raymond.

"Pardon me, ma'am?"

"How many civilians were killed at SC Charlotte?"

Raymond shook his head. "I don't know yet. At a guess…thousands."

For a moment neither of them spoke. Charlize ran through the facts in her head. Albert had been shot, but he'd found his sister and he was coming home with a young boy plucked out of the chaos. For the first time in days, she felt conflicted optimism. With the Chinese sailing toward the United States, Charlize had to hold onto the hope that the country could turn things around.

"MS-13 and the Latin Kings appear to be responsible for the organized attack in Charlotte," Raymond continued. "Perhaps those Chinese soldiers will come in handy."

Charlize stopped short of nodding. Those gangs weren't the only domestic terrorists threatening the lives of innocent civilians and the restoration effort at the survival centers. Dan Fenix and his Sons of Liberty were still out there. They wouldn't slip through her fingers again.

She stood and jerked her chin at the door. "Let's get back to it, Colonel. We have a lot of work to do."

***

Colton didn't sleep a wink that night. As soon as they got back to the station, Jango led him to the jail cell, where Colton had remained sitting with his back to the wall until the sun came up. It gave him far too much time to think. He'd made some poor decisions, but in the end, each one was made to protect his family, friends, and Estes Park to the best of his abilities.

At the end of the world, a man could only be expected to do so much. Colton had done everything in his power to save those he loved.

And he had failed.

He lowered his head and put his hands on the back of his neck, resisting the urge to scream.

"Hey, friend," said a voice.

Colton knew it was Clint Bailey, the prisoner across the hallway, but he wasn't in the mood to talk. He wondered if Clint had suffered a head injury that scrambled brains, or if he'd always been a bit odd. It didn't matter, really; the man still didn't know when to shut up.

"I said 'hey,'" Clint said.

Looking up, Colton glared, ready to snap. But when he saw Clint had suffered another beating during the night, he couldn't bring himself to yell at the poor bastard. Thompson and his men were animals. In some ways, they were worse than Brown Feather and his brother, because they had the power to commit murder on a much wider scale than the two psychotic Sioux brothers.

Colton lowered his head again, sinking into the hopelessness of his situation.

"It's okay, friend," Clint said. "We can help each other."

The guard at the other end of the hallway let out a long snort and then went back to snoring regularly.

"Don't give up," Clint whispered. "We're going to get out of here, me and you."

"I'm not giving up," Colton replied. And to his surprise, he found it was true.

Marcus Colton wasn't the type of man to quit. Never had been. He had been a soldier and a fighter for most of his life, from the boxing ring to the mountains of Afghanistan. Now wasn't the time to despair—now was the time to kick some ass and save the people he loved.

He slowly scooted over to the bars, meeting Clint's eyes. The man may have smiled, but Colton couldn't tell because of how bruised Clint's features were.

"Tell me how we can help each other," Colton said.

Clint scratched at his forehead, then looked to the right. The guard continued snoring down the hallway.

"I know things," Clint said. "I know their weaknesses, and most importantly, I know how to get out of here."

Colton paused to think. He was exhausted, and he had no idea if he could trust this man. But what choice did he have? No one was coming to rescue him, and Thompson wasn't going to just let Colton go. He had to find a way to escape and get back to Estes Park. He wouldn't let anyone negotiate with Thompson, that was for sure.

He had only one choice. He would have to trust Clint—not just with his own life, but with the lives of everyone else in Estes Park.

"Okay," Colton said at last. "Tell me everything you know."

***

It was noon on the day after Raven had shot Don in the face on the trail near Storm Mountain. The night had been full of ups and downs, but Creek had pulled through. The dog now slept peacefully on the floor of Chief Colton's office at the police station in Estes Park. After hammering out the terms of an alliance with John Kirkus and his fellow preppers, Raven had returned to Estes Park with Lindsey and Creek earlier that morning.

Raven hadn't known if anyone would believe him about Don's betrayal, which was why he let Lindsey do all the talking. While Raven waited for everyone to gather at town hall, he watched Creek sleep.

A patch covered the dog's eye, and a bandage marked his shoulder where the doctor had removed more pellets. The Akita wouldn't be back to work anytime soon, but he was alive. Thunderer had told Raven he'd lose more loved ones, but at least the universe hadn't taken Creek from him. Raven wasn't sure he'd be able to keep going if that happened.

Instead, he feared that Colton had been lost. Don had seemed certain that the chief wouldn't be coming home. With Don and Hines dead, Colton missing, and the people they'd lost during the raider attack, the town was defended by a dwindling band of officers and volunteers. Their list of allies was growing thin while their enemies seemed to multiply.

Raven groaned as he shifted in his chair. Creek wasn't

the only one in bad shape. Raven had scored more cuts and bruises, and he was pretty sure his ear was about to fall off. Aside from the threat of infection, he wasn't too worried. The injuries were just more scars on his already scarred body. All that mattered was that he was here to fight another day.

A knock on the door made Raven flinch. He turned to see his sister and Allie outside the office. He opened the door, and Sandra reached out to embrace him. She hung back at the last moment and scanned him up and down instead.

"Sam, you look like shi—" Sandra stopped herself from cursing and hugged Raven instead, embracing him in a bear hug that made him groan even louder.

Sandra pulled away. "I'm sorry, I didn't mean to hurt…" her words trailed off again when she saw Creek stir on the floor, tail wagging.

"Oh my God," Sandra said.

"Stay down, and don't try and move, boy," Raven said.

Creek rested his head back on the ground, his tail still whipping the carpet.

"What the heck happened to you guys?" Sandra asked.

Raven put his hands in his pockets. "It's a long story. Don ambushed me and Lindsey at Storm Mountain. Apparently Don was behind the burning of the Stanley Hotel, and he also betrayed Colton by sending him to Fort Collins."

"Allie, stay here with Creek," Sandra said. She put her hand on Raven's shoulder and turned him around, directing him into the hallway.

Great, another lecture.

Creek's remaining eye followed Raven out of the room.

"It's okay, boy, I'll be right back," Raven said over his shoulder.

As soon as they stepped into the hallway, footfalls sounded and Lindsey rounded the corner. She forced a smile and said, "Hey, Sandra."

Sandra didn't return the friendly gesture. "One of you needs to tell me what the hell is going on."

"Detective, would you like to answer that?" Raven replied.

"I will in a bit, but right now we need to get to the conference room," Lindsey said. "Sheriff Thompson is on the radio, and he wants to talk to the person in charge of Estes Park."

"Stay here with Allie and Creek," Raven said to Sandra.

"But…"

"Just listen to *me* for once," Raven said.

Sandra let out a frustrated huff and walked back to Colton's office while Raven followed Lindsey into the conference room. Mayor Andrews, Administrator Feagen, Detective Ryburn, Officer Matthew, Margaret, and several other staff members were inside. The shock on their faces told Raven that Lindsey had already broken the news about the previous night. He was glad not to have been here for the majority of the conversation.

"Who's going to talk to Thompson?" Lindsey asked.

"Colton would want you in charge," Officer Matthew said.

"Yeah, but Mayor Andrews is in charge of the town until he comes back," Lindsey replied.

"Me?" Mayor Andrews asked, pointing at her chest. "I…I…"

Lindsey rolled her eyes and grabbed the radio receiver.

Raven stepped up next to her.

"This is Detective Lindsey Plymouth," she said.

"Never heard of you," Thompson's voice replied. "I'll keep this very short. We have Chief Colton. And I'm told you have one of my men, Jason Cole."

"Cole is the raider that hit us the other day," Raven said quietly when Lindsey's questioning eyes met his.

"If you don't return him, then I'm afraid I'll just have to keep Chief Colton. I've got a spot picked out for him right next to the former sheriff. If you ever want to see him alive again, you'll do exactly as I say."

There was another pause full of more shocked looks, and then Thompson added, "Oh, and we're also going to need half of your medicine supplies, half of the elk meat, and the majority of your weapons. Then we'll get scheduled drops each week. You will drop off the first load with Jason halfway down Highway 34 in three days. I'll give you a few minutes to talk it over."

Lindsey looked at Raven for guidance, something he'd never thought would happen.

"Do we comply with the demands?" Ryburn asked.

"Hell no," Raven said. "That would leave us unarmed, and we need those supplies to get through the winter."

"If we don't, they will kill Colton." Lindsey shook her head. "What do we do, Sam?"

Everyone else looked at Raven as if they expected him to lead them. Colton was being held prisoner, Jake Englewood was dead, and Gail Andrews was too flustered to organize a PTA meeting, let alone take charge of a town in crisis. He locked eyes with Lindsey. If anyone here should take the lead, it was her.

The radio crackled and Thompson's voice surged back over the channel. "What's your answer?"

Raven stepped over to Lindsey and whispered, "Tell them we'll comply with their demands."

"Are you crazy?" Lindsey asked, her eyes uncomprehending.

"Just trust me," Raven said. "I have a plan. Don't worry. We're not handing over Cole and we're not giving Thompson jack shit. We're going to fight, and I'm going to get Colton back."

He grinned at Lindsey. It was the smile of a man with a plan that was just crazy enough to work. After a moment, she smiled back at him. Together, they would protect the town and get Colton back safely. They would not allow Estes Park to fall.

Let the storm come, Raven thought. *We'll be ready.*

—End of Book 3—

Read the epic conclusion to the Trackers series

Trackers 4: The Damned

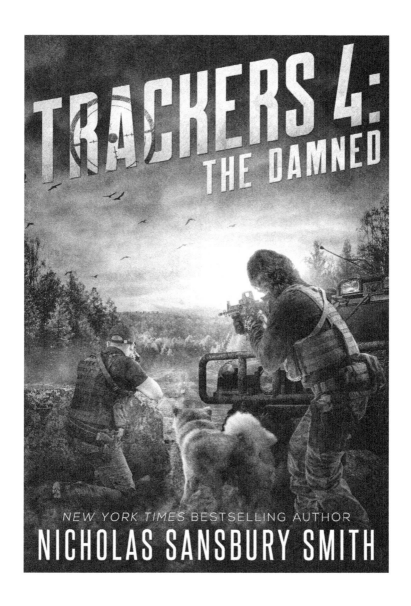

TRACKERS 4:
THE DAMNED

NEW YORK TIMES BESTSELLING AUTHOR
NICHOLAS SANSBURY SMITH

About the Author

Nicholas Sansbury Smith is the New York Times and USA Today bestselling author of the Hell Divers series, the Orbs series, the Trackers series, the Extinction Cycle series, and the new Sons of War series. He worked for Iowa Homeland Security and Emergency Management in disaster mitigation before switching careers to focus on storytelling. When he isn't writing or daydreaming about the apocalypse, he enjoys running, biking, spending time with his family, and traveling the world. He is an Ironman triathlete and lives in Iowa with his wife, their dogs, and a house full of books.

Printed in Great Britain
by Amazon

22066439R00169